Bearly Snowed In

Kiera A. Reynolds

Contents

CHAPTER ONE
TAKING CHARGE

GRETA

Life always has a way of surprising you. You work hard to get to where you want to be. Nice place to live. Steady work. A loving fiance. Puts you on the top of the world before crashing down around you.

That's about where I am right now.

"What do you mean you slept with Jeremy? He's your boss!"

"You're just against this because I slept with another man."

"I don't care if the person you slept with has a penis or not, Damian. We were supposed to get married in a month."

"What do you mean 'supposed to?'"

I squeeze my eyes shut. This conversation has been replaying in my mind on constant repeat that gets worse with every repetition. Each time is crueler than the last. This has been my life. I thought I was in love. Well, maybe not love, but fondness, sure. Feelings were developing.

Images of me dropping the enormous diamond ring back into his palm flash through my mind. My eyes fly open to try to clear my vision, but it doesn't work. The confusion and hurt in Damian's eyes still shine through the white walls of my home. He was always quick to anger, so I saw that in his gaze as well.

"I'm not marrying someone who is going to have an affair with his supervisor, Damian."

"You can't do this. Father says if I don't marry you, I lose the company. Just admit that it's the fact he's a man that's bothering you."

"It's not! Committed people don't sleep with anyone else."

"None of my other girlfriends cared about the other women in my life, so why else would you be making such a big deal over this? I give you everything you could possibly ever want."

Except a man that respects me and doesn't sleep around. Why couldn't I have said that then? Pinching the bridge of my nose, I drop onto my couch. How did things take such a terrible turn? I was marrying the future owner of the biggest tech corporation in the city, who was currently working his way through departments to learn the process. We were to have a big beautiful wedding, then produce lots of babies. It was all planned.

I've put up with a lot from those I have loved in my life, but I'm drawing a boundary with cheating, particularly with his supervisor. The last thing I need is an entire city laughing at me because I can't keep my husband in my bed and STDs popping up randomly. I deserve better than that.

My phone rings, showing a picture of my mother. I lick my lips and wish I could simply ignore the phone call. She won't stop though. Next, she'll bang on my door. If I don't answer, she'll get the manager because my nice home is in one of Father's hotels. No one wants to upset Bridget Parks, wife of the man who owns Parks' Hotels.

Before it can go to a cut off voicemail to make room for another frantic call, I answer. "Hello, Mother."

"Don't you dare 'hello' me. What's this I hear about you cutting off the engagement?"

I wince at the disapproval in her strict tone. This isn't going to be pretty. "He was cheating on me."

"I highly doubt it. Don't smear his name because you got cold feet."

"Mother! Someone sent me a very explicit video!"

"Fabricated. You always do this. Take something tiny and blow it way out of proportion."

Tears sting my eyes at her appraisal of me. Nothing I've ever done has been good enough. I'm always too lazy, don't tend to my appearance enough, embarrass her, and overreact. Emotions are for the weak. That's what my beloved mother has always told me. I live every day trying to make her proud, earn her love. It's never enough.

"What would you do if Father slept with someone else?" I say, trying to reason with her.

"It would never happen. I have as much power in the relationship as he does, so he'd come to regret it. I'd destroy him, which he knows. If this isn't one of your insane overreactions, you probably did something to deserve it. You've always been weak-willed."

The tears fall now, and I hold back a sob. Crying is always met with derision. Only weak women use tears to get what they want. What would Mother say if she knew I've been crying since an anonymous someone sent that video to me? I don't care who or why; there's no way it was fake. Absolutely none. I saw faces and recognized his office.

"Mother—"

"Don't even try to argue with me. Drive back over there and get your ring back. I don't care if you have to beg to do it—just not in public. You're a Parks and need to start acting like it. Put your silly immature feelings behind you. This man is good for you. The next time I hear from you, it better be from his loving embrace."

She hangs up before I can reply. Dejected, I stand to do as she says. Mother will never take disagreement from her children. The first thing I do is go to the bathroom to see how bad the damage is. I wince at the woman looking back at me in the mirror.

The clip holding my blonde hair in the back is lost in a tangled mess. Mascara and eyeliner leave dark trails down my raw cheeks. The light blue of my eyes is a stark contrast against the dark red consuming the whites. Mother will kill me if I return to Damian looking like this, so I wash my face the best I can and put eyedrops in. The clip is a bit harder, and I'm shocked I don't have a bald spot on the back of my head by the time it's out.

When I'm semi-presentable, I walk to the door. My phone buzzes. My best friend messaged me.

What's up, girl?

Nothing.

Uh oh. I can hear sadness.

There is no way to hear sadness through text.

I can. What's going on?

Nothing.

My phone rings, and I sigh while answering it. "I swear. It's nothing."

"Stop lying to me. I can hear the sadness even better now."

"I broke up with Damian."

"It's about time."

I clench my jaw for a second. "I know you never liked him, but this really hurts."

"I'm sorry, sweetie. I didn't mean it like that. Grab yourself a pint of ice cream, find some movies with bad endings, and laugh at fake people who are worse off. If I was closer, I'd join you."

Dana had to move away for a job three months ago. She's not far, but no one wants to drive two hours to console a broken-hearted wretch like me. Besides, she can't.

"I have to go talk to Damian."

"What? Why?"

"Mother—"

"Say no more."

"I can't when you don't let me."

She laughs. "I don't need to when your excuse starts with your mother. That woman—I swear it. You are a twenty-six-year-old adult, Greta. She has no say in your life. You are worth so much more than she is. I wish you'd see it."

"I'm so much less than her. That's why she doesn't like me, let alone love me."

Great, now I'm crying again. I'm going to have to do my makeup all over again before heading out. I really wish I could hibernate away from everyone. Why does stuff like this always keep happening? Why am I never good enough for anyone? I'm not enough for my mother. Father barely pays attention to me at all. Damian had to find his pleasure in the arms of another.

"Don't do that," Dana says through the phone.

"Well, she doesn't."

"That's not what I'm talking about. Don't go around blaming yourself for her shortcomings and thinking about how you're not good enough for anyone."

"You're a mind reader."

"I'm not. I just know you too well. Promise me you won't go groveling to the sleazeball." Her voice pleads heavily with me to see things her way.

"But—"

"No buts. He doesn't deserve you, Greta. Turn your phone off and go to a different hotel if you don't think you can't hold off your mother. Just don't go apologize to the man who wronged you."

"Maybe I should just take some vacation time and come see you."

"I'd love that, but you can't. That big storm is coming in tonight."

My eyes narrow. "What storm?"

"I swear you live under a rock. They're calling it the storm of the season. Feet of snow within a couple of hours."

"Oh."

"Don't go see him. If you feel your resolve weakening, I'll be here to talk you out of it. Give me a call."

"Fine."

"Good. I need to get going because I'm sitting in the grocery store parking lot. Love ya, girl."

"Love ya too."

We hang up. It's hard, but I force myself to sit again. Dana's right. It's time for me to stand up to my bully of a mother. I'm better than this. I can withstand the pressure.

I think.

Despite my determined defiance, I keep looking at my keys. Maybe if I do this one thing, Mother will see that I'm more than she thinks. Just one more time.

No. I can't. This is impossible. An entire life of programming is hard to ignore. One way to do it would be to leave. I know Dana mentioned the storm, but I've driven in snowstorms before. Course set, I jump up and grab my keys and wallet. After a short debate, I leave my phone, eliminating my mother's only way to contact me. If I get stuck, I can easily find somewhere to get help. There isn't much between here and there that's not settled besides one short stretch. I can do this.

When I get to my car, I notice it's not snowing at all. It's probably just one of those big storms that is predicted but not going to happen. Happens all the time. Jumping in, I start the car and drive. As long as I'm focused on this plan, I can keep Damian out of my mind. I'd much rather spend a few days with my best friend than sit at home crying or being forced to pursue my dead-end relationship.

For once, I'm taking my future into my own hands. No one is going to tell me what to do anymore. Won't Dana be surprised to see me? A silly snowstorm that might not happen won't keep me down. I'm finally feeling positive again, and I won't give that up.

About halfway, the snow starts. Wind tries to push me off the road. I come to a town, and for a moment, I consider stopping for the night. If I stop, I might get stuck here. Dana isn't too much further, just over the mountain and through the small strip of forest. I'm sure I can make it, so I keep on.

At the first intersection out of town, a tree blocks the road. There has to be a way around it. I turn and try to keep myself going in the direction that will lead me back to the main road. My tires slip from time to time, causing me to grip the steering wheel hard enough to turn my knuckles white. After a few turns, I feel defeated and like I need to turn around. I'll go back to the town I just passed through and stay there. Mother won't know I'm there if I don't use my credit card.

Trees surround me on all sides, but I find a place to turn around. Disappointed that my adventure is done before it truly began, I blink tears from my eyes. The moment of distraction moves my car too far to the side. All four tires slip. No matter how I turn my steering wheel, I can't control the slide.

Screaming, I find myself heading straight for a pile of snow. Nothing works to gain control. A puff of white explodes into the dark when

I hit, my bumper getting stuck. I throw the car into reverse, but all my tires do is spin. I'm stuck.

Reaching for my phone reminds me that I left it at home due to momentary bravado. What was I thinking? I'm an idiot. Looking around, I see nothing but trees and fast accumulating snow. Stuck in the only wild stretch between me and Dana. I don't think I should walk in unfamiliar country during a storm in the dark. My gas tank is still mostly full. All I have to do is make sure the tailpipe is clear, and I can stay warm tonight.

I'll leave first thing in the morning. The light of the sun will make the trek less dangerous and warmer. All I need to do is wait it out. I'll be fine. No matter how many times I tell myself that, my anxiety rises further. This is what happens when I go against the grain.

Mother is right. Nothing I do is ever good enough. I overreact and act like an idiot, which leads me to make stupid decisions. Now I'm stuck in a snowy forest, all alone and with no one around to help. Why do I feel so dizzy?

CHAPTER TWO
BROKEN PEACE

SILAS

Snow falls around me, unbroken and fresh, like my hopes for this place. It's clean and pure, untouched by those who want to hurt and destroy. When I look down, I realize my paw breaking the snow represents the reality of my existence. I leave a mark that defiles the purity of the world around me. It seems like I always have.

It's why I came here, after all. Somewhere I belong; that's what I need. I don't fit in anywhere, which is understandable with my mixed lineage. What I am makes me unwelcome anywhere.

Looking down again, I dig my large paws into the snow more. It's falling heavily, so of course I need to come out and enjoy it. I hate when snow only comes for a few months out of the year.

After taking a few steps, I stop at the sight of cougar prints and lift my top lip from my sharp teeth. They're almost filled in, so the cats are long gone by now. The cougars watch me intently, looking for any kind of weakness. So far, I've proven too strong for them. It's not like I meant for what happened to happen. It was an accident. New territories take some getting used to.

Not that the cougar shifters will listen. In their eyes, I've wronged them. I'm a malicious bear shifter who doesn't belong here and smells odd to them. If they only knew...

Huffing a loud breath, I feel my thoughts sour the moment. The snow no longer looks perfect. Too much like home, a place I don't belong. According to the cougars, I don't belong here either. They're right, but this is the first undisturbed place that's called to me, and I'm not willing to give it up yet.

Turning, I follow my disappearing prints back through the worsening blizzard blowing between the thick trees. I feel it collecting in my fur, giving me a pleasant chill. By the time I reach my cabin, the prints are gone, lost in the fury of the winter storm that reminds me of my childhood.

My cabin in the woods isn't far, and the light cast through the windows from the fireplace looks inviting. It's a small home, built with my own two hands, quaint and welcoming. To me, at least. No one else would fall in love with this simple solitude, but it's home and a nice change.

I take one more look at my giant paw, grimacing at the brown hair sprinkled through my white fur. Polar bears tend to stay in colder climates. Too bad they don't want me. The light brown in my fur makes me an outcast anywhere.

Annoyed by my own thoughts, I growl and force my paws to turn into hands. Even in my naked human form, the cold is no more than a gentle chill. A proper shifter can change with clothes. Not this one.

My bare feet trudge across the wood of my small porch. The railing will need to be fixed again in the spring, coming loose at the opposite end this year. The only things on the porch are my old rocking chair and the barrel to catch rainwater. Walking over to the barrel, I chip away the layer of ice, cup my hands, and dip a drink of water in my palms. Cool and refreshing. It's low, so I'll need to start melting snow.

Heat blasts me when I walk inside. My fireplace crackles in a friendly way, greeting the return of its builder. I can smell the stew in the pot that I left to cook on the flames. A wreath, my only Christmas decoration, falls. With a grumble, I replace it and close the door.

There isn't much in here; only a table, a bed, and a couch. A few boxes of supplies sit along the wall. My latrine is outside because it needs to be re-dug often. Living in excess leads to feelings of grandeur and a false sense of superiority. I much prefer this to bright lights and sparkle. No one needs more than what I have before me.

I settle in a rickety chair at the table, one that almost doesn't want to hold my bulk, with a bowl of stew. The tastes of rabbit and wild carrot explode on my tongue, leaving me to moan with my eyes closed. Shifting and running as a bear always leaves me hungry. After the first bowl, I grab another and another until the pot is empty.

Cleaning is quick and simple, and I find myself settled by the fire with one of the five books I own. This one has probably been read over a hundred times, but this is how I spend my evenings. It's not like a bear shifter living on the land can afford to buy new ones. I don't mind. I like the five books I own.

Unlike most evenings, the pages can't hold my attention. I find my eyes drifting to the window, which I lifted from outside a hardware store in the closest town, over and over. More specifically, the snow. I press my lips together and take a deep breath through my nose. It doesn't snow enough in this place to suit me, but it's the best I could find while putting distance between me and where I was born. You can take the bear out of the snow, but you can't take the desire to frolic in the white fluff out of the bear.

Grunting, I place the scrap piece of cloth that I use as a bookmark between the pages and stand. Another run won't hurt. I still have some deer jerky if I make myself famished again. Stripping, I step outside, letting the cold air caress my naked skin. For a few moments, I simply stand and watch the magic world of white.

A snarl escapes my lips. There is no familiar magic in this land because this isn't home. The snow is deceitful in its attempts to convince me otherwise. My fingers clench, and the change takes over me without thought. Within seconds, I'm on my paws, shaking my white and brown fur out.

The peace of the night storm calms my anger enough that I don't move for a bit. I watch the flakes fall and brighten the dark landscape. The sun's down, so night predators will be out, including cougars. I chuff a laugh. They've tried many times to take me down. The thought of their presence in the trees still gives me pause.

Maybe I should move again. The doubt is fleeting because I looked all over before I found this secluded place. Everywhere else suitable was inhabited by wolf shifters or grizzly, neither wanting to allow me the quiet I desire. The cougars are a pain, but they're an inconsequential pain. I'll deal with them for now.

My head turns to observe the small area around my cabin. There are at least three feet already. By the feel in the air, this blizzard will last until dawn. It's barely even started. I lift one paw and push it into the undisturbed coldness. All hesitation is blown away with the sensation, and I find myself jumping in the snow like a young cub. I've missed it.

By the time I stop playing, I realize I've wondered a ways from my home. Worse, I'm close to the road. No paths or streets come close to my home, but my peace means being relatively near civilization, if you can call humans that. Still, very few have braved the wilderness far enough to find my cabin. They leave quickly.

I don't like being this close to the road. It makes my skin itch beneath my fur, so I turn to head for home. That's when I hear a strange rumbling. I pause and look toward the sound, then back in the direction of my cabin. My ears turn backward. Whatever it is, I should just ignore it. Trouble can't find me if I don't go looking for it.

Despite my conviction to return home, I find myself looking back at the sound. What if it's some kind of threat? It's better to know now than to be surprised. Emitting a low growl, I walk in the direction of the rumble. As I draw closer, I realize it's the purr of a car engine. That almost makes me turn around, but a look around tells me no one should be out in this weather.

Annoyed at my instinct to check, I trudge forward through the growing snow. The smell of exhaust turns my stomach long before I find a small vehicle embedded in a snowbank. Cautious, I move slowly until I'm beside it and push the snow off the driver's window with my nose. A small blonde woman sits with her head in an uncomfortable position that will leave a nasty kink in her neck. She doesn't open her eyes at my approach.

My claws dig into the snow as I debate what to do next. Moving to the back, I snarl annoyance. Don't humans have any idea how dangerous this is? Apparently not. I dig the snow away from the back of the car and the exhaust, then look back toward home. I did all I could.

As I start walking back, I halt with a sigh. What if she's hurt? She might not wake in time to turn off the car before she suffocates herself when the snow gets too deep again. Walking back to the window, I lift a paw and scratch at the glass. The woman still doesn't move.

I dig the door out of the snow with my paws and shift to open it. Nothing wakes her. First, I turn off the engine and wonder if that's enough. The cold wind hits me, making me shake my head. Humans don't do well in the cold, and one look around the inside of the car tells me this one wasn't smart enough to brave the storm with preparation. There are no blankets or any source of heat.

Dumb human. They never take mother nature seriously.

Reaching a hand in, I shake her shoulder. The woman still doesn't stir. I grab her chin and move her face so I can examine her. Blood mats her light hair on her forehead, obscuring parts of her face. It looks as if she hit her head, so she may have a concussion. Growing annoyance makes me snarl once again. I should leave someone not smart enough to stay in during a storm to her fate.

Something inside me keeps me from acting on that threat. With another sigh, I lift her from her seat and cradle her in my arms. She feels so tiny against my chest. Closing her door, I turn toward home. My peace and solitude are about to be broken because I don't have the heart to leave her. For the first time since leaving home, I'm going to have company in my residence.

Not just any company. A human. A disenchanted adult that I'll have to hide my true nature from. Unlike a child, she won't believe in magic and the supernatural. What did I get myself into? Getting home takes longer with the deepening snow and bare feet, but I make it in one piece.

I nestle my patient into my only bed and cover her with every blanket I have before I get dressed. After throwing a few more logs on the flames, I settle on my bench by the fire and feel the heat slowly increase. I watch the delicate creature breathe beneath my covers.

The wind picks up, whistling through the cracks around my door. I'm not going to be able to get her back to the road until the snow melts. I'm going to have a mangy human stuck in my small cabin, prying into secrets she doesn't deserve to know. This is just great.

Who's the dumb one now?

CHAPTER THREE
RUDE AWAKENING

GRETA

My head hurts.

That thought comes echoing through the drowning blackness that is my current state. I moan. At least, I think I do. Hearing sounds, even if you make them, is difficult to accomplish when semi-conscious. I attempt to open my laden eyelids, but all that does is make it feel like I'm spinning out of control.

It's like the time at the fair. I rode some kind of easy-looking ride, only to be spun in circles by my friends until I almost threw up. Mother did not like hearing I went. A Parks is not to soil the name by going to civilian events. Fairs are stinky and beneath us. I still had fun once I was done feeling awful. My friends found it hard to get me on another ride because of their deception. Trust was broken.

Get a grip, Greta. More important things to worry about.

Just like then, I learn my lesson now. No more prying my eyes open before they're ready. Why does my head hurt so much? And why does my environment smell like smoke, wood, and musk? Stranger and stranger.

I can figure this out if I can just open my eyes. This attempt goes a little better. Mind numbing pain but not spinning. I close them again and take the time to just breathe. What is the last thing I remember?

Giving my ring back to Damian. Tears and pain. Mother trying to bully me, and Dana talking me down. Getting into my car.

That's all I remember. There's more, but my mind can't access the memories at the moment. Maybe when I get some time to clear the fog from my brain. First, I need to find a way to open my eyes without my head splitting in half.

This time, it works. My headache increases but doesn't cripple me. Blurry vision doesn't help me discern what's going on. All I know is that I am not in my car. Maybe I made it to wherever I was going. I feel a mattress under me and a mound of blankets creating too much warmth.

When I try to push some of the heat off of me, it doesn't budge. Either they're too heavy or I'm too weak. The latter wouldn't surprise me. Isn't that what got me here in the first place?

A burst of memory hits me. No, it was my defiance that got me out here. My stupidity drove me into a dangerous situation. Details are still fuzzy, but I'm getting that much.

A few blinks clear some of the fuzz from my vision. Wood. That's the impression I get. Walls and ceiling made of wood. Soft flickering light that's low enough not to hurt my straining eyes. I guess that explains that part of the scent mixture I noticed upon waking.

Looking to my right shows me a table with an empty bowl. At least, I think it's empty. When I turn to look the opposite way, I almost jump out of my skin. A very large man sits backwards on the couch in front of a fireplace. His dark blue eyes flash as he watches me, so deep they almost look purple. What an odd color. Dirty blond hair looks shaggy and unkempt, like he cuts it with a razor. Broad shoulders flex as he turns his head to the side, as if I'm some huge mystery to figure out.

"What happened?" I ask, keeping my voice soft for fear of angering this strange man. I'm so used to well-kept men with perfect hair and clothes. This man is gruff and shirtless, making me hope he at least has pants on. Mother tells me to avoid these types of men. They only want one thing and are uncivilized to the point of being feral. If she's right, I'm in danger.

"I found you in your car."

His voice is rough, as if unused to being used. A glance around the one-room cabin I can finally make out in all its bare splendor makes me think company isn't common. A loner; even better. I'm in so much trouble.

"Where's my car?" Simple questions. Keep him feeling unthreatened. As if someone about a third his size could be threatening.

"In the snowbank you decided to park it in."

"Oh." Not the best reply to keep the conversation civil, but I'm at a loss for words. What do I even say now? Questions swirl in my mind. None of them feel smart to ask at this point. I need to know more about my situation.

"Why would you leave during such a nasty storm?"

His question forestalls my need to ask one, and I only stare at him for a moment. When his eyes narrow, I shiver and hurry to answer. "I wanted to visit a friend. Am I far from my car?"

"You left safety during the storm of the year to visit a friend?"

I feel my cheeks warm. I'm not making a good first impression. "I didn't think it would be that serious. The weathermen are rarely right."

A look of confusion passes over his fascinating eyes; I swear they're almost purple. "Well, I guess they were."

"Seems so. I apologize for any inconvenience. If you can take me back to my car when it's light out, I'll be on my way."

He cocks his head to the side again and leans more on the back of his couch. Bulging muscles twitch with the movement. The sound of the couch squeaking under his strength sets my nerves on edge. There's no way out of this if he plans on anything nefarious. There's no way I can withstand those savage muscles. I swallow hard.

The man who is either my savior or captor takes a deep breath. "You don't need to fear me. I'm not going to hurt you. If I wanted you hurt,

I'd have left you there. You were close to asphyxiating by the time I found you. Don't you know not to keep your car running when snow can cover the exhaust?"

"I thought I could keep it clear."

"That gash on your head says otherwise."

I open my mouth to argue but close it when his words fully register. Gash? Shaking fingers work their way out of my pile of blankets to my forehead. The tips touch a piece of gauze.

My brows furrow. "I hit my head? I didn't feel it."

"Could have been the adrenaline. You've been out for a while."

Lifting the covers, I check to make sure I'm still clothed. My breath comes out in a deep sigh of relief. No evil doings happening while unconscious. That's a plus. I look for a window, finding a low glow outside. Dawn?

"Well, I'm awake now. If you can take me back to my car..."

"Won't do you any good."

My fist clenches under the blankets. "Why is that?"

"We got about four feet last night. Your car isn't moving. Probably buried."

Great. I take a few deep breaths to hold in my panic. "Do you have a phone I can use?"

He laughs. "Does it look like I do?"

I glance around to see my space completely devoid of electronics. "How do you communicate with people?"

“Who says I want to talk to people?”

"Well, point me in the direction of the nearest town."

His strong shoulders move with his deep breath. I'm sensing annoyance. "Listen, whoever you are. I live in this cabin to avoid people. The nearest town is hours on foot during good weather. Triple that with this amount of snow, and that's being generous. The road is the closest, but it'll be unpassable."

So, I'm trapped here with someone who wants to be away from people. Why? Don't strange serial killers who hunt humans for sport hide in the forest? I can't see any reason for hiding away from civilization in this hovel that isn't suspect. I can't let him know that I think that. Keep playing dumb.

"Why?" Stupid freaking question. If I want to be dumb, I shouldn't ask him to enlighten me about my situation further. I need to be so much smarter than this if I want to get out of here alive and unharmed.

"That's none of your business."

His reply doesn't make me feel any better. Not only is it rude, it enforces that he's hiding something. I need to get out of here. Sitting up brings memories of the fair roaring back. Gasping, I lay back against the flat pillow and do my best to will away the dizziness and pain. Quick movement with a head injury is not a good idea. Noted.

When I can see straight again, I find the possible murderer standing next to me. I jump, making my head hurt even more. At least he's wearing pants. That mystery has been solved favorably. Strong hands brush the sore spot on my head gently.

"Sudden movement in your condition isn't advised. Are you cold?" he says.

I try to scooch further away from him. "What are you doing?"

His concern turns to annoyance. "Taking care of the idiot who drove in a bad storm and disturbed my solitude. Are you cold?"

I press my lips together and scowl at the blankets to keep from angering him more directly. "No. I'm actually very hot."

When he sticks his hands under the blanket, I squeal and pull further away, earning another glare. He removes his hands to show me heating pads before grabbing a few more from under my cocoon. If I wasn't already roasting, my cheeks would be on fire.

"For the last time," he says, "I'm not here to hurt you. I want to get you well and on your way as soon as possible, so I can go back to peaceful solitude. Or maybe I should have left you out there to asphyxiate, then freeze?"

"No. Uhh, thanks for saving me."

He grunts and tosses the heat packs on the table. The solo bowl bounces when they hit. Returning to his couch, he stares into the fire as if I no longer exist. I'm not sure whether to be happy or unhappy about this turn of events. Even if what he says is true, I can't stay in such a small space with a strange man. People will talk if I'm found like this, and Mother will come down with an iron fist.

I still don't trust him, but I decide to offer an olive branch. "My name is Greta Parks."

"Silas."

"Silas..." I prompt.

"Doesn't matter."

Huffing, I position myself against the rough wall behind the bed. I'm not lying prone with someone who can't even follow common courtesy. His lack of manners tells me all I need to know about him. Can I trust his words that he won't hurt me?

"Thirsty?" he asks, breaking the silence.

"A little."

He stands, grabs a plastic cup that's seen better days from a box under the table, and fills it with water from a pitcher I didn't notice near the couch. When I take a drink, it tastes of ice and decaying plastic. Still, I gulp it down, surprised at just how thirsty I really am. Silas waits and takes the empty cup from me.

"More?" he asks.

"No, thank you. I'm feeling better."

"I still have a little stew leftover from supper. Not much, but it should fill someone as light as you."

I clench my teeth, wondering if he's insulting my size. He should be happy I'm small since he carried me here. "I don't think my stomach would tolerate food."

Nodding, Silas turns away, walks over to the fire for the pot hanging over it, then eats what's left while standing. I stare with wide eyes. Lack of manners doesn't fully describe this man. Who eats like that? What if I am hungry later? This man needs lessons in being a good host. A child does better than this.

Something on my face must convey my thoughts because his eyes narrow when they meet mine. Talk about lack of manners. This situation has me out of sorts. I need to do better. Watching the fire over his shoulders after he sits back down makes my eyes grow heavy. Fine. I'll sleep to recover from my ordeal and gain strength, but I still don't trust him.

CHAPTER FOUR
ROUGHING IT

GRETA

This time, waking is easier. The headache isn't gone, but it doesn't try to punish me harder for being alive like before. I open my eyes and stare at the wooden ceiling above me. Maybe if I don't move, Silas won't realize I'm awake. I need to think without him staring at me or questioning my life choices.

So, I'm here. Regardless of how I feel about that fact, it's not changing. Silas promises he doesn't want to hurt me, but someone without my best interests at heart wouldn't tell me they are going to torture and murder me. The fact remains that I'm still here and unharmed.

He'd surely have acted already if he had dangerous thoughts about me. Wouldn't he? Unless he's fighting those urges or is sadistic enough to want me awake to see my reactions. Okay, now I'm letting my imagination get away from me. Silas is either a master manipulator, or he's sincere.

But he still doesn't want me here.

That thought intrudes on my emerging calm. How long will he put up with my annoyance before making me disappear? That would give him the peace he craves, the calm I've disturbed with my idiotic decisions. It's obvious I'm nothing but a nuisance. Ask my mother. Not only will she agree, but she'll point to Damian's infidelity as proof of that. How long until Silas is tired of my presence as well?

Lifting my head brings a lightness that makes me feel as if I'm floating. My skull hovers a couple inches over the pillow for a few moments while I wait for my vision to clear. Is it the injury or hunger?

The twisting of my stomach tells me it could be either. A discomfort further down tells me I need a bathroom soon.

When I can see clearly, I look around the small space to see it empty and without any doors indicating a bathroom. There's nowhere to hide, particularly for someone as large as the man who owns this tiny home, so I know he's not in here. If only an extra room with a toilet would appear. That feels safe and definitely needed.

Silas said the snow is too deep for travel, but he's out in it. Does that mean he's lying? Maybe there is very little snow, and he's just outside laughing at my foolishness for believing him. I try to look out the window from where I sit in the bed, but there's a square of leather covering it. Without the little glimpse of outside, I begin to feel highly claustrophobic.

Standing causes another needed moment to remain still until I feel I'm steady on my feet. I glance between the window and the door. The door will lead out and to possible safety, but Silas might be right outside. The window will give me a view to determine if he lies or clues to where he might be. After a short debate, I decide the window is the smarter move. I can hide better by only peeking out the leather covering.

I only make it three steps before the door opens, letting in a gust of freezing air that paralyzes me as much as the man who must have opened it. Midstep, I stop moving completely, almost losing what's torturing my bladder. This is ridiculous. I'm not some animal that freezes as the bright lights come barreling closer.

Annoyed by my reaction, I swallow the fear and turn. Silas closes the door behind him and examines me. It takes everything I have not to hop around doing the pee dance. I need to go.

Seeing Silas all at once while not being dizzy proves to me that he's even bigger than I thought last night. A coat covers his strong muscles now, but even that hints at the bulk beneath. There's no doubt about it; I'll need to look up if I get too close to him. The man is a mountain. My mouth goes dry at the thought of him trying to take something I'm not willing to give. No way can I go up against a man this large.

Something in my face must make my thoughts apparent. He huffs out a breath. "How many times do I have to tell you that I mean no harm?"

I clench my hands and rub the tips of my fingers over my palms while taking a deep breath. Mother told me all about men like him. Not that I can tell him that.

"Mother told me we can only trust men that are well-groomed and gentlemanly. She says that unsophisticated men mean danger."

What the hell, Greta?

So much for not revealing my thoughts to the subject plaguing them. Now, my nails dig into my palms as I wait for his reaction. Will he realize I'm onto him and drop the act? Will he be angry? Insulted? Kick me out? Go into a blind killing rage?

None of those options are pleasant, so I hope none of them are right. Nothing like sticking my foot in my mouth during a dangerous situation where it's needed to help me run. How do I backtrack my running mouth? Is it even possible to do so?

So far, all he does is cross his arms over his broad chest and turn the corners of his mouth downward. I've done it now. He is deciding how best to make me disappear. I've worn out my welcome, even if the welcome was for nefarious purposes.

"Do you always listen to everything your mother tells you?" he asks instead of rushing at me and tearing me limb from limb like I imagine.

"What?"

"Do you always do what your mother says?"

A new type of unpleasant discomfort shudders through me. I want to tell him no. I can tell he expects me to because what twenty-six-year-old still follows all their parents' rules? Telling him that the answer is yes isn't a good idea.

Once again, he reads me easier than I expect. "I see."

Silas cocks his head at me again, giving him an even wilder appearance than I first noticed, which is saying something. I swear his ears would be perked forward if they could be. Something about this situation intrigues him enough to be curious.

Shaking his head, Silas walks over to the table, drops a rabbit on it, and pulls out a large knife. The sight of the incredibly large killing instrument makes me squeak and look toward the exit.

He scowls. "This isn't for you. How else do you expect me to skin the rabbit? With my nails?"

"Skin what?"

"Have you ever been outside of the city in your life?"

The derision in his tone straightens my back. "We have a camping cabin outside the city. We go there every summer."

"Let me guess. Electric. Indoor plumbing. Comfort and expensive things to do. Restaurants and food delivered."

It's my turn to frown, forgetting my fears enough to be insulted. "There is no need to be uncivilized just because you're roughing it."

"*Roughing it*," he mumbles before turning the rabbit over to stab it.

I turn with a gag, which causes him to grunt. Not focusing on him gives me the chance to be reminded of my surroundings. No wonder he used that tone when he repeated roughing it. There's no hint of electricity, no sinks or tubs, and nothing elegant or comfortable. He might as well be sleeping outside on the ground and using trees as his bathroom..

That reminds me. "Where's your bathroom?"

"Outside."

Forgetting the scene behind me, I turn to gawk only to spin around away from the bloody mess. "Do you have to do that here?"

"Easier than doing it in the snow. I know how to clean it up. Do you need me to show you to the latrine?"

Latrine? Please tell me whatever he's talking about is enclosed and heated. Another twist of my bladder orders me to not be so picky right now. "Yes, please."

"Put your coat on," he says.

When I hear the sound of the knife falling onto the table, I turn but not enough to see the rabbit. Again, I curse my stupidity. Never turn your back on a strange man you know nothing about.

I find my coat on a rusted nail by the door. Grimacing at the weird bubble from where it was hanging, I slip my arms into the sleeves. When I look at Silas, I notice his hands are still covered in blood.

"Don't you want to wash your hands first?" I ask.

"To take you to pee? I'll wipe them in the snow if you're that squeamish. I'm assuming you're hungry as well. This is how you're going to eat."

I press my lips together and open the door. If I don't want to touch blood during my escape, I'll need to do this much. Holding it open, I motion the man through first. The better to keep an eye on what he's doing.

As if he knows my thoughts, he shakes his head before walking past me and through the door. When I step out onto the rickety porch, I stop to let my mouth hang open a bit. He wasn't lying. The snow is so high.

There's a path shoveled off to the side. He must have been hunting and shoveling while I slept. The walls of the path are taller than I am. As promised, Silas stops to wipe his hands on a pile of snow, turning it from pristine white to blood-red. I almost gag again, but I don't want to give him more reason to insult me.

Without looking, Silas walks forward. I follow, feeling like I'm trekking through a white cave. Above, the treetops are visible, naked and trembling in the wind. I pull my coat closer around me.

Silas's coat isn't very thick, and I see holes in some places. "Aren't you cold?"

He glances over his shoulder. "I grew up in true cold. This is nothing."

Is anything about this man soft? Muscles. Attitude. Impervious to the freezing temperature trying to eat through my only source of warmth.

When he stops in front of a structure that looks no bigger than the box our large deep freeze came in, my brows knit together. "You have to be kidding me. It's an outhouse."

"Surprised you know what that is. I built it myself, thank you very much."

Of course he did. "Isn't it freezing in there?"

"It has walls and keeps the cougars out."

My eyes widen. "Cougars?"

"You're in the wild, Ms. Parks. There will be predators."

His voice is quiet as he says the last part. The tone of his voice sends shivers over me that have nothing to do with the frigid air. I examine him as he looks at me. There's something hidden here, something I'm not sure I want to uncover.

"It's either in there or climbing over the piles of snow to find a tree," he says.

I lick my lips, regretting it immediately in the cold, and hurry into the tiny box that makes me feel like I'm entering a coffin. The "toilet" is nothing more than a hole dug in the ground with a bucket for a seat. I stare for a moment before deciding I have no choice.

The holed bucket lid almost freezes to my thighs as I sit after maneuvering in the small space to pull my pants down. As I unleash the liquid threatening to explode my bladder, a loud moan escapes me. I clap my hand over my mouth and hope Silas didn't hear that. Something else I regret when I wonder what all this hand has touched on the trip out here.

Finishing as quickly as possible, I hold back a groan when I see large leaves to use as toilet paper. This man is nothing more than a very large animal. Why would anyone subject themselves to this torture if they're not hiding something?

I slip out to find the hints of a grin on Silas's face. "Feel better?"

Damn it. He heard. "Much."

"Did you survive the outhouse?" With a huff, I stalk past him toward the cabin. He follows with a chuckle. "Wait until you see how you'll need to bathe."

My feet falter. "What? Don't tell me you have ice baths?"

"Not quite that rough. A pale of warm water, a rag, and a sliver of soap."

I press my lips together and wonder if I should just brave the wilderness. "Would you hold me here if I wanted to leave?"

A little more straightforward than I wanted, but it works to wipe the smugness from his face. He replaces his amusement with a scowl. "You aren't a prisoner, Greta Parks. If you want to go, you're welcome to. It's my advice that you don't."

"Why's that?"

"One, you have no idea where to go. It's very easy to get turned around in these woods. You'd freeze to death. Two, even if you know where to go, you'd still freeze to death. You're a bit far from your beloved civilization. Three, predators. I trust you remember that part. Not only cougars, but wolves as well. Lucky for you, most bears are hibernating."

"Most?"

"I've seen one or two still roaming. What will it be? Trust that I won't hurt you, or brave the wild forest?"

I turn away, unable to look him in the eye. He mutters that it's as he expected before brushing past me on the path through the snow. When it's safe to look, I follow his strong back with my gaze. There is no way I'd survive out there, but that doesn't mean I have to trust him. All I need to do is wait for the right moment. I can learn from him and use that knowledge to gain my freedom. Because one thing is for sure; he's not holding me here by force, but I'm still trapped.

CHAPTER FIVE
UNCULTURED

GRETA

Sizzling meat leaves a scent hanging in the air that makes my mouth water. I'm starving, but it will take time for the rabbit to cook. As it is, I'm avoiding looking at the naked animal on the spit over the fire. If I do, I won't be able to avoid the comparison of the meal awaiting us and the fuzzy animal it once was.

I'm not a vegetarian or anything. I love a good steak or roast chicken. Something about rabbit turns me off though. I've always thought they were adorable. Mother always turned my request for a pet down, but bunnies were at the top of my want list.

To keep my attention off the fire, I flip a page in the worn book. Silas has a small collection and has allowed me to choose one to my liking. I was never allowed to read anything uncivilized. There's that word again. As I remember all the times Mother used it, I grit my teeth. As a small act of defiance, I have chosen horror.

It's not easy. This has to be one of the worst ever written because I'm on the edge of my seat, and I'm only three chapters in. How do people read stuff like this? I'm going to have nightmares for days. For some reason, I can't put it down. Logic tells me I should, but whether it's defiance or the fact I might actually like this, my fingers keep flipping from one page to another.

Silas sits at the table, avoiding placing his presence too close to mine. That's fine because I'm still not sure how to feel about the man. While I'm still guarded, I'm a little more at ease. If he wanted to do something to me, it would have happened by now. The long game doesn't seem to be present enough to make me believe what I first thought.

I do my best to keep my mother's voice out of my head, which is extremely hard to do. She's been criticizing and forcing me to do things for so long that it's like she's living inside my skull. Everything I do, that voice comes to life and tells me I'm an idiot or not worthy. I wish I knew how to evict her from my mind.

Another page flips in careful fingers. The binding is creased and makes turning the pages easy. The top corner of the cover is missing, and the bottom has a crease. Some of the pages are crinkled. There was a food stain of some sort a few pages back. Whatever he feels about horror, Silas must have read this book many times. It's obviously well-loved and utilized.

My heart skips a beat as our main character hears a noise outside the bathroom during her shower. My entire body tenses as I worry about what it might be. Eyes rivet on the words while my breath stops. I can feel my heart beating in my chest.

"Enjoying the book?"

Crying out, I jump and drop the novel onto the floor. I glance around in search of danger with my hand over my heart. Silas stands in front of the fire with one light eyebrow raised halfway to his shaggy hairline. For a moment, I force down my mother's voice. I don't really trust him, but I'm losing my fear of this large, wild man.

"What?" I ask.

"I'm going to take that as a yes; you're enjoying the book."

"Sorry, but yes. I was riveted to the scene where Alice sees someone behind her in the bathroom mirror."

He laughs. "Have you never read or watched horror before? That's a pretty cliche moment for a jump scare."

"Jump scare."

"And I'll take that as a no to my previous question. Anyway, glad you like the book. Hungry?"

My stomach chooses that moment to grumble aggrieved agreement to his question. I can't remember when I last ate. I was too upset yesterday afternoon, so maybe breakfast? Hard to remember in the mess that my life has been for the last twenty-four hours. Silas takes my growling stomach as an answer and walks back around the couch with a motion for me to follow.

That's when I realize the rabbit is no longer over the fire. I must have been really lost in my reading to not have noticed him removing the searing meat. Standing, I brace myself for the sight of a charred rabbit.

My brows furrow. "You did that fast."

"Did what fast?"

"All I see are pieces of meat. Where's the rest of it?"

Silas settles into a chair and uses his fork to place meat on my plate. "I figured you didn't want to see it because of how squeamish you are, so I cut the meat off and disposed of the skeleton while you were engrossed in the bathroom horror scene."

"I'm not squeamish. I just think that bunnies are cute."

"They're delicious too."

I glare at him but give no response. When I gingerly place a piece on my tongue, I realize it is really tasty. Either that or I'm just really hungry. Maybe a little of both. Avoiding telling him he was right, I focus on chewing and looking around the bare cabin.

The silence gets to be too much. "What time is it anyway?"

Silas shrugs. "Judging by the amount of light outside, maybe a little past noon."

"Don't you have any kind of clock?"

He takes another bite, chews, and swallows before answering. "No. There's no point in knowing what time it is. I wake when I'm done sleeping, eat when I'm hungry, and sleep when I'm tired. It's a simple life that doesn't include harsh schedules. It's freedom to follow my instincts and not what others tell me I should be doing."

I fall silent for a few moments. I don't think I have any idea what that's like. Since birth, Mother had me on a strict schedule that only changed in activity as I aged. Up at six in the morning, follow the to-do list promptly, then bed at nine. What would it be like to live in the freedom of doing what you feel like without regard for others? I shake my head. That way leads to chaos.

Which leads me to my next conundrum. How am I going to keep a productive schedule without a clock? I glance around for anything that may be helpful.

My perusal ends with a frown. "Don't you like any conveniences? How do you know about the weather without having at least a radio?"

"I look outside. If you spend enough time outside, you get a feel for the change of weather. I knew the storm you blindly drove in was coming hours ahead of time. I don't need anything to tell me more than that."

Such a simple life, propelled only by instinct. Isn't that the definition of uncivilized though? Mother says that way lies chaos, but I may need to embrace it for a while. Only until the snow melts enough to free my car.

"You don't have much here though," I say, unable to keep myself quiet. "The little luxuries in life are what make it worthwhile."

Silas scoffs. "The little luxuries make you crave the larger ones. I have my books. I have my forest. I have my chores. That's all I need in life. Anything more threatens to consume all time for introspection. That's where the death of instinct comes in. Do you have any instincts?"

"Well, yeah. I'm finding I can't always trust them though. My instincts told me it was safe to drive. My instincts also told me you were dangerous, which you contest."

"That's not instinct. You're using past experience and things others tell you to determine what's best. Do you ever just sit and listen to your mind?"

I feel my brow furrow. "What in the world does that mean? My brain says what I think."

"Exactly."

"I don't get it."

"Your instincts are so far suppressed that they can't be heard. You rely so much on other people and things to tell you what's going to happen that you lost all ability to hear what your mind and heart say."

Why does this man feel he has the right to judge me? He's the one living in the middle of nowhere like he lives in the pioneer times. "I listen plenty to my heart. It told me to break up with my fiance, so I did."

"Before or after something bad happened?"

"Why does it matter?"

His dark blue eyes flash purple again. "It matters a lot. Leaving before a situation gets too grave spares a lot of pain and damage. Waiting too long leaves you at the mercy of the consequences."

"It's not my fault he cheated on me with another man." My hand covers my mouth. Here I go again. Overreacting and being impulsive. Mother is right about that much. I let his judgment of me get the better of good sense. Silas doesn't need to know the darkest secrets in my heart. Why did I say that?

The man across the table watches me for a few seconds without a hint of what he's thinking. "How did you find out?"

"How is that any of your business?"

"It fits our current conversation."

I scowl at Silas. "Someone sent me an explicit video."

"So, you didn't catch any signs?"

"What signs? Do not try to make this my fault. You don't have the right to judge me."

Leave that for my mother.

Silas stares at me, and I continue to glare at him in challenge. He says, "I didn't say it was your fault. I'm simply trying to make a point. No one is responsible for the actions of others. Did you not see any signs? Have any feelings that something wasn't right?"

I bite my tongue to keep from answering because he's right. There were hints, but I just didn't listen to them. If I even entertained the fact that something was wrong, Mother would step in and tell me I was just being stupid.

Instead of all that, I say, "We were planning a wedding. Everyone gets a little off with something that big."

"So you did feel something and ignored it. That's not trusting your instincts."

Crossing my arms over my chest, I stare down at my empty plate. I'm not pouting. I'm simply ending this insane conversation. Besides, I'm too impulsive and emotional. Mother tells me that all the time, and she's right. Those two flaws are how I ended up here in the first place. It's better to listen to her than my impulses.

Accepting my silence as an end to our talk, Silas grunts, picks up our plates, and washes them in the melted snow from over the fire. I sip my water that probably came from the same source and ignore my wonder if his method of cleaning actually cleans or not. It's not my place to question him when I've never lived a life like that.

"I need to chop more wood," Silas says when he's done. "Would you like to come out?"

"I'll go back to my cliche horror story since I'm obviously too uncultured for you."

With a roll of his entrancing eyes, he throws on his threadbare jacket and walks out the door. I look around to see if there's something else I can do besides read. When nothing presents itself, I settle back onto the couch and open back to the bathroom mirror. My eyes start to grow heavy, but I force them open to keep reading.

I start losing the battle with my eyelids, thanks to the warm fire and quiet, when Silas bursts through the door. I jump up, dropping the book on the floor for the second time due to him startling me. Angry, I turn my head to give him a piece of my mind, but what I see snaps my mouth shut.

"What happened?"

CHAPTER SIX
ROUGH AND WILD

GRETA

My jaw twitches as my eyes rove over his panting body. Silas lost his coat somewhere, and the muscles between what used to be a white tee shirt flex with each heavy breath. He's soaked from head to toe in melted snow. Rips in his clothes are accentuated by growing red spots.

Even his face isn't left untouched. What looks like claw marks cover his left cheek. His purple—definitely purple now—eyes are wide and feral. I'm not sure if I'm seeing anger or fear or a mix of both. Something heavy hits the porch, making Silas jerk.

My eyes move to the wooden barrier separating us from whatever did this to him. A loud scrape sounds on the other side, which makes him press his back harder against the splintery surface. He grits his teeth and lets out a rough growl that sounds like it comes from a wild animal.

"What happened?" I ask when the outside world remains quiet for a while.

"Cougars," he gasps.

I feel my eyes widen, looking at the door behind him to gauge its ability to keep large cats at bay. He warned me they're out there, but I'm not sure how well I believed him. Judging by his current state, I'm going to say he wasn't lying. Dana had a cat when we were little, which Mother hated because it rode home on my clothes in the form of fur. Those look like cat scratches. Bigger than the domesticated ones, yet still the same.

Taking a step forward, I look over him. "Do you need a hospital?"

"No," he says, shaking his head.

"Rabies?" Silas laughs and shakes his head again. I'm not sure why he's so sure of that, but I'll focus on the here and now. "First aid kit?"

"I'm fine."

"You are not fine. I'll help." Standing, I look around.

When Silas realizes I'm not dropping this, he grunts. "Behind the firewood box."

I rush over and find another small box of meager belongings behind the one holding our source of heat. A short rifle through brings a dirty kit out. Scared of how little I might find, I open the latched box, surprised by a full supply. That's lucky, considering the state of everything else in this cabin.

Silas still stands by the door, so I grab his arm, marveling at how thick it is. He follows my guidance without argument or fighting against my touch. Once the man I once considered a captor but now look at as a host is seated, I take a closer look at the damage. I don't think I'm qualified for this.

"I'm no doctor, but the wounds on your face look like they'll need stitches. You really should go to the hospital," I say.

"I've dealt with worse than this."

Pinching the bridge of my nose, I take a few deep breaths to cool the frustration his determined jaw clench brings me. If I push too hard, he might not let me help. Maybe I can pay him back a little this way. It's not like I'll change his mind. Why are men so stubborn?

"Fine," I mutter, hurrying to the boiled water. I fill a large bowl with clean liquid, grab some soap and a cloth, then return to the couch.

Squatting, I take his chin in my hands, careful of the deep cuts in his cheek. As I clean them with warm water and soap, I can't help but wince at how deep they are. "Tell me more about what happened while I work?"

This man must be made of steel. He doesn't even flinch at my touch. "Not a lot to tell. I was chopping wood when I was ambushed. They've had it out for me for a while."

My brow furrows as I move to his forehead. "They're animals."

"Animals can hold grudges as well as any human."

"What did you do that you think they are out to get you?"

"Not something I want to talk about with someone who doesn't trust me."

I frown but take the point without dispute. While I feel he isn't keeping me for nefarious reasons anymore, I don't totally trust him. He's too wild and... And what? Free? I hold back a roll of my eyes and keep my head from shaking back and forth. Freedom is no reason not to trust someone.

Mother would argue that point. I know she'd tell me that we can't be trustworthy and good without strict rules and order. Maybe I should keep the distance I've created between me and Silas. No one has as much freedom from rules and order as someone left alone in the woods. Something makes me wonder if I should keep thinking that, but I can't isolate the feeling enough to identify it.

He saved you.

There it is. Maybe rules don't equal good. They do mean predictability and order though. That's enough to remain wary. I can be wary without fear.

"Thinking awfully hard there. Have you decided I don't need your help after all?" Silas says into the silence.

I jerk a bit at the intrusion to my thoughts. "No, no. You need to be cleaned up and bandaged. How did you escape?"

"I can handle myself. Although, it's easier if I don't need to risk an audience."

Curious, I settle back on my heels for a moment. "An audience? Are you saying my presence made this happen?"

The flinch he makes turns my mind even more inquisitive, but I see his expression close off. Mother does that all the time. I've learned over the years that means not to push further, or there will be consequences. Silas isn't my mother. That doesn't mean I'm willing to spark the ire of a wild stranger from the woods who can *handle* himself.

I swallow down the ready question and find some antiseptic and bandages. When that's done, he tries to stand. I frown. "Don't even think about it. I'm not done."

Sighing, the hulking man settles back down. "I can guarantee the others aren't bad."

"Shirt off," I say. When he quirks an eyebrow, I feel myself blushing. "So I can see the wounds."

He chuckles and pulls the destroyed material over his head. Gasping, I feel my lips make a long-lived O shape. These are bad, so they aren't as okay as he told me. I touch the skin close to the big set of gashes in the center of his sculpted chest. The muscles twitch beneath my fingertips.

I look up at him. "These are worse than your face."

"Again, they aren't that bad. I've had worse. Don't you dare try to talk me into going to a doctor, or we're done here."

My mouth snaps shut on my urge to say just that. "Why are you so adamant on this?"

The only thought that makes sense is that he doesn't want to be found or recognized. While he may not have evil plans for me, something keeps him hidden in these woods. What secrets is he hiding?

"Don't look at me like that," Silas says.

"Like what?"

"Like I'm some giant puzzle you're determined to figure out."

I huff. "You are a puzzle, but lucky for you, I've never been interested in puzzles."

After I wet the rag in soapy water to dab at the mess of his very attractive chest, he says, "What are you interested in?"

"Getting home to civilization. Don't look at me like that. You may be fine living without the most basic conveniences, but it's not the world for me. Besides, you've already told me before that you're ready for me to leave and let you return to your peace. My occupying your space is simply a necessity born from bad decisions."

"Fine, keep your secrets."

I almost laugh. As if this man has the right to talk about secrets. He has an entire group of cougars after him for reasons he won't say. He hides away from the world in solitude and *peace*. He didn't defend himself to the fullest because of the risk I might see.

Yep. Silas has absolutely no secrets whatsoever. Me not wanting to talk about my real life has nothing on him, so he better get used to it.

For the first time, Silas releases a soft hiss as I try my best to clean a stubborn spot. Mud is embedded in the cuts, and I need to make sure it's clean.

"You seem to know your way around healing," Silas says into the tense silence.

"What I know comes from books and TV. I really am an amateur."

"I'll remember that for next time."

My gaze finds his. "Next time."

"I told you. They have a vendetta."

I let out a pent out breath and shake my head, dabbing at a part that's bleeding worse than the others. Once that's clean, I move to his arms. His legs are thankfully free of injury, so I don't need to ask him to take his pants off.

"Did I get everything?" I ask once all I see are clean.

Silas flexes and points to his shoulder. Standing, I look and flinch. A cat tried to bite a chunk out of his muscle. I bite back the desire to mention the doctor again. There's no way he can clean that himself.

"This bite is deep," I say instead.

"Cougars have long teeth."

Nodding, I go back to work, dabbing at the wound that goes from the top of his shoulder to halfway down his shoulder blade. This one must hurt because he twitches as I gently swab the mess clean. Once done, I use more antiseptic and bandages.

After the worst is covered, I move back to his arms and chest. Those go a little easier. When I'm done with his chest wound, my fingers trail down his hard torso, looking for anything we both may have missed. They find nothing, and I let them fall and glance up to lose my breath.

The look in his dark blue eyes is smoldering. My mouth grows dry at the intensity he gives me through his eyes. There's a hunger I've never seen before in them, and I find my entire body heating in response. Eyes locked on him, I lick my lips and watch his gaze follow my tongue.

That's when I realize that while I dropped my fingers, they're still touching his hard stomach. I jerk them back, stand, and turn away. "All done."

The falseness in my voice sounds rough to my ears. Silence stretches a little longer before he says, "Thank you for your assistance. I'm going to try to gather the wood I cut, then I'll be in. I will make some stew."

I spin back around. "What if they're out there?"

"Worried about me?"

"Well, yes. I owe you for saving my life, and I have no idea how to survive in this place without you."

Silas watches me as if waiting for me to say something else. When I don't, he only grunts and nods before turning for the door. "I'll be careful. I simply let my guard down last time."

The door closes behind him, and I find myself staring at it a little longer. What else could he have been waiting for? There is nothing more between us than a rescue and forced proximity to each other. The lingering warmth in my stomach reminds me that I felt something more than that before.

With a scoff, I turn and start cleaning up the mess. He'll need to get more gauze when the weather clears enough to let him. Nothing I think about distracts me from what just happened.

Did he want me? Something in me felt like it wanted him more than I've ever felt before. I shake my head. Living in the rustic woods must have put weird ideas in my head. He's not the type of man to be chasing. One, he's quite wild, which I'm embarrassed to say might be part of his appeal. Two, I know nothing about him. Three, I'll be leaving for my world once this is over. I know he won't follow me, and this isn't what I picture the rest of my life being.

I will say one thing though...

No one has ever looked at me that way before. I should be appalled that this rough man did, but I'm not. Not even close. Something in me feels wild in return. Part of me feels alive at the mere thought of letting order go and see what happens.

CHAPTER SEVEN
HEALED WOUNDS

SILAS

As the axe splits the wood on the block, something unknown reaches my ears. It was hard to hear when I was chopping, so I stop to listen. Straining my hearing, I focus it in all directions. Just when I think I was imagining it, a crunch in the snow sounds. It's faint, and I wouldn't be able to hear it if it wasn't for my inhuman hearing.

I turn, feeling something hit hard on my right side. That's when the scent hits me, musky and feline. I roll by instinct, coming up ready to fight. The next attack hits me head on. Grabbing it by the throat, I throw the cougar to the side.

There's no way I can fight them like this, so I yank my only coat off and toss it aside. I care less about my other clothes. Reaching down into myself, I feel the animal within. Before I can do more than locate the second part of me, I stop and glance toward the cabin.

The distraction is enough to allow another cat to sink its fangs into my shoulder. Teeth scrape across bone, and I find it difficult to hold back a quiet yell of pain. She can't come out here. She can't see this or be targeted. Worse, I can't properly defend myself from the attack in this form. Changing isn't an option with the chance she may look out and see me doing it.

That woman already fears and distrusts me enough.

Instead of continuing the fight, I dodge and deflect as much as possible, slowly making my way to the porch of my only shelter. I stumble when one rakes its claws across my face. The next one catches my chest. After many more minor injuries, I make it to the porch and burst through the door.

My eyes open to the view of the firelight flickering over the wooden ceiling. A glance at the flickering flames tells me that I need to add more wood soon, but I can wait a few minutes. Thoughts of the attack consume me after dreaming about it.

That felt close. Greta isn't part of this world and never will be. She can't know what really resides in these woods, what I am. I once lived in a world where hiding only worked with bullies. Everyone knew of magic and shifters. Not anymore.

The human world is so much different. They don't know what hides in their midst. If they did, they'd be scared of what they can never feel and understand. My father dealt with humans indirectly. His warnings served well to keep me safe and alive when I left.

How can such a small woman cause so many troubles? First, she breaks into my blessed solitude. I couldn't shift and defend myself for fear of discovery. I had to suppress my magic to keep her from seeing my fast healing long enough for her to finish her useless ministrations. She makes me feel things I shouldn't.

I'm not sure what happened yesterday. Her gentle touch stirred something in me I didn't know I had. Those soft fingers grazing my skin left fire in their wake, a heat that couldn't be cooled by the pain of my unhealed body. The discomfort of my arousal added more reason for me to go outside to cool off.

In that very moment, I wanted her. What is wrong with me? I find her annoying and weak. Why would my body want to lie with someone like that? She's human and not part of my world. I'm glad she pulled away because that would have been a monumental mistake.

I hear her rolling around in bed and sit up to see if she's awake. This couch is not the most comfortable, but at no point did I ever think that

I should make her sleep on it. Her sleeping form twitches in dream. She's still oblivious to the world.

Lifting my shirt, I look beneath the bandages to see smooth skin. Once hidden away, my magic took care of my healing quickly. That's one of the reasons I like where I have settled. Not everywhere has magic coursing through the soil, and I can't call my bear without it. I found a pocket void of magic and decided to live in it for a bit, forced to interact with humans. My bear has caused a lot of trouble, and I wanted to be rid of it. I went stir crazy.

This place, the magic is strong. I can feel it churning through the dirt and trees. That's also why the cougars chose to settle here. It's a prime location for anyone who depends on magic. I always wonder what disperses the power here. Not enough to go searching for it with enemies near. Once again, I wonder if I should move.

Shaking my head, I prepare to remove the bandages, stopping to look over at the tiny woman in my bed. I better not. Seeing my unbroken skin would only make her ask questions. While I no longer think about kicking her out to fend for herself, I can't reveal that part of me. I guess I'm stuck with useless bandages to hide healed skin. I can only hope that the weather clears enough to send her on her way. I'll take her to the nearest town because I need more supplies anyway. She can be home long before Christmas that way.

I hope.

It's best for her to be with her own kind and for me to be alone once more. I'm not accepted anywhere, not even where I was born. She has a family and friends that she needs to be with. The world of magic is nowhere for a human to be. It's best if she's gone as soon as possible.

That stirs a painful feeling in my chest. After so long in solitude, it's nice to have company, even with someone as clueless as Greta. I deserve to be alone, but that doesn't make it easy. I have missed interacting with others.

Greta's tiny body stirs, so I return to watching her. Slowly, those light blue eyes that remind me of ice covering a frozen pond open. She brushes her light blonde hair back from her face and sits up. I watch all this in a strange fascination. When she isn't talking, she's quite beautiful. Her eyes kept me entranced while she ran her fingers over my abdomen.

I grow hard, looking away to keep my frustration hidden. She's human. The only reason I'm reacting this way is because of my determination to hide away from the world. Having company is doing things to me. The snow needs to melt enough for me to get her car out of the pile she plowed into.

As I stand, I glance at her to see her arching her back in a glorious stretch with a huge yawn. Even more uncomfortable, I shift to the side and adjust the stiff rod in my pants to be less noticeable.

"I need to use the little girls' outhouse," Greta says, her voice husky from sleep and stirring something deep inside me. She warms a part of me I promised to leave frozen over. This can go no further. I'm encased in ice for a reason.

"Do you need me to come with you?"

"No. I can find it. Unless you're worried about the cougars."

"They don't tend to move around much at this hour. They're most likely hunted out and need to rest through the early dawn. It should be safe. Leave the door open and yell if you need me."

She glances between me and the exit. "Are you sure? That will let all the heat out."

I shrug. "Cold doesn't really bother me. When you come back and shut the door, the heat will build quickly."

Nodding, Greta slides from bed and bundles up to go outside to relieve herself. I throw a few more logs on the fire and look through my meager food stores. I've been keeping mainly to caught food and veggies, but we need a little something more. I still have some eggs and bacon I pilfered from the farm before the storm. It's not enough to satisfy two for long. Yet, a treat will be nice.

As I take a few eggs and a few strips of bacon out, I notice that I need to refill the box with fresh snow to keep things cold. There isn't much left in here to preserve, but it might be best to gather more. I close the box, grab a skillet, and take everything over to the fireplace.

I hang a rack on the bar over the fire. The skillet warms quickly, and I throw the bacon on it to sizzle and pop.

Greta returns and closes the door behind her. "Is that bacon?"

I glance back to see her hair a mess of light strands glistening with moisture. "Yeah. I had a little. Figured it would be a treat. Is it snowing again?"

"I thought you could tell the weather."

My attention refocuses on breakfast, turning the strips and getting bit by their grease. "Not from inside."

"No, it's not snowing. The wind picked up and blew some into my face. I've never had bacon before."

Startling, I look back. "Never?"

"Mother says it's a vile meat that clogs your arteries."

With a shake of my head, I pull out the eggs. "I've been eating bacon and eggs for my entire life. I can promise I'm in top shape." I don't add that I'm also magically healed, but that's not something she needs to know. "Indulging a little never hurt anyone anyway."

"You're definitely in shape," she mumbles at a level I think is meant to pass by me. My hearing catches it, but I let it drop. Too many questions might arise if she realizes I can hear that well. She continues on, "Doesn't it come from pigs? Are there boars around? I've heard those are dangerous."

"No boars," I assure her. "I bought some from a local farmer. Do you want some?"

I leave out the part that I didn't actually buy the meat as I crack the eggs next to it. The less she knows, the better. It'll all be in the past soon. The weather seems to be holding at sunny. Snow melts slower in the forest, but I can get her to her car by the time the warmth of the sun frees it. That's all that matters.

I check my bread to find green fuzz growing on it. With a grimace, I toss the moldy pieces onto the fire. My fault. I took the bread and forgot how much I love butter, so it was plain. Now I wish I still had it.

Greta watches me fry the greasy food for a bit before breaking the silence. "How are your wounds? I should change the bandages."

I cough a little to buy time and pull out two plates. Once the food is on them, I say, "I checked while you were out. They're fine for now."

"I doubt that. You were still bleeding. If they're dirty, you could get infected."

Oh, how little she knows. Infection doesn't touch my blood and never will, not as long as magic continues to flow through my veins. Besides, the wounds stopped bleeding as soon as they were hidden away enough for me to let them. She doesn't need to know that though.

"I promise, they're fine. I checked. We also don't have a lot in terms of first aid supplies. If I need help changing them, I'll let you know."

To emphasize my point, I grab a shirt to tug over my chest. I can't hide the one on my face, but that seems to work when she huffs out an annoyed "fine" while sliding into her chair by the table.

Her insistence to help me annoys me, so we both get to feel the emotion. I told her no, so that should be enough. Grunting, I slip into my own chair and slide her plate over. We eat in surly silence, and I'm reminded why it's better to be alone.

I don't need people to worry about me, and I don't need people to worry about in turn. Privacy is important. My boundaries are not negotiable. Melted snow can't come fast enough.

CHAPTER EIGHT
STALKERS

GRETA

I insist on cleaning since Silas cooked. It's not like cleaning is difficult here. Dishes remain few, and liquid soap doesn't seem to be an expected commodity for the hulking man. It turns my stomach a little, but it's not like I have a lot of choices in front of me right now. I can always get examined when I get home. Mother will most likely expect me to anyway once she knows where I've been.

That thought makes me flinch inwardly. The explanation for this will turn heads and increase tempers. A Parks woman spending however long I'll be here with an uncivilized man in a cabin that lacks basic hygiene means. This will be something Mother will fight to keep the public from knowing. She definitely won't tell Damian about it.

I frown. Damian. The man who betrayed me that I need to reconcile with to appease my most volatile parental figure. This is a huge mess without an easy situation. It's sticky to the point I'll be dealing with the consequences long after I'm home again. Can life get any worse?

"I'm going out to check the traps for lunch."

Startled, I jump and splash myself with heated snow. My hands feel greasy after the bacon, which I enjoyed much more than I expected I would. I wouldn't mind having it more.

"Can you wait until after I finish cleaning up?" I ask.

"Why?"

General curiosity infects his voice, and I realize what a terrible guest I have been. "I'd like to come with you."

When I speak, I can see him bending over to poke at the fire. My words make him jerk his head up and hit it off the rough stone. I wince and determine that I am definitely a terrible guest if my wanting to do something companionable with him causes him a concussion. The thought almost makes me giggle, but I quickly stifle it. I'm doing everything wrong.

Maybe I misread his growing friendliness toward me. "Unless you don't want me to."

Silas's wide dark blue eyes find mine. "No, it's fine. I just didn't think you'd want to go walking through the snow-covered woods with me. It's pretty hard to move around."

"Oh. I'd still like to come."

With a nod, he says, "I'll let you borrow my clothes. Yours need to be changed anyway, I think."

Taking my eyes off him, I turn toward myself and sniff. I do smell like body odor. No basic enmities also means no deodorant. Not only do I smell sweat but also the distinct scent of unwashed flesh. It's terrible.

"Can I wash before I change?" I ask.

"Sure. I'll warm some water while you finish there. Then I'll find some clothes and go out to cut some more firewood while you wash. We can head out when you're ready. Just come out and find me."

He does as he said he would and leaves. I dry the frying pan before moving to disrobe. I pause for only a second at the thought he might come bursting back in, but I don't believe he will. Silas seems to be a gentleman, if a little rough around the edges. Unless he gets attacked by cougars again, I'm safe from prying eyes.

I still wash as quickly as I can. The soap looks like a toothpick, but it's enough to get me smelling less like a cavewoman. Why does Silas smell musky, but I smell like death? I enjoy his scent on everything. I can clear a football stadium.

My hair causes some difficulties. I soak it as best as I can and use the tiniest sliver of soap to wash what I can from it. A hot shower and proper shampoo sounds like it should be the first thing I go in search of when I'm home. Mother will take one sniff and find me scandalous. That thought makes me giggle and makes me think I should force a hug out of her. I learned long ago not to hug her, but I can pretend that I'm so happy to see familiar faces that I can't contain myself.

The scene of my mother recoiling from her filthy daughter in public makes me laugh. She'd never forgive me. I let the fantasy fade from my mind, knowing I won't do such a thing. It's nice to think about though. A girl can dream.

Silas's sweatpants hang on my hips. I pull the strings as tight as possible, but they still hang loosely. The sweater makes up for it when it falls to my knees. If it wasn't for the snow, I wouldn't even need the pants. Although, he doesn't have underwear to replace my gross pair, so I'm commando at the moment. A slip may show too much without the pants. It still might when they fall down as I slide on the icy ground.

Oh, well. Nothing for it. I can't hide away in this cabin until the weather is agreeable. I need to get out to do more than relieve myself in a bucket over a hole. A walk will be nice, even with all the predators Silas mentioned. For some reason though, I feel safe around him. I've gone from fearing his nefarious intentions to trusting him to save me from a bear.

What does that say about me?

I push all the possible answers down. My shortcomings can wait until I'm forced to confront them. With a sigh, I forcefully pull my coat over the fluffy sweater that seems to want to keep bunching up.

Even then, my hands are covered by the ends of the sleeves. That's fine. The more protection the better.

The steady thunk of an ax biting wood brings me to the side opposite from the outhouse. I stop to see the metal wedge send the pieces of wood flying in two directions. This man is strong.

He notices me, wipes the sweat from his forehead and moves to stack the wood he split while waiting for me. The stack grows quickly. I want to be surprised at how much he cut and split, but I just saw how easily he did that last piece. What else can those strong hands do?

Blinking, I try to dispel the strange thought. I need to focus. That was a crazy thing to think. Silas saved me and is housing me until I can get to safety again. It's really not proper to be thinking about his hands in that manner. What is wrong with me?

"Ready?" he asks, breaking through my growing self-loathing.

"Yep. Where to first?"

"This way."

Hitching up his pants on my hips, I follow him into the snowy wilderness. The snow is deep, but he makes a path as he walks. Besides, the path between traps seems like it might be worn enough to keep me from getting too cold and stuck.

~~~

After trudging through snow for so long, I'm chilled too much for conversation. As expected, the path made from Silas checking traps multiple times a day makes walking easier than elsewhere. My toes are still numb, and even the long sweater can't help my fingers now. I'm scared to look at them. Not to mention how quickly pulling his pants up to a more secure position has become really annoying.

"This is the last one," Silas says into the silence.

Good. I'm ready to turn around and head back. Not that I'll admit that to him. This is important, and we need to eat. I'm out here at my
~~~

insistence, so I better suck it up and cope. This last one means we get to go back to the warm fire and a nice worn book.

"Got a squirrel," Silas says. The glee in his voice makes me smile.

I can't blame him for the excitement. All other traps held nothing but snow or blood. A few were destroyed completely. Each time he found blood or a trap made into a mess, he would look into the distance as if trying to find the free animal that left these traces. Each empty trap left me worried we'd go hungry. Luck at last.

Silas bends down to release the trap, tying the squirrel to his belt. As he stands, he turns his head quickly away from the path. My gaze follows his, and I can't see anything that may have grabbed his attention. Straining my senses brings nothing to be worried about. What is he looking for?

That's when I hear it, the sound of something breaking in the distance. Unfamiliar with the outdoors, I ask," What was that?"

His tense muscles belly his alertness. "A cougar stepping on a branch. We need to get home."

Thinking of how long it took us to get here, I tremble while following. "Will we make it?"

"We aren't far."

"But we were walking forever."

"Mostly in a circle," he says, motioning me to walk faster. "As we went around, we worked our way outward, but we aren't as far as it might seem. Walk quickly though."

"You make it sound like that's easy. You have longer legs than I do, and even following the path your giant feet make doesn't ease it more."

"Are you asking me to carry you?"

My shoulders stiffen at the suggestion. "Most certainly not."

"Then keep walking."

Another breaking branch echoes in the distance, closer than it was before. I startle, swallowing my argument and quickening my pace. The next crack almost makes me squeal.

"How far?" I ask.

"Almost there. Move it."

The tone of his voice sets my back straight. Who does this man think he is to order me around? I'm moving as fast as I can. What more does he want from me? I'm not letting him carry me, so he can get that thought out of his head. A Parks lets no man carry her. Mother would have a royal fit.

Another snap precedes a not so distant thump and crunch of snow. I force the whimper back and practically start power walking behind Silas. As I remember the wounds they gave the big man in front of me, my imagination goes wild. If they can do that to someone like him, I'm sure I'll get much worse. We need to reach safety, and we need to reach it now.

It's not until I run into Silas that I realize I can, in fact, move faster. The sudden impact forces a scream out of me, but Silas turns and covers my mouth with his hand. It muffles the sound but doesn't stop it. Even covered, my mouth makes more sound than I want it to.

Instead of berating me as I expect, Silas simply scowls at me, flips his gaze around, and turns to walk briskly away. I hurry after, my heart in my throat and my lungs begging to pull in more oxygen. I'm sure the large cats can hear my breathing, so I keep it shallow when I can't hold it outright.

The closer we come, the harder it is not to panic. The sounds come closer with each step. It feels almost like they're playing with us. I've heard of pet cats playing with their prey, but do wild felines act the same way?

Ahead, the square of light that is our window comes into view. I let out a deep breath of relief without relaxing. My heart races with the need to walk through that door and shut it between us and the predators stalking us.

At last, Silas's boots echo on the wooden landing of the porch. As he opens the door, the ratty wreath falls to the floor. He kicks it inside and motions for me to hurry. I almost dive through the door. He replaces the wreath on the outside, making me want to scream at him that it's unimportant. The door finally closes between us and outside.

"Take your coat off," he says, making me realize I've been standing and staring at the inadequate barrier for an indeterminate amount of time.

"I'm still cold."

"Your coat is frozen from the wind. Take it off and huddle by the fire with a blanket. I'll start gutting the squirrel. I assume it's okay for me to do inside?"

"Of course. I won't make you go back out to be attacked."

"Good."

Without sitting, I get as close to the flames as I dare, holding my hands out like I see the less fortunate do throughout the city. I need to be nicer to them if this is how they feel all the time. My fingers have no feeling.

Once I'm warm enough, I walk over to the window, carefully avoiding looking over at the gory table. I glance outside to see nothing out of the ordinary. Maybe we were imagining it. As I prepare to turn back to the fire, something catches my attention. A long brown tail disappears behind the closest tree.

CHAPTER NINE
CHOPPING WOOD

GRETA

The light fades above the trees faster than it does outside of them. It's the same in the city though. The skyscrapers block out the rays just as thoroughly, if not more, than the trees do. It might already look dark from my apartment windows.

The table chair I brought out to the porch squeaks a bit under my shifting weight. I have a book in my lap, forgotten and unread. It's another horror. Mother will not be pleased with my new hobby, but I feel myself drawn to it still. Something about this genre makes me feel better.

My eyes scan the trees, looking for any sign of the animals that were hunting us earlier. Silas assures me they're gone. Although, I'm not sure how he can be so confident about that. He didn't know they were there until we heard them. How can he know now?

It's my job to keep watch while he chops wood. Not that it's official or anything. In fact, I'm sure he'd laugh at the notion and talk more about my suppression of my natural instincts. He doesn't need to know I'm watching his back.

The wind has calmed, so while cool, the air isn't frigid like before. If we can have a few days like this, I'm sure I'll be able to get home soon. How I long for hot showers, television, my phone, and a heated bathroom. My butt is still cold from my last trip to the bucket.

A loud thunk brings me back to the subject at hand. I sit at the very edge of the porch, able to see Silas and the woodpile from here. He's coatless but wears a threadbare sweater. It does nothing to hide the rippling muscle beneath the flat fuzz. I lick my lips, feeling them instantly freeze and causing regret. That wasn't a good move.

I can't help it. Watching him move causes strange feelings to blossom within me. Don't get me wrong, I'm no innocent. But this is something unfamiliar. Yes, hot guys have driven heat into me. This is different. This feels almost feral.

Each twitch of his back as his strong arms swing the ax down sends new shivers over me. Each time the wood splinters and sails away in two pieces, an animalistic urge grows deep within. I can't explain it because it's such a foreign feeling for me.

Turned on is one thing; this is something else entirely. My body responds to each movement. My mind wonders what it would be like to lie awake in those strong arms. His musky scent must be so much stronger when close. I'd love to experience that.

Shaking my head, I force my eyes away from the large man chopping wood and triggering my desire. This isn't right. He's not a gentleman. Yes, he saved me. Yes, he's keeping me alive and returning me when the opportunity presents itself. None of that makes a gentleman. Mother told me that gentlemen open doors for you, buy expensive presents, and protect you from failure.

Opening doors? Not happening. Expensive presents? I almost snort. He protects me, but not from financial or PR failure.

Those answers should be enough for me, but I feel confused—conflicted even. Could Mother have been wrong? She never seems to any other time. She makes sure we all know how right she is.

So, why am I so confused by this man? He doesn't meet the description of the personality men like this should exude. Uncivilized? Most definitely. Unkempt? No question. Rude? Sometimes. Yet, he seems to respect my wishes, even if they exasperate him. He keeps me safe.

Silas doesn't fit into any category as I understand them. So, who is he really?

My eyes move back to his flexing form, letting my mouth go dry at the sight of his strong body moving. I should fear this man—I did fear him—but I don't now. Why is that? Am I really as stupid as Mother says I am? She's only been telling me I'm an idiot my entire life.

Silas drops the ax onto the chopping block and looks over at me. His elbow leans on the handle as his massive chest expands and retracts over and over. He really is something to look at.

"You don't have to babysit me," he says.

"I don't mind. It's not that cold now. Do you really think you should be doing this with your wounds?"

He looks confused for a moment before shaking his head. "If I don't do this, we'll die of hypothermia. Unless you want to try."

I look at the ax and pile of unchopped wood. "No, thanks. I don't think that would be possible. I have like a quarter of the muscle mass you do."

He smiles, making his eyes gleam that strange purple shimmer again. I must say, he really lights up when he smiles. It doesn't happen enough, and it takes my breath away as I watch it happen now. I'm starting to think it takes more than well-groomed and well-dressed to make a man something good to look at. He's rather beautiful under the roughness. I'm fascinated.

Silas turns back to his work, and I settle in to watch. My mouth makes conversation without warning me first. "Where's home? Like, where did you spend your childhood?"

His arms jerk at my words, throwing off his next chop. The edge of the ax hits the wood off-center, and it flies up and over the pile. Silas glances back at my shocked expression while he grabs a fresh piece. The other one is now lost.

"Up north," he grunts.

I purse my lips, but him turning his back to me tells me that's all I'm getting. Fine. I'll open up and see if he follows. "I've always lived in the city. I love this time of year. The white snow. The large Christmas tree in the park. All the lights everywhere. It's beautiful."

He laughs. "I've seen it. It's not that impressive."

"You've been to the city?"

"Once, but it was a huge mistake I'll never make again. Too many hu—people."

I cross my arms over my chest in challenge. "Oh yeah? Where have you seen better?"

"Home."

When I realize that's the only word he's saying, I sigh. "What was Christmas like at home?"

Silas glances at me again and slams the sharp edge into the wood before answering. "Bright. Lights everywhere. People caroling endlessly. My family lived for Christmas. You can say it ran in their blood. Compared to that, your city is no more than a dying stoplight."

I cock my head to the side and watch him split another log. My gaze travels back to the lone wreath on his door. It seems to be important that it remains in place to him, but there are no other decorations anywhere on the cabin hidden within snowy trees.

A frown takes over my face. "Seems this apple falls far from the tree."

Silas straightens, gazing at me with narrow eyes. After a moment, he catches my meaning. "I didn't like home. I don't want to be reminded of it."

"Why not?"

"Isn't important."

Sighing, I let my curiosity on the subject drop. That doesn't mean I'm completely done with this train of conversation. "Then why bother with the wreath if you hate it so much?"

"Can take the man out of the festivities but not the festivities out of the man."

I snort softly. A single wreath is considered festive? Does he even know the meaning of the word? Oh, well. To each their own.

"Did you celebrate a lot?" he asks after a pause.

"As much as I'm able. Mother keeps me pretty busy. She always had a big tree with lots of lights but not much else. There is no time for festivities on a large scale when there are so many more important things to do."

Silas casts another glance my way, leans his ax on the old stump, and gathers the wood into his carrying sling. "How old are you?"

"Twenty-six. Why?"

"And you're still doing as mommy tells you?"

He's smiling, but the tone of his voice sounds judgmental enough to raise my hackles. "You have no idea what it's like. My family expects me to act a certain way to bring the right attention to the Parks name. You don't know what it's like to have the pressure of such a lofty name weighing you down."

Silas laughs hard. "Shows how little you know."

"What?"

"Nothing important that you need to know. You can't always follow the rules of someone else. No one, not even family, knows who we are deep down, who we are meant to be. Just because they tell you who they expect you to be doesn't mean it's the path you should take. Sometimes, you aren't meant to follow in their footsteps. Sometimes, you're meant to forge your own trail."

He trudges past when I jump to my feet. My mouth opens, but I have no response that I feel is appropriate. He's crazy if he thinks I'm fated to be anyone but who I am. If I was, I wouldn't be a Parks. Shaking my head, I follow him into the cabin with my chair.

While I watch, he pulls some food out of the containers. He grumbles about being low on potatoes but digs out wild carrots and onions. A few strips leftover from the squirrel come out next.

So far, I've been nothing but a burden. Despite his obvious annoyance, this man doesn't push me too far from my comfort zone. Just because he doesn't need my help doesn't mean I don't feel useless.

"Teach me," I say as he puts everything on the table.

Freezing, Silas looks up at me. "What?"

"Let me help. I don't know how to cook because Mother told me that's a job meant for people with less importance." When he scowls, I realize my error and hurry on. "Not that I think you're less. It's just the reason she used. Teach me to cook, so I can help you."

He shakes his head. "Teaching you how to be proficient will take all the time you're stuck here, maybe more."

"Then help me be more independent. You say I shouldn't listen to everything my mother tells me. Maybe this is an easy place to start. I may not become some five-star chef, but I can take some tasks off your hands."

"If that's what you want. Want to try chopping carrots? I'll do the onions because they are more difficult to work with. Then I'll teach you how to saute everything together."

"Looking forward to it."

Silas drops a few wild carrots in front of me and hands me a knife. He shows me the best way to hold the knife, shocked that I don't even know that much. I feel heat rise onto my cheeks with embarrassment.

I push the discomfort away. This is what I asked for, so there is no reason to be embarrassed.

As soon as Silas starts chopping onions, I find my eyes burning. Soon, I can barely see through the tears. Pain bites into my finger. Crying out, I drop my knife and wipe at my eyes. My injured digit bleeds profusely.

"I'm going to lose my finger," I say with a yell.

Silas comes over to take a look. "It's deep but not quite that dramatic. I think I have some butterfly bandaids in the first aid kit that will work. Hold on and stop squeezing it like that. You'll make it wider."

By the time he gets back, the tears rolling down my cheek are from more than the onion vapor. Silas is gentle but firm as he cleans the wound, then frowns at the cut gushing blood.

When he pulls something else out of the kit, my eyes widen. "Is that glue?"

"The butterflies won't work with the way this is. We need to glue it first. This may burn."

I cry out and hiss in pain as he glues the two sides of flesh together. As he blows on it to dry, the pain lessens. It's not until I open my eyes that I realize they were scrunched shut. His lips are pursed right above the skin, mere inches from my finger.

For some reason, this view sends warmth trickling through me. Silas moves closer until I can feel the heat of his lips as well as his breath. I swallow hard, wondering how this man can have this effect on me.

Silas looks up, catching my gaze. His eyes widen at what must be a very interesting expression I carry. He stares into my eyes for a long time, color turning to a dark purple. I look at the lips that were drying the glue on my finger and wonder what they would feel like on my skin.

As if my thoughts bring the injury back to the front of my mind, a bad burn runs from the wound to my wrist. Moment gone, I suck in a sharp breath of pain. Silas quickly finds some pain relief ointment with disinfectant to smear over the cut, covering it with a bandaid. Clearing his throat, he stands to finish the chopping. I decide to watch instead of participate this time, looking over his work and wondering why I keep having these strangely strong desires for this rough man.

CHAPTER TEN
SHATTERED CALM

GRETA

A spider makes a web in the corner of the cabin furthest from the bed. I watch it weave its masterpiece, hoping it stays far away. While I respect its right to life, I don't want to wake to find it on my face. All eight legs work diligently, and I wish I had skill of that level with anything in my life. I always feel so awkward and dramatic.

My finger decides to choose this moment to remind me that I can't even tie a string right now, let alone weave a web. My gaze falls from our inconspicuous roommate to my throbbing digit. Silas assures me that it will heal well, but I worry about infection in a place like this. He told me a doctor wouldn't have done stitches. I'd still like to have one look at it. Stupid snow.

Not that I want to leave right now anyway.

A horrendous snore reminds me of one of the reasons why. I lift my head enough to see the back of the couch, one long leg hanging over the arm. How Silas can sleep on that thing, I'll never understand. It's not even that comfortable to sit on.

It's strange to think some wild stranger makes me wish the snow would stay a little longer. It makes no sense to me. I barely know this man. He was rude and insulting when we first met, and judgment still fights for dominance in his strangely beautiful eyes at times. How can I feel like he's pulling me to stay? Something about him makes me want to learn more.

How would his strong hands feel in the sensitive areas only men my Mother would approve of have touched? What would his tongue taste like? How would it feel to be pinned to the mattress beneath his bulging muscles? Does he make love differently?

Sighing, I push further into the pillow. Has anyone ever made love with me? Mother hates the word sex. She thinks it's vulgar and uncultured. If there is no love, how can it be making love? It is what it is. Sex.

I wonder if his version is rougher than I'm used to. That thought sends a thrill through me that leaves me questioning who I really am. I wasn't raised this way, so why am I thinking these crude thoughts? Visions of him chopping wood and blowing on my injured finger come to my mind.

Oh, yeah. That's why.

My uninjured fingers twist the blanket that covers me as I revel in those very graphic memories. Even the time where we ended face to face while I was bandaging him spends some time living in my mind. This man is everything I've been told to avoid, so why do I feel drawn to him?

Maybe that's the cause; I was told to avoid men like him. I've always heard of children who do the opposite of what their parents tell them, and I've always marveled at their courage. Then again, isn't that the reason I'm here now? I decided to grow a backbone at the wrong time.

Was there a better time? Damian slept with his boss while being engaged to me. His remark about other women not bothered by his straying makes me wonder who else he was sleeping around with. The bigger question pushes its way to the front of my mind.

Who sent me the video?

Whoever did it must have really wanted to ruin Damian's life. Or they wanted to save mine. There I go, being dramatic again. Mother would have a fit if I said something like that. Our union was best for the two wealthy families. I would have had more than I could have ever asked for, so much luxury.

A glance around my currently humble abode makes those words ring less true. Sure, I could use running water and electricity, maybe a good medical facility, but is it really that much better? Sure, there is no material luxury to be had. There could be other kinds of luxury.

Like privacy from paparazzi trying to find their next story to twist for the drama-loving citizens. More control over my life. Freedom to do as I want. A man who doesn't see some kind of opportunity out of spending time with me.

There's no doubt about it; Damian was all about opportunity. No love was ever possible, no matter how I once wished it might be in the future. It was simply a profitable deal that he went along with to ensure rising in his father's business. Love doesn't stray like he did. That was probably yet another opportunity Damien recognized and snatched.

I'm not sure when I decided so, but I deserve better than a husband who sleeps with anyone. How would Mother handle the PR once his affairs were exposed? There's no doubt they would be because he's in the news as the biggest business sensation to come. She would've blamed me for him straying.

My thoughts sour. Could she be right?

Snoring rises in pitch, and I lift enough to look at the back of the couch. Now, one of his arms hangs over the back of it. That cannot be comfortable at all for such a large man. I'm beginning to feel guilty for taking his bed. It's big enough for two, but can I control myself if my thoughts keep going in this direction simply by looking at him from a distance?

My eyes find the spider in the corner again. Web finished, it seems content to sit in the very place the walls and ceiling meet. Contentment is something I've never felt. Maybe the spider is right. I need to understand that home is not where I am told to reside but wherever I want to make it. That's what Silas seems to do, and he seems happy for it.

Birds tweeting pull me from the slumber last night's thoughts dragged me into. Strange dreams dissipate slowly, giving way to the reality of my current environment. I stretch, loving the feel of my spine straightening out and my muscles loosening as always. With a yawn, I sit up to find Silas reading a book. The novel that would be huge in my hand looks like a pamphlet in his.

"Outhouse," I say, slipping out from under the blankets and pulling up my borrowed sweatpants.

"Need company?"

"Nope. I feel confident I can find my way and back. I'll scream if I'm attacked."

"I'm sure you will. Just keep your eyes open."

After bundling up, I let myself out into the wilderness. Around me, all is still. The birds chirp in the trees, but nothing else disturbs the peace within the forest. As far as I can see, it's calm. I run around the side of the house and let myself into the makeshift bathroom to relieve myself. Once done, I stand in the fresh air and take it all in.

The snow really is beautiful when I'm not ramming my car into a pile of it. The world sparkles outside the paths we've worn into the white blanket with our comings and goings. Sunlight brings a glimmer that isn't ever evident inside the city. I'm sure the snow and ice would have already been taken care of the morning I woke up here. Only dirty slush would have remained, and then only for a day or so.

Here, it still hangs from branches. Although, it's currently dripping, which makes some very impressive icicles. They only add more beauty. Living in the city all my life, I never got to experience life this way, live in a world of glitter. Even our cabin trips were highly sheltered.

Instead of returning inside, I decide to walk around the cabin a bit. Thanks to the warmth brought by clear sky, much of the snow is melting. I traipse through the thinning layer with much more ease than before. For a moment, I consider letting Silas know I'm going for a walk, but I shake my head instead. I'm not leaving sight of the cabin.

I need not have bothered with the thought. As I walk along the trees in the back, Silas circles around from the front. "There you are. Are you alright?"

"Yeah. It's almost warm out here, and I wanted to take some time to enjoy it."

"Okay. Need company?"

"I wouldn't push the offer away."

He falls in beside me for a few moments of silence before speaking. "Snow's melting."

I hum an agreement and enjoy our peaceful companionship. Not long ago, I feared and distrusted the man that saved my life. Now, I enjoy his companionship.

When I don't say anything else, he continues. "We may be able to reach your car soon."

Stopping, I look up at his dark blue eyes, looking for the purple I sometimes see in them and consider what he's saying. "Do you think my car will be free soon?"

For a brief second, he looks uncomfortable. He brushes the emotion away with a shrug and looks to the sky. "That was a large pile you drove into, but it should melt enough that I can get you out soon. As long as the weather holds, of course."

His voice sounds sad, which makes no sense. I thought he wanted his solitude back. That's what he told me when I first woke in his cabin anyway. Does his heart conflict around the inevitability of my departures as well? I almost snort at my fantasies of him wanting me around. I'm nothing but trouble, so he's probably sad he can't make me leave right now.

"Go for a walk?" Silas says after a bit.

I laugh. "Isn't that what we are doing now?"

"I'd like to show you something."

"Okay."

Shocked when his warm hand wraps around mine, I look up to find his eyes almost purple again. He gives me a smirk that makes my heart stutter. "For your safety."

I have to try twice to speak. "Of course."

Without hesitation, I walk where his hand pulls me. While rough, it feels good enough that I wrap my fingers in his without looking to see his reaction. In his presence, I feel safe. Nothing can get to me. Holding his hand somehow enhances this feeling.

We walk for a while in silence until he brings me to a clearing with a small pond. My eyes widen at the sight. "I had no idea this was here."

"We didn't come this way when looking through the traps. It's one of my favorite places to sit and think."

My fingers loosen around his as I step closer to the frozen pool of water. He releases me, but it feels reluctant, which makes me want to scoff again. I'm seeing things I want to see—feel in this instance.

It's not large, about a hundred feet across or so. Frozen solid, the surface reflects the light from the sun. It's surrounded by trees of various sizes, covered in white. When I look up, I can see old birds' nests frozen in the branches.

"This must be absolutely beautiful in the spring," I say with wonder.

"Even better in the fall."

"I bet."

A sound I'm beginning to recognize as branches breaking echoes on the other side of the pond. Instantly alert, my gaze travels toward where the sound came from. When I see or hear nothing, I look to Silas for reassurance. His handsome features seem to be straining, and he cocks his head to the side. The look on his face turns to anger. The snarl on his lips completely changes the beauty of his face.

"Move," he whispers.

"What is it?"

"Cougars. They're always watching me. I should have known this would be a bad idea. Move."

I turn to follow our path back while he watches behind us. Each sound is closer than the next. I try to run, but Silas holds me back, telling me how dangerous it is to run from a predator. A sharp growl makes me yelp and turn around to see the line of cougars coming out of the trees between us and the small pond. Silas pushes me behind him and adopts a protective stance. I can't help but clutch the back of his shirt.

CHAPTER ELEVEN
THE FRIGHTENED FAWN

SILAS

The cougars stop not more than ten paces away. My entire body tenses with the need to shift and fight. There is no way we will make it back to the cabin with them this close. Glancing around shows me that they're not moving in. They simply wait. For what, I'm not sure.

Greta peeks out around my back, earning a hiss from the one in the front. I snarl back at the feline. Protective instincts are kicked into overdrive, and I won't let a single claw harm a blonde hair on her head.

I feel my muscles strain against my sweater. Forcing my change to halt is difficult. Something primal in me wants to attack. Something feral will rip these cats to shreds to keep the woman behind me from their jaws. They won't have her.

As one takes a step closer, Greta clutches my shirt tighter. Her fear is so strong I can smell it, making the shift harder to refuse. If I don't get her out of here now, she'll know what I am. I can't let her know the magic that exists in this forest. She has to get out of here.

"Run," I growl.

"Excuse me?" she whispers back.

"Go."

"I am not leaving you. Besides, you told me running would get me killed."

"It's me they want. So far, they haven't tried to flank us. If you go now, they'll leave. I'll block any that decide to try to slip past."

"I can help," she says with a stubbornness that makes me force the next growl down.

"How? With what weapon? They're not tiny house cats, Greta. These are vicious predators that will rip the flesh from your bones without thought. I'll be fine. This isn't the first time I've gone against a group of them. I know what to do."

While she fights with the decision to listen to my advice, I do my best to sound confident that I can, in fact, take this group. It's larger than most of the groups they've sent to kill me. I don't want to hurt any more of them. Why can't they just let me be?

"Fine," Greta mumbles, almost too low for me to hear. "But we are going to have a talk about why these cougars are after you when you get back." She takes a few steps and pauses. "You better make it back."

The pain and determination in her voice stiffen my back worse than the cats already have. I want to risk a glance back at her but know that's not a good idea. The minute I turn my head is the minute I feel claws dig into my back. I wait and strain my senses to hear her until I can't any longer.

Digging my feet into the crushed snow, I prepare to transform. Stripping would be best to keep her from asking awkward questions, but there is no time for even a quick removal of clothes. This isn't some playful romp in the woods.

Before I can do as I wish, a man dressed in jeans steps from the trees. I grimace at Ande with a growl. If the leader of their group is here, he means business this time. I know just how strong this shifter is.

"Silas, I've been looking forward to a visit," he says with a growl in his husky voice. "You've been evading this talk for too long."

"Talk," I say, ready to release my inner animal the moment it's needed. "That's funny because it never feels like a peaceful visit when your furballs are chewing on my neck."

Ande smiles, a cynical lift of the corners of his mouth. Two fangs are already protruding behind them. Powerful shifters can start the shift but not complete it until ready. I don't have the ability to shift that far without completion, but I fill my body with the power, feeling the animal strain against my human side. Any further, and I will lose control completely.

"Cute female you have with you. She's as skittish as a young fawn, isn't she? Have you tasted her yet?"

I can't hold the growl back, ready to bite his face off at the mere mention of Greta. I rein it in to keep my feelings hidden from my enemies. It seems I'm not successful. Ande smirks, devious and predatory.

"She's simply a human that I saved from freezing the night of the storm. She will be heading home as soon as her car is cleared enough to do so," I say with as much detachment as possible.

"The way you stepped in front of her? The way you reacted to my threat? There's more there. Who are you trying to fool? I can smell the feelings on both of you. Storm, huh? Moving quickly."

I bite my tongue to keep from showing my hand. Part of me wants to revel in the fact he smells emotions about me on her, but now is not the time. Cougars have a greater sense of smell than the hybrid in me. Again, now is not the time.

Ande chuckles at my silence. "Why don't you just give yourself to our justice? Maybe we'll let her live."

"Justice or vengeance, Ande?"

"Is there a difference?"

"I've always thought so."

Instead of answering, Ande's muscles ripple with the shift. I call my power forward, letting the bear take over. As much as my animal is a hybrid, it looks bear enough to be considered one. Not like these kitties know anything of my past. Massive paws with razor claws replace my hands as my muscles twitch and twist to accommodate the transformation. My head expands, sharp teeth leaving the taste of blood on my tongue.

As soon as it's done, I let out a ferocious roar of rage. It's cut off when the first cat hits me. Teeth tear through my thick fur, ripping into the flesh of my shoulder. I growl and bite the cougar's flank, tossing it into a tree. As mentioned earlier, I don't want there to be any more blood on my hands, but I can't lose this. Who knows what will happen to Greta if I don't return?

Two more hit me from behind, climbing my tall back with sharp claws. The cougar that is Ande holds back, watching and assessing how his kill squad works. I'm sure he'll find any weak spots and do what is needed to fill them in to throw them back at me again.

When he notices me looking, his lip lifts to reveal a fang in warning. Pain in the back of my neck keeps me from reacting. Another is rushing at me, but it flies away when I hit it with one massive, clawed paw. Dropping back to all fours, I flop to the side and roll. The two on my back jump away before they can be crushed by my superior weight.

One of those that were on my back stumbles, and I use my claws to open its back leg. With a yowl, it wobbles away. Triumph is short-lived when the other pounces. It digs its teeth into my head, scraping my skull. When it hits the bumps I hide under the hair by my ears, it jumps away in shock. I use that momentary lapse to snap my jaws over a front paw.

Crippled, it hops away, leaving a trail of blood through the snow. Three more overwhelm me together. From what I can see, this is all, except Ande. He still waits for the outcome, now sitting with his tail wrapped around his front paws. The king cougar doesn't see me as a threat, so he waits and watches the skill of his fighters.

A bite sinks into the lower section of my back leg, causing me to almost collapse. I twist to reach for the cat, but it dodges away, leaving me open for another set of claws down my other shoulder. My back paws move as if trying to get away from the pain. Another cougar trips me. My foot steps on a tail, and it can't get away before I fall on top of it.

That still leaves two, and a patient Ande who could end this at any time by joining the fray. There's no way I could take him on top of these two when I'm bleeding as badly as I am. The two remaining cats jump on top of my prone form. One gets too close to my face and loses an ear for it. As it tries to yank away, I hit it with my claws.

My last opponent rakes powerful back nails into my stomach. I roar in pain and try to rip the cat from my body. It dodges and bites into my flesh. There is so much blood matting my white and brown fur that I can't tell which wound is the worst.

After more struggling, I'm able to knock my assailant off me. This time, it jumps at me, and I'm able to hit it hard with my paw. The final cat stumbles to the side before falling unmoving in the snow. Its chest still moves up and down, so I won another battle without death.

Turning, I stare down at Ande from my greater height. He cocks his head to the side but doesn't move out of his relaxed posture. Their leader yawns at me, his whiskers twitching. While staring at me, he slowly stands and sends me the best sneer he can from his cat face. As if to say I'm no threat at all, he shrugs his furry shoulders, turns his back on the bleeding bear, and walks away with his back hips swaying.

He doesn't worry about the injured members of his assassins because he knows they'll heal and return home. Their wounds are much less than mine. I'll heal as well, but I can't do it here.

Swaying, I push onto all fours and take some time to just breathe for a bit. The movement makes me realize that there are some deep scratches in my sides as well as everything else I actually remember hurting. The first step is agony, but I'm able to make it. Then the next. And the next.

Blood leaves a trail behind me. It's not like I need to worry about predators seeing it. My greatest enemy already knows where to find me. Why did Ande let me go? What is his angle? What do I need to wait for?

As I draw close to home, I slow. I'll need to shift. Taking a deep breath, I can smell her here. She's alive, but that's all I can tell. Unlike the cats, emotions aren't detectable to me. Happy humans smell the same as frightened. Angry the same as calm. I take a moment to enjoy simply knowing she's still alive before doing what I need to do.

This is going to hurt because my body will not want to transform with the bleeding wounds plaguing me, but these wounds will take time to heal. Each bone breaking and each muscle reshaping send agony through my body. I try to hold in my roar of pain, but that only makes it worse. It feels as if my entire body is being torn to shreds as I change. By the time my shift is done, I feel like an eternity has passed by.

Lying in the bloody snow, I let the frigid cold of the padding numb any wounds it touches. I take deep breaths to calm the raging fury within me. Why can't they accept that I mean no harm? Why can't they understand it was an accident?

After a quick moment of self-pity, I stand with great effort. Stumbling forward is harder on two legs. Somehow, I manage. Seeing Greta waiting for me on the porch is enough to make my struggling heart beat even faster than it already is.

Her glacial eyes brighten at the sight of me before widening. "Where are your clothes?"

I look down to see the nakedness I forgot in the midst of my agony. "Cougars tore them to shreds."

"Oh! You're bleeding so badly."

"I'm fine," I say with a grunt as I take the first step.

She helps me as best she can, her so tiny versus my largeness. "You are not fine. Let's get you to the couch. I'll do what I can. You need a doctor though."

"No doctors."

"Silas..."

"No!" Momentary strength forces the single word from my mouth with so much force Greta takes a step back. For a second, I regret yelling at her, both because of her fear and the pain my body uses to tell me to take it easy.

Gasping, I let Greta move me toward the couch with mutterings calling me all kinds of words that are synonymous with stubborn. I don't care. A doctor isn't a possibility for me. I'll heal on my own, without giving up the secret of shifters. I don't make it to my couch, collapsing onto my knees halfway.

Why am I still alive? These wounds won't kill me, only hurt for a while. Is he torturing me? Will he drive me to the edge of death, only to let me heal and do it again? That's when Greta drops to her knees in front of me. "Silas?"

"Oh, no. It's you."

"Well, that's not very polite. Wait, why do you look so frightened? What about me?"

"An eye for an eye," I whisper, confusing her further.

CHAPTER TWELVE
HIS BED

GRETA

Getting Silas onto the couch isn't easy, and I can see lots of new stains being added. It doesn't matter. It's not like I can go back out into the cougar-filled snow to look for a tarp. This is as good as it gets.

The wounds covering his body are grotesque, making me unsure that I can do anything to help this time. Any thoughts of asking for him to see a doctor stay inside after the way he exploded when I asked earlier. It's been a while since I feared this man, and I felt it worse than ever then. He was like a wild beast in his defiance of outside help.

Fear of him dying replaces that of his earlier anger. What if I can't keep him alive? I can't survive out here alone. The cougars probably will pick me off quickly without him to protect me. I'll starve. The only thing I know how to do is cut carrots, and my bandaged finger tells me that's not enough.

I take a moment to step back and take in his panting form, skimming over the large appendage between his legs. There's nothing small anywhere on this man, and I file that observation away for later. I should throw it out completely, but I've proven that I don't always do what's best or smart. I'm sure I'll review this sight with a little less gore later.

After taking stock of all his injuries, I place a towel over the log between his legs and go in search of more bandages. My first instinct is the first-aid kit.

"Are these all the bandages we have?" I ask, eyeing the very inadequate supplies we have left after the first attack and my carrot accident.

"Yes," he grunts. "It's fine. I'll heal."

"No. You'll bleed out. And if you don't, you'll end up with a nasty infection. You really should let me help you to—"

"No! No doctors. I will not negotiate with this, and asking will only anger me."

Jumping at his harsh tone, I brush away the fear it brings to level a glare at him. "I'm not skilled enough for this."

"Then leave it be."

A quick glance at him shows me he'll die if I don't help in some way. He probably will still die if I do because I'm not a doctor. "Then you'll die."

Dark eyes look at me, devoid of any hint of blue or purple. The sight makes me shiver, but I don't back down. Silas grits his teeth and speaks through them. "You are not taking me anywhere. There's no way you can without my cooperation anyway."

Huffing, I grab the meager bandages and walk over to him. I look through all I need to do and choose the gashes at the base of his throat to start on first. I'll bandage the larger wounds, then see what I can do for the rest. Not much more I can do.

"Maybe I'll wait until you pass out and go in search of help on my own," I mutter beneath my breath.

Silas must have excellent hearing because he grabs my wrists. "Don't you go outside. It's too dangerous."

My fingers still over the bleeding skin below his throat. Terror replaces anger from this bear of a man. In response, my heart stops. "We've gone out before."

"Not now. It's too dangerous. Promise me!"

I want to argue, but something in his voice stops me. Silas is terrified of me going outside. "Why?"

"Why can't you just promise me?"

"I need to know what has you so anxious. How much danger am I in right now?"

"None. I will protect you from the cougars."

My lips press flat in annoyance. "And if you die from your wounds?"

"I won't."

Exasperated, I pull my wrists free. "That's not good enough because from where I'm standing, you're knocking on death's door right now. Don't you dare act like this is going to be alright. You can't see what I can right now."

"I know my body."

"Obviously not that well. Why am I in so much danger?"

When Silas tries to stand to avoid this conversation, I push him back down. We both look surprised when he plops back down without a fight. I know I'm not strong enough to hold him in a place he doesn't want to be.

"They have a vendetta," he says after a bit.

I move toward cleaning and bandaging his wounds. "They're animals."

Frustration makes me less than gentle, as shown by him jerking away from my touch. I simply glare at him, then hold him still. When I run out of bandages, I find an old tee shirt to tear up.

Silas refuses to respond to my further prodding, the skin beneath my fingers becoming paler and paler. "If you die, I won't survive."

"I'm not going to die."

How can someone's voice be both gentle and annoyed at the same time? He somehow manages it, and I don't dare look into his eyes.

Some of these wounds need stitches, but I'd probably only make it worse with my lack of homemaking skills. Tears of fear and frustration fill my eyes, and I stubbornly wipe them away, probably leaving a trail of blood on my face.

Shaking hands grab my chin and pull my vision to his bandaged face. The gashes in his scalp are particularly worrisome. "I'm not leaving you. I promise. Rest is all I need right now."

From the way he's swaying, I can tell he's telling me half truth. He needs sleep. My issue is wondering if he's going to wake up. At this point, I doubt I could even get him anywhere fast enough to save his life. The helplessness of this situation brings more tears to my eyes.

"Let me rest," Silas says, trying to collapse on the too-short couch.

I grip his bicep to keep him upright. "Wait. At least take the bed."

"I gave the bed to you. I'll be fine. Besides, the couch is covered in my blood. You don't need to sleep in that."

"Nonsense," I argue. "It's big enough for both of us. You stay on your side, and I'll stay on mine. This couch is too small for you during a regular sleep."

"Fine," he says.

When I help Silas to his feet, his body leans forward from the blood loss. I grit my teeth and support some of his weight on my shoulder. Together, we stumble him over to the mattress. I flip the covers back, let him climb in, then pull them up to his chin. The man is out within moments.

For a few minutes, I simply stand and stare at his prone form, trying to drink him in while I can. The hopelessness of my thoughts becomes too much, and I release a light sob while biting my lip to try to keep from disturbing him. It's not just fear of survival scaring me. It's losing him altogether. Sure, I'll be leaving soon, but I can't fathom him dying.

What am I going to do?

Shaking myself, I purposely turn away from him, which is harder than it should be. I return to the couch and survey the mess. One step at a time, I pick up the packaging for the supplies I used. Extra shirt strips go next to the washing bowl for me to use to clean him when he wakes—if he wakes. I take a deep breath and push the dark thoughts away.

I should be trying to think hopefully, but I can't find it in myself to do so. Not after what I saw. Those wounds are too vicious. Unable to think anymore about it, I feel myself let the tears spill over and sob. I'm as quiet as possible, but I cry it all out.

All the fear from the cougars catching us in the woods. All the pain of seeing Silas in agony. The feelings of being helpless. And finally, the grief.

It all spills down my cheeks, into the hands covering my face, and onto the floor. I know I barely know him, but I don't want to lose him. If he makes it through this, I won't act in a hurry to leave anymore. I swear this to myself and to the sleeping man that fights for his life while I weep on the floor. Regrets flood through me. Not just putting myself in this position, but also the regret of being in a hurry to leave this man behind.

A soft snore pulls me from my misery. At least he's sleeping. I can only hope the slumber ends. Standing again, I stare at the couch and decide it's a lost cause. I put what's left of our first aid away and return to the bed to look down at him. Silas sleeps so peacefully.

As if to prove me wrong, he twitches, which produces a pained moan from his throat. Grimacing, I look away. Even asleep, he's in pain. Not that I blame him with how bad the wounds were. Touching his face doesn't bring healthy warmth. Cold, clammy skin meets my fingers instead. That's not good.

At least, I think it's not. Once again frustrated, I growl and walk to the other side of the bed. This is ridiculous. I'm not a doctor. I'm not even sure I did what I did for him right. For all I know, I did something terribly wrong that will kill him. How do I always put myself into these kinds of situations? This might be the worst one yet.

Silas jerks and rolls to face me. He mumbles and yelps in his sleep, obviously lost in a nightmare. How could he not? After what he's just been through, it's to be expected to have bad dreams. Awake, Silas is a formidable rock. Asleep, his guard releases. He does fear.

Feeling oddly embarrassed to be witnessing what he probably sees as a weakness, I walk over to the window and look out. Shadows stalk the trees, despite the fact that it's still early enough to be brightly lit. There is no doubt in my mind about what's out there.

"You're lucky I don't have a weapon. If I could, I would..."

I would what? Get shredded to pieces? Run away screaming like a little girl? Even Silas can't take on a group of cougars; his current state proves that. I wouldn't last twenty seconds before I'm ripped limb from limb. There's no vengeance to be had.

With a huff, I move to the table to get a drink of water, gulping it down quickly. I turn back toward the bed. Silas kicks softly and whimpers, still struggling with slumbering demons.

It's still early, but the events of the morning took a lot out of me, so I slip into bed on the other side. Once settled in, I place a hand on his uninjured cheek. Hope that he heals quickly assaults me, making me disgusted at myself for ignoring reality to live in fantasy. I push it all away.

My touch seems to calm him, so I leave my hand on his face. The pained lines around his eyes soften, and he stops jerking and moaning. If I can give him this little comfort after my absolute failure as a medic,

I'll do it. It's the least I can do, considering all the times he's saved my life since I got here.

Not that I believe the cougars will attack me just because, as he seems to think, but I don't trust wandering the wilderness alone with them in it. They definitely seem rabid, which gives me a new worry. Can they get rabies? If he survives this, will the rabies take him?

I shake my head against my pillow. This should be the least of my worries because his likelihood of survival doesn't look promising. If he dies here, I probably will as well.

In more ways than one.

CHAPTER THIRTEEN
QUICK HEALING

GRETA

Snoring pulls me from a slumber I didn't realize I fell into. Blinking brings focus, but I remain confused about my surroundings for a moment. Memory returns, and I let out a soft sigh. I'm not home in my peaceful apartment, dodging calls from my mother. I'm snowed in a cabin in the middle of the wilderness by a man I'm beginning to look at as hot and sweet.

My eyes find the window to see the sun is still up. This much sun must be good for melting the snow. My heart falls when I think that, and I have to fight to remind myself that this world isn't mine. I didn't grow up roughing it, so I'm nothing but a liability and an annoyance. It's best for me to return home.

A strong arm wraps around my waist, almost causing me to squeak in alarm. Another snore tells me that Silas is still sleeping. It's not conscious thought that causes him to spoon me. My mind goes over ways to mitigate this position while my body longs to stay in it.

My body wins out. Instead of pushing him back, I snuggle into him, and I'm rewarded by a tightening of his embrace. How can a man who feels like he's made from stone feel so good against my body? This feels perfect, like it's meant to be. I could lie like this all day.

I try to shake those thoughts away without disturbing the man pressed against me. The snow will be melted soon enough. I can't get lost in those ideas. Soon, I'll be home, and Silas no more than a distant memory. Why does that make my chest ache?

Silas' hips press further, making my eyes widen when I feel him poking into my backside. I also choose this moment to remember he's naked. For a moment, my imagination gets the better of me. While trying to avoid looking yesterday, I managed to steal a few glances anyway. His entire body is beautiful from head to toe. His cock may have not been hard, but it was still quite impressive.

I've never been with anyone that big. What would it feel like to be so full? My body shivers at the imaginings, and I press further again, no longer caring what's wrong with me. Silas groans through the next snore, making me feel warmth pooling between my legs. What would he do if I reached around and grabbed it?

No, that's not a good idea. Silas doesn't look at me as anything but a nuisance, even if he's better at hiding it than when we first met. I'm not stupid enough to think his hard-on has anything to do with me. This is just how men are when they wake. That doesn't mean I can't imagine; I just can't get myself too riled up.

As if hearing my thoughts of possible assault from the woman in bed with him, Silas rolls away. The loss of his warmth against my back causes a grief I didn't expect. The snoring gets even louder, but I long to have him back against me. Maybe if I pretend to be asleep, I can cuddle him without him getting upset.

Rolling over, I take some time to peer at him without making my move. The color of his face looks much better, no longer looking like he's on death's door. My brows scrunch together in thought. There's no way he has healed that much yet. He almost died.

Careful not to disturb him, I touch his cheek with cautious fingers. He turns into the touch while still snoring, giving me a better feel. I pull away, shocked. He's warm, but not the heat of fever. It's almost like he's all better.

I reach up and touch the bandage over his shoulder. Stopping, I wait to see if he stirs. When he doesn't, I lift the patch hiding what I know is a grizzly wound. My mouth drops open. Less cautiously, I lift another.

Shocked to my core, I jerk back and put distance between us. I take it too far, falling from the bed with a squeal. By the time I regain my feet, Silas is standing by the bed with a wild look in his eyes.

His gaze falls on me. "Is there danger?"

My hands are shaking as I twist them in the sweater I borrowed from him. "It's not possible."

"What's not possible?"

Ignoring the question, I go over what I saw in my head and what I remember. Silas was barely alive when I laid him down, and I figured he wouldn't wake again. Despair had taken me. I felt lost and hopeless.

How is this possible?!

"You're healed already," I gasp. "There's not a scratch on you, not even from the previous attack. Everything is completely healed over. I didn't realize your old wounds were gone because I was so worried about the new ones. How is that possible?"

Fear threatens to take over, and all my willpower goes into not running into the wilderness as the sun sets. Who knows what might be outside besides the cougars. Well, I don't even know what's inside with me right now. I never should have let my guard down.

Silas winces; whether from the fact his secret is out or from the fear I feel, I can't fathom. This isn't right. No one heals that fast. How is he even standing right now?

"Greta, please calm down. I'm not going to hurt you."

"What the hell are you?" I ask, making him wince a second time.

"I can't talk about that with you because it reveals the secrets of others besides myself. Please, trust me."

"How can I trust you?!"

"You did before."

I roll my eyes. "That's before I knew you are whatever you are. No one heals like that. I thought you were dying!"

I am not sure which of the two statements at the end makes me more upset. He takes a step toward the end of the bed, and I take one toward the door. My movement makes him go limp like a very large deflated balloon.

"Greta..."

"Don't! Don't act all sad that I figured out you aren't normal. You've been lying to me. What are you?!" I feel like a broken record repeating that question, but it's one that I desperately need answers for. How much danger am I in now?

"I can't go into details, but I can tell you that magic exists," he says.

I laugh but stop when I realize he isn't joking. Swallowing, I give the exit another glance, wondering if I'll be better with the cougars than in here. Magic can't be real. My eyes move over his naked torso to remind me he's giving me proof just by standing there.

That's when it hits me. "You're going to sacrifice me."

Confusion creates lines in his forehead. "What?"

"You said magic made you heal. Don't you need like my blood or life force or something? You know, a sacrifice."

Silas almost looks amused beneath his caution. "Not that kind of magic."

"What kind then?"

He sighs. "Can we sit?"

"I'd rather not. Since you're not bleeding to death now, you can't use that as an excuse. Please put pants on." I'd rather stand because I want the route to the door open. He doesn't need to know that because then he'll expect it. Surprise is my ally.

Silas does as I ask, leans against the wall and rubs his hand over his face. "The world is infused with magic, Greta."

"Prove it?"

"You've just seen my super healing. Do you really need more proof?"

He's got me there. Frustrated, I fold my arms over my chest but keep my feet ready to run. "If it's infused, why don't I heal like that too?"

"As I said, I can't go into details. Not everywhere has magic, and those that weren't born with magic can't access it. Those born with magic still benefit from any pocket they move to. I'm one of those people."

This time, I do laugh. "That sounds like a fairytale. How do I know you're not going to kill me for learning your secret? This is just a ruse for me to let my guard down."

When he stands straight again, I take two more steps backward. "There's more, but I can't tell you without jeopardizing too much. I have no intention of killing you. I wouldn't hurt someone I feel such a strong sense to protect."

Protect. Okay, he's got me there. He could have let me die of asphyxiation in my car. He could have left me to the cougars. I truthfully believe Silas won't hurt me because he's had many chances to do so. That doesn't mean I trust him anymore.

Something in my posture must make Silas think I'm no longer a flight risk because he walks toward the end of the bed to turn toward me. My body tenses, ready for flight. When it comes to fight or flight, I'm definitely choosing to flee.

He stops again, sadness turning his eyes a darker blue. "I'm sorry I kept secrets from you. I didn't trust you either at first. Our world must stay hidden for us to remain safe. Please, accept that I don't plan on doing anything to you."

"Stay hidden? As in, kill any normal person who finds out?"

Silas sighs. "No! I'm not going to hurt you. All I ask is that when I get you home, you don't tell anyone."

"Like anyone would believe me. My mother would have a field day with that one. I can just imagine the publicity and my punishment for causing it."

His eyes darken, frightening me. He holds up a hand. "Don't be scared. I'm not mad at you; I'm mad at the woman who makes you live in fear as you do."

"I don't fear anyone but you right now."

"You know that's not true."

I bare my teeth at him, mostly because he's right. Mother scares me no matter how far away she is. "What can you possibly know about me? We've barely spent any time together."

"I can see it in your eyes every time you speak of your mother."

"My relationship with my mother is none of your business."

"You're the one bringing her up," Silas argues. "Granted, you do it less than when you first got here, but you still do—multiple times a day. That woman lives in your head, and her attitude toward you holds you down."

Every fiber of my being wants to argue with him, but he seems too good at reading people to believe me. Instead, I clench my teeth and speak through them. "Take me home now."

"Your car isn't going to be free yet."

"Then I'll go myself."

Silas moves faster than expected. He's in front of me in seconds, holding my arms with gentle hands. I pull away from him but don't make any more moves toward the door. I have a feeling I won't make it.

"I thought I wasn't a prisoner," I say.

"You aren't, but I can't let you get yourself killed. The cougars aren't the only predators out there. It's not safe."

"It's apparently not safe in here either."

He makes to reach again but stops halfway. "You're always safe with me."

"I can't trust you! I don't even know who or what you are! Do you think I'll trust someone who heals like you do and keeps secrets from me?"

"No, I don't, but I can't tell you more. It's going to be dark soon. Your car might not be free, but I can walk you to the closest town. Please, wait for tomorrow. The darkness is more dangerous than the forest during the day."

I want to argue. I want to rage. Most of all, I want to be out of here. I can do none of that because he's right. Going out into the forest during dark isn't smart. Defeated, I say, "I still don't trust you."

"I know, and I'm so sorry. I promise any additional secrets have nothing against you and don't put you in danger."

For some reason, I doubt that. How can he say that? Everywhere seems to be dangerous, even home. Resigned, I grab my horror book and return to the bed. Silas asks if I'm hungry, but I shake my head. I can't believe he thinks I can eat right now.

Tomorrow morning. I just need to wait for then. Once I'm in town, I'll call my mother. For once, I don't fear her reaction. If it means I'm out of these woods, I'll be happy to get yelled at. This ordeal is almost over.

CHAPTER FOURTEEN
CHANGE OF PLANS

SILAS

Greta snoozes on the bed with the book on her chest while I sit on the floor and feed wood into the fire. I glance over at her again, watching a sliver of drool slip from the corner of her mouth. Apprehension fills me, accentuated by the wind whistling through the door frame.

A storm is hitting again. I promised Greta I'd lead her to safety tomorrow, but this storm may make that impossible. We're in the mountains, so the snow tends to pile up quickly. The sun rising isn't going to go so well for us.

I turn back to the fireplace and jab the smoldering logs with the poker. The weaker ones beneath collapse, sending sparks into the chimney. I set the poker down and stare into the flames, mourning the loss of companionship I didn't know I wanted.

Greta's company has brought out something I didn't know I still had in me. Hope. The need for socialization. Happiness.

And I'm losing her because of what I am. Not that this isn't something I'm used to. The whole reason I'm wandering the world is because I'm different. Just when I feel again, it's taken away from me for the same reason. I should be angry that she's pushing me away like anyone else, but I can't blame her. I don't belong anywhere, particularly not with her.

I bury my face in my hands and take a deep breath. Complacency causes pain. I know this and still let it happen. People don't like those that are different from them, which humans do better than anyone else. My own people wouldn't accept me, so why would she? Why would a human not fear me and want to be away as quickly as possible?

It's not like I can tell her everything. That will only bring more questions I dare not answer. The world of magic and shifters is not for humans. They'd never understand it. It would only bring danger to those like me. Even what I told her may cause trouble.

This is impossible. Greta has every right to want to get away from me. She can't trust what she doesn't understand, and I can't tell her enough to make her trust. This is one giant mess. Taking her home is the only remedy. Her car might not work, but she can find a way home in the town to the south. If only the snow would stop.

The sun should be coming out now, but the snow still hasn't stopped. I can feel the end in the air. Too late now because I can also feel all the fresh snow lying on the ground. Greta will not be happy.

As if summoned by the thought, I hear little noises coming from behind me. Taking a deep breath, I prepare myself to give her the bad news. It's best to wait until she's fully awake, and it gives me more time to think. Not that the last few hours gave me anything but that.

I've been too busy trying to find reasons for her to stay that aren't dependent on the weather. That's as hopeless as wishing the weather to turn favorable again.

Greta slips from bed. "I'm going to use the outhouse, then you're taking me out of here." I turn and open my mouth, closing it when she glares. "Don't even try to argue. You promised me!"

She's out of the cabin before I can think of the best way to mention the weather. Screams of frustration reach my ears. I'm about to stand to check on her when she stomps back in, the snow caked up past her knees. Her scowl burns a hole straight through me.

"The snow's back!" she yells, slamming the door shut.

I spare a quick thought for the fact that she didn't go to the bathroom but hold back bringing that up. I'm sure she'll make her way there once done yelling at me.

"I don't control the weather," I say. "I promise to take you as soon as the paths are passable."

"What paths? There are no paths in this forsaken forest."

"There are, but they're really far away. I know these trees like the back of my hands."

She stomps the snow from her pants and points a finger at me. "You also said you could tell the weather, but you still promised. You tricked me!"

"I didn't trick you. The storm moved in quickly after you fell asleep. Before, I couldn't sense anything because there were other things to worry about, like the attack and you finding out what you weren't supposed to know."

"Don't you dare put this on me."

Exasperated, I find my voice rising. "In what world does what I say imply that?"

"You fought with me, so you missed it. I've been told everything is my fault all my life. I can tell when I'm being gaslit."

"I am not your damn mother, Greta. My promise was sincere. There's nothing I could have done about the storm. Why can't you understand that?"

"Because everyone always tells me what I should do and how I should do it. I thought you were different, but I guess I was wrong."

She turns and stomps out the door. I flinch when the door slams again. It must have been one time too many. A thump and her shriek tell me she just got hit by snow from the roof. I take a few deep breaths to calm myself. Greta is so lost in the way others treat her that she can't seem to understand I'm not the same. I'm not blaming her for anything. The circumstances simply haven't worked out for what she wants me to do.

Standing, I decide to keep myself busy. I hang the pot over the fire and add some melted snow. Our squirrel is almost gone, so I'll need to check traps again soon. I throw what's left into the water, pull out some carrots and our dwindling supply of potatoes. They won't last much longer.

I grunt, wondering when I started thinking of my things as ours. Maybe this is for the best. She belongs with the other humans, and I only seem to bring danger to her. It's easier to just feed myself. I'm sure she won't like the fact that a lot of the food I have didn't come to me from ethical means. I'm better off alone.

By the time she returns, the potatoes are peeled and in the process of being cut. Greta glances over at the table, grabs her books from the bed, and moves to the corner furthest from me. She slips down the rough wall to the floor and opens the pages. I find myself missing her attempts to help, even if the last time ended with her being hurt.

I glance at the bandaged finger. That should probably be changed because she got my blood on it, but I don't have the nerve to bring it up. I go back to chopping and putting everything together in one pot. Once that's bubbling away, I stir it and take my seat in front of the fire.

Another glance tells me it's not just my blood that's saturating her bandage. After a short debate, I decide it's best to mention it. "You should change the bandage on your finger. I can help."

She shoots me an angry look. "That simply isn't possible. Your fake wounds used up the last of the bandages."

"We have more shirt strips. And my wounds weren't fake."

"Whatever. They aren't there now. No, I don't want your help. I can do it myself."

Standing, Greta moves over to clean the wound on her finger. Even from here, I can tell it's bleeding again when she removes the bandages. I feel guilty knowing that the bleeding is because of me. If she didn't feel the need to help my wounds heal, she wouldn't have reopened it.

"Do you need me to glue it again?" I ask, trying to get through to her that she can depend on me still.

"It's not bleeding that bad, so it's fine. Not everyone is used to their cuts closing quickly, but I do know that I'm not in any danger from this little bit of blood."

The anger and sarcasm mixed in her voice makes me sigh. I turn back to the stew for another stir. I wish I had something else to offer her. I've heard upset women like chocolate. I haven't had any kind of candy for years.

Once done, Greta returns to her book. She continues to cast glances at me that range from angry, to curious, to fearful. I can only imagine the conversation she's having with herself in her head. Probably worse than mine. We sit in silence until the stew is done.

"You have to be hungry," I say, spooning out two bowls.

I can see her debate about whether she needs to eat or not, glad when the hunger wins out. My heart aches when she grabs her bowl and goes back to her corner to eat. With a deep breath, I walk over to the table to sit down. The stew is a bit bland with fewer vegetables than I usually use, but it will fill us up.

The silence gets too loud. "You know, we are stuck here until the snow melts again. The best we can do is at least be civil."

"I'm not yelling at you. That is civil."

As much as I don't want to admit it, she makes some sense. That doesn't mean I'll accept it. "We have to share the same space until I can get you home. The best thing would be to at least act like you don't hate me."

"I don't hate you—much—I don't trust you anymore. I don't know who you are, and you won't answer questions. That's enough for me to keep my distance. I'll be out of your hair as soon as you get the weather right and get me back to civilization."

The stubborn set of her jaw tells me that I won't win this argument. "Hate or no hate, we can still be civil."

"What more do you want from me? I'm trying my best not to freak out and run out of the cabin. That is all you'll get from me."

Giving up, I forcefully shove another spoonful into my mouth. Fine. If she doesn't want to talk, there's nothing I can do about it. Greta is stubborn and childish. I guess that's what happens when you're handed everything you could ever want. Maybe her mother isn't really that bad. Maybe she's just spoiled.

With my next bite, I let out a huff. That's not fair. I'm pushing my anger into judgment. She may be spoiled, but it's clear her mother is a terrible person. That doesn't give her the right to treat me like this. They aren't just my secrets, so why does she feel entitled to them?

When she finishes her bowl, she grabs mine while ignoring my protests and takes them to wash. Guess she still does want to help. It'll just be done without talking. She returns to her corner.

Despite the fact that I have a bunch of wood chopped already, I head outside to do more. I need physical exertion to work off my anger and hurt. I've done so much for her, but she still doesn't trust me because of one secret. I guess I should be glad she is staying in the cabin and not running into trouble that I'd need to bail her out of.

That doesn't mean her treatment of me doesn't produce anger. Losing myself in the repetitive rise and fall of the ax melts away some of the tension in my muscles. I pretend each piece of wood is a different annoyance and obstacle, then chop it in half. Perfect representation. Try to shrink one annoyance, and it simply multiplies.

Not once do I look up and search for any hint of the cougars. If they want to cause trouble, they can go ahead and try me right now. I dare them.

CHAPTER FIFTEEN
FROZEN DINNER

GRETA

The snoring doesn't wake me because I haven't slept. It's still dark out, but it has to be close to morning. Doubt battles with my hope for light. Not sleeping tends to make the night much longer.

I can't believe I fell asleep before. How could I do that with everything going on? I went from reading my book to waking up. Everything going on surely forced exhaustion upon me, but I should never have closed my eyes while alone with him.

Magic. For most of my life, I never believed in it. It's a thing of fairytales and myth. Silas is making me a believer. How can he heal that quickly without magic? Humans can't heal from life-threatening injuries in a matter of hours, so there is something else at play here. Genetic enhancements could be a pliable reason. His muscles definitely make it seem possible. Much more plausible explanation.

So why would he go with magic if it wasn't true? This is stupid. Why am I actually considering this?

Because you saw it with your own eyes.

Snoring covers my groan as I rub my eyelids. If he hid something this big from me while living in the same cramped cabin, what else might he be hiding? Other secrets may be worse, and I don't even know the full extent of this one. I could still be in danger.

Yes, I'm angry, but fear is the emotion that clouds all others. This isn't normal; none of this is. I need to get out of here, and I need to do it now. Who knows what will happen next, what secrets will come to bite me in the ass. Dealing with my mother is safe. Mother is predictable, unlike this situation. How can I predict what I can't know?

Slipping from bed, I make up my mind. Silas snores away, covering any noise I might make. I slip my coat over my arms and cover my hands with gloves. Next, I cinch my hood as tight as it will go over my face and lace my boots over my ankles. Cold air blasts me as I crack the door, so I'm careful to only open it as much as needed for me to squeeze through.

Once surrounded by the frigid air, my determination falters. It's so cold. Maybe this isn't such a great idea. No, I need to get out of here before I find out what the consequences of this strange magic are.

But which way?

I spin while shoving my gloved hands into my coat pockets. My nose already threatens numbness. Okay, that way leads to his pond, so not going in that direction. Behind the house leads to the furthest traps. There's only one way I can think of going. Turning right, I start walking—or shuffling.

Every few steps, I glance at the sky in hopes that it looks a little lighter. It does not, increasing my frustration and annoyance. Bright and warm sunlight can't be all that far away. The snow isn't as high as the last storm, but it almost reaches my knees. A little warmth would be welcome to both dispel the freezing and melt the snow a bit.

My hopes go unanswered, so I continue to trudge along. Everything below my knees burns, not protected at all by Silas's sweatpants. My teeth chatter with a violence that hurts. I haven't even been out here that long.

I need my car, or the road. One or the other will do. There's the possibility my car isn't salvageable, but a road will lead somewhere and might put me in a position to be spotted by another person. I can only hope I'm going the correct way.

The wind picks up, as if it wasn't terrible to begin with, throwing snow into my face and making me stumble. I wobble and curse before falling to my knees. The snow is now up to my waist in this position. Frustration strains against my will to continue. The only other way is back, and I'm not that desperate yet.

Pushing myself to my feet, I glance around to make sure I'm still heading in the right direction. Walking becomes more difficult the further I go. My nose is no longer the only issue. My entire face is numb, and tears from cold eyes freeze on raw cheeks. I keep going.

Gasping, I lean against a nearby tree to regain my breath. I can't tell how long I've been out here and would kill for a watch, but the sky is still dark. No stars tells me clouds may be delaying daylight. Wouldn't the sky still look lighter in one direction if the sun was rising?

Maybe it wasn't as far into the night as I thought it was. After a few deep breaths, I decide I better head back. I'm clearly nowhere near the road and needed to go a different way. I wonder if Silas has noticed my absence yet. He was snoring pretty hard when I left. Magically healing must be exhausting.

I grit my teeth and consider continuing my numb journey into nothingness. That way surely leads to death, and pride isn't worth killing myself over. I'll take any scolding he gives me, hoping that's all he does in retaliation for my defiance. Who knows what a man that can heal himself from the most grievous wounds is capable of. Time to find out.

Going back should be easier because I've already made a path. I only make it five steps before I freeze and listen to an eerie howl in the night.

Please, tell me that was the wind. It has to be; it's windy enough to be. I take a few more steps.

The howl picks up again, this time from a different direction but still in front of me. There is no doubt in my mind what it was this time. That's not wind. Wolves.

And they're back the way I came from. Going back will surely mean my death, so I turn around and continue trudging ahead, looking for any kind of shelter that may help me continue to live. All frozen limbs are forgotten in my hurry to get away from the hunters that may be stalking me.

I continue to hear them as I use my shins to plow the path ahead. They come from all over, behind me and to the side, and they're getting closer. I no longer doubt who their prey is. Another solution needs to be found.

My eyes scan the dark forest, finally seeing a tiny brightness difference ahead. Nothing presents itself for my survival, making me pick up my pace. The issue with walking through a snow-covered forest involves the fact that I can't see the ground, a point that makes itself apparent once again when my foot catches a root.

If my face wasn't already numb, it would be now. Gasping, I push myself up, snow melting on my tongue. My hand finds something beneath the white blanket obscuring my visibility of the ground. I dig furiously with frozen fingers.

The object I desperately grasp is a large branch. I almost throw it away in frustration—I don't know what I was expecting—but I stop with my arm still braced behind me. It may be a stupid branch, but it is still the only weapon I have, so I let my arm come back to my side. Grasping a low branch beside me, I pull myself to my feet. The next howl sends me forward again.

A tree would be a good idea. Wolves are like dogs, and dogs can't climb. With the little feeling I have in my lower extremities and my fingers, neither can I. Instead, I keep moving as fast as I can in the deep fluff that's making a nuisance of itself. I need to find somewhere to hide.

A shape blurs between the trees beside me, slowing my feet while I look for what I think I saw. Snow crunches behind me, and my heart picks up its pace. My feet follow my heart's lead. I'm practically running and stumbling on numb legs. Sharp barks and yelps surround me. It's hopeless.

Desperation fuels me, but it may not be enough. As I push forward, a furred body brushes my hand, making me yelp and pull it away. The wolf disappears behind the trees beside me again. I wonder what they're waiting for.

Are they playing with me? Are they testing me? What are they doing?

As if hearing my internal monologue, one jumps out in front of me. I skid to a stop, my fingers tightening on my branch. The animal in front of me growls and raises the fur along its neck. It lunges.

I swing, hoping I have enough of an aim to at least put up a fight before becoming a meal. The yelp coming at the same time as the jarring sensation in my arms leads to relief. The wolf stumbles back into the trees. When no more attack, I assume this was to test my defenses, and start running again.

Howls pick up around me once more. I'm completely surrounded. A weight hits me from behind, and a sharp pain pierces my shoulder. I scream and somehow manage to roll the weight off me. The wolf that was on my back comes for me again, grabbing my hand in its jaws. I cry out and sob.

My branch is a little ahead of me. Reaching through the snow, I wrap my unencumbered fingers around the only weapon I have and twist with all my strength. Wood connects with skull, and I'm able to pull my hand from its jaws. It lunges again, but I get it with the pointy end this time. The wolf leaves a trail of red spots during its retreat.

Growls echo around me, and I fight to find my feet again. More move in closer, but my feet carry me forward. Agony throbs through my aching hand and up to my elbow. I try to find some way to put distance between me and the predators stalking me. They remain too close.

That's when I see a large boulder ahead, wedged against a tree with another trunk leaning against it. The sight gives me a new surge of adrenaline. A wolf passes in front of me, tripping me, but I manage to keep my feet.

I grasp the fallen trunk and try to climb up it on all fours while holding my stick. A wolf barrels into my side, spinning me around the rough log that holds my only salvation. I scream and wrap myself around it. I almost fall but manage to scramble back upright.

Shaking, I hug that fallen tree like my life depends on it, which it does. I slowly climb to all fours. Panting catches my attention, and I notice another wolf launch itself at me in time to flatten. The animal digs claws into me without finding purchase. This kicks me into gear.

Almost falling multiple times thanks to my numb limbs, I manage to scramble the rest of the way. The boulder appears beneath my downturned face. I clamber onto it and stand. It's not terribly high, but it might just be enough. Enough to what? Give me a vantage point to freeze from?

Holding my branch out in warning, I spin and watch the wolves surrounding me. One thing's for sure, they aren't letting me down without tearing me apart. The branch shakes in my grasp. Why did I come out here alone? Why did I risk it when I knew how dangerous it was? I stupidly convinced myself that the sure danger I know of is better than the unknown within the cabin.

And now, I'm going to pay for it. "Go away! Leave me alone!"

The wolves' ears twitch back, but they make no move to depart. I chuckle. As if that was going to work. Now, I'm stuck between a rock and a hard place, on a freaking boulder. Freeze to death or feed the wolves. I should have stayed with Silas.

CHAPTER SIXTEEN
UNGRATEFUL

SILAS

I jerk awake, unsure of what pulled me out of my slumber. The cover I used to hide the bloodstained couch bunches with my movements and falls over me. After I clear my face, I sit and listen, all senses straining hard. I'm about to give up and go to sleep when I hear the noise that must have woken me.

"Wolves," I mutter.

Other howls answer the first, and it sounds like they found prey to chase. Oh, well. Wolves deserve to eat as much as any other creature in this world. Shrugging, I snuggle back down. I hate how deep wound healing saps my energy. I feel like a real bear in need of some deep hibernation.

I should mention the wolves to Greta. Even if they're chasing prey, stragglers won't mind attacking her if she's using the outhouse. As I consider doing that, the exhaustion tells me it's not important. She won't go out in the dark.

Will she?

She is pretty upset with me, and I know she's back to not trusting me. It's not like I can do anything about that. I'm not sure what else I can tell her that wouldn't expose more than she can handle. This mess is too much. I should go back to sleep.

When the next howl comes, my anxiety rushes up. I better tell her. She's never gone to the bathroom in the dark, but there's a first time for everything. Greta would never survive the wild without me because she's too much a city girl. Besides, her anger might trigger pride that won't let her wait to ask me to escort her to relieve herself.

Mind made up, I groan and sit with a yawn. The bed's empty. Full wakefulness washes over me, and I jump up from the couch. My eyes scan the small cabin, not finding her hiding in any of the corners. She wouldn't.

How sure are you of that?

I have to admit, I'm not sure at all. This woman is stubborn and way over her head. If those wolves find her, she'll be torn apart in seconds. There's no way she can hold them off. Muttering a few long curses, I burst into the cold without thought for slipping on more than my shoes. My bare chest tenses as the icy wind touches it, but only for a second. I grew up in much colder than this.

Scanning the snow tells me she did not head in the direction of the bathroom. Her footprints lead away from the cabin, deeper into the woods. When another howl rends the air, I panic. Please tell me she isn't their prey.

I dash into the trees, following her tracks. Slowing part way in, I try to decide my actions. If I find her, I won't be able to shift in front of her. Wolves aren't any easier to fight than cougars, and I don't need more wounds to freak Greta out. But, if I go as a bear, she won't see me shift, and I'll be able to take on an entire pack if needed.

Decided, I strip and hide my clothes in the branches. Once on four paws, I follow the trail once more, sniffing and listening for any attack. A stray wolf would think twice about attacking a bear, but cougars may take this advantage to finish me off.

My clawed feet eat away the distance at a fast lope. I stop when I realize that the path isn't straight. Greta seemed to walk one direction for a while, then veers off. She's getting further and further from the cabin, just not in a straight line. Does she have any idea what she's doing? Was she lured out here?

I sniff the air, continuing to follow her trail. No other scent assaults my nose, so I know she wasn't being tracked. A little further, I begin to notice paw prints in the snow as well as her footprints. This is where the wolves found her trail. She *is* their prey.

Furred paws carry me even faster. I can hear yelps and growls in the distance, and I hope with everything I have that they aren't victory noises. Please keep the wolves from killing her. I'm not sure who will hear my pleas, but I can't help but ask for help from the inevitable. If only I would have woken with the first howl instead of trying to go back to sleep. Every second counts.

When I draw close to the sounds of snarling canines, I slow. I look through the trees to decipher what's going on and come up with a strategy that will hurt the least. The wolves circle a large boulder, growling and snapping up. Glancing in the direction they're focused, I find Greta standing on top of the large rock with a branch in her hand. From this distance, I can see blood on the end of it.

I guess she isn't as helpless as I thought, but she still needs to be saved. Shivering tells me she's already cold. If she goes too numb, she'll fall right off that boulder. A glance around gives me a direction of attack that will cause the most damage before they turn on me.

Running straight for two younger males, I bowl over one and dig my teeth into the shoulder of the second. The first receives a back claw to the skull that cracks bone. Two wolves down, plenty more to go.

I turn to place my back to the rock right when another attacks. I manage to knock this one down with a powerful swipe, but two more hit me from different sides. Pack animals strategize too well together. I can't fend off two attacks from opposite directions.

Teeth penetrate fur as I turn in the opposite direction to take out the other wolf. A third hits me the second I turn away from the rock. When a stick knocks the one off my back, I send a quick, grateful glance up to Greta. She may seem like a helpless doormat, but it looks like there's more to her. I curse her mother for beating her down until she hides her strength. There's no doubt about the fact it's her fault Greta's inner fire is contained.

Spinning, I throw the other wolf attached to me into a tree. The third hits me again, and I manage to squish her against the rock. She yelps, lets go of my fur, and drops. A swipe to the face takes her out for good. These are regular wolves, so I feel less apprehensive about fighting for keeps. It works, and the rest of the pack starts to retreat.

One straggler remains. He snarls at me, hackles raised. I roar my fury in return, causing a second of hesitation from the canine in front of me. Only a moment because he's then lunging at me, and he's fast. My oversized body can't dodge in time. My claws barely miss him.

He's on my back before I can follow with a second attack. His teeth attack my spine, but he can't get proper purchase through my fur. Still, it hurts. Greta reaches down with her stick again. This time, she misses and tumbles from her perch. I can't break her fall and fight this predator off at the same time, so I hope that she remains unbroken.

Landing causes her to cry out in pain, which feeds my fury. This time, I roll. The wolf jumps off me to avoid being flattened before going for the weaker target. Greta screams, and I leap into action, grabbing a furred tail in my jaws and pulling.

The canine yelps in pain, then turns his fury on me. His rage is no match for mine, and I pin him with my claws and tear his throat out. The fight in my final enemy dies as his blood stains the snow red. To keep from frightening Greta later, I release enough of my magic to heal my wounds while fur hides the action.

She stands, stumbling a little on her one leg. "Please, don't eat me."

I chuff at her and shake my head. This woman cannot trust a good thing when she sees it. If I was hungry, I'd eat the dead wolf in front of her, letting her run off in peace. To show her, I nudge the body of the predator in her direction.

"No, thank you," she says, misunderstanding the action.

When I huff my annoyance, she jumps, so I sit to show that I'm no threat. Communication is much easier in human form. How do I tell her she's safe?

Greta doesn't give me the chance to figure it out. "Thank you for killing the wolves, Mr. Bear, but I should be moving on. It's a little cold out here without fur."

While keeping a close eye on me, she circles the boulder with a frown on her face. She looks confused and frustrated. "If I can figure out which way I need to go to find my car."

Irritation at the statement makes me growl, startling her again. I feel less guilty about her reaction this time. Why can't she trust me when I tell her I'll lead her out? Well, I'm not doing it now. Climbing to my feet, I watch her cringe.

I turn toward the cabin and look back to see her watching me. After a few steps, I stop and look back again. Greta still stands in the same spot, uncertain. How do I get her to understand? It's not like I can shift right now. I take a few more steps and swing my head to indicate she should come.

"Oh, you want me to follow you?"

Relieved that something got through, I nod. Hesitating a short moment, she takes a few steps. I take a few more as well and glance back to see her following with a little more confidence. I don't need a cougar sense of smell to know she's afraid of me, but at least she's listening—for once.

With a limp, Greta trudges behind me. Instead of following her crooked path, I lead us straight toward the cabin. By the time we draw near, I can tell her ankle is paining her. I hope it's merely a sprain and not a broken bone. Sprain, I can help. Broken bone, not a chance. Since she's able to walk on it, I'm going to guess it's a sprain.

When the cabin comes into view, she groans. "Back to where I started from."

I growl my own frustration out, causing her to hold her hands up. The increased fear on her face annoys me. I swing my head toward the cabin that she rejects, hoping she'll get the point that it's safest for her there. Greta glances at the lightening sky and nods.

Careful to stay out of reach, she walks around me, then continues while still facing my direction. When she trips over the step because she's looking at me instead, I snort amusement. Serves her right for not trusting me. I wait until she's inside the cabin, looking out the window, to turn back for the trees.

To keep her from knowing where I'm heading, I return the way we came from, keeping my hearing out to listen for her trying to run again. I circle around, shift, and pull my clothes out of the tree I left them in. Dressing in the snow is never easy, so I throw more annoyed grumbles her way for letting her distrust put her in danger and put me in this situation.

Why can that woman not understand that I mean her no harm? Because of her unfounded suspicion, Greta put us both in danger, hers almost fatal. It's dangerous out in the forest in the dark for anyone, even a predator. She could have gotten herself killed.

Fury builds in me. So far, she hasn't tried to flee again yet, so she's still waiting inside. Wait until I lay into her for her obstinate stubbornness and ungratefulness.

CHAPTER SEVENTEEN
SURVIVAL

GRETA

I watch from the window as the strange bear returns to the trees. I'm not sure what kind it is, but I'm not very versed in bear species. It's white, like I think a polar bear would be. That's all I know. I'm pretty sure a polar bear wouldn't be here though. Besides, it had some brown shadings to its fur as well.

It's strange that it led me back here. Why would it do that? Does it know this cabin? Maybe Silas feeds it.

Oh, my. Silas. Spinning, I look at the couch to find it empty. He's nowhere in the cabin, which means he must've woken up and found me gone. As much as I don't trust a man that heals like magic, I hope the wolves didn't get him.

I look out the window again, finding his tracks in the snow, right beside mine. He followed me out into the wilderness, so it's possible he found the wolves too. Despite my anger at him, I worry about Silas's safety. He's taken on cougars; surely wolves wouldn't pose a challenge. If he comes back in here covered in more grievous wounds, he will get no sympathy from me. He can heal on his own.

Not that he needs me. I don't need him either. The only reason I'm back here is because I followed a stupid bear. Why would a bear know where I wanted to go? It was stupid of me to follow it. Although, it's a pretty smart bear to get me to follow it and bring me back to shelter. Wonder if there's a circus in the area.

That doesn't matter, and I shouldn't take my mind off the subject at hand. Silas needs to learn that he can't keep me hostage like this. He should have let me go without following. I hope he did get attacked by wolves. Would serve him right for not letting me be.

When I see him walk out of the trees, I move to the table and sit. I won't show him that I'm upset over him, but I will let him know my displeasure that he thinks he can control my life. He better be ready for this discussion.

The door opens, admitting the large shirtless man. He opens his mouth to say something I can tell I won't like, but my shock beats him to it. "You went out in the cold without your shirt?"

He stutters to a stop, staring at me in confusion. "What?"

"Why would you go outside without a shirt?" My entire argument derails by a set of hard abs. I watch his chest move with the deep breath that comes with an emotion I can't tell because his face feels miles away. The only feeling I get from this moment is a heat in my core. The snow melting and running down the grooves between muscles isn't helping one bit.

Why was I mad again?

"I went out without a shirt because you left in the middle of the night to put yourself in danger," Silas says, cooling my heat.

Oh, that's why.

"You aren't in control of my life, Silas. No one is?"

"No one? You seem awfully rushed to follow your mother's orders."

"That's not fair," I argue, my anger rising. "She's family. You're a stranger with some sort of magical secret that might lead to something dangerous."

"How many times do I need to ask you to trust me?"

I scoff. "Trust isn't something that just happens because the other person says so. You earn it. Keeping secrets doesn't instill trust."

"It's not just my secret. Why can't you understand that?"

"It's not just a secret, Silas. It's something impossible. You heal like a freaking unicorn."

His dark blue eyes narrow. "Unicorns aren't real."

"Are you sure about that? Seems a lot of things I didn't know are real are."

"I heal quickly. How is that lots of things?"

It doesn't pass me over that he didn't answer the questions. "Wait. You don't really know for sure if unicorns are real?"

Silas sighs and squeezes the bridge of his nose. "There are a lot of things I don't know, Greta. Focus. The point is, you ignored my warning about the dangers out there and went anyway."

Unicorns forgotten, I let my anger climb again. "I'm my own woman. I can come and go as I please. Or am I a prisoner? You promised me I'm not."

"You're not. That doesn't mean I'm going to let you hurt yourself. Why do you seem to be determined to do just that?"

"I want to go home, where things are normal. There isn't as much danger."

The anger on his face falls away, and he turns to face the opposite direction. From behind, I watch him lift his hand and rub it over his face. "I told you I'd get you home, Greta."

Silas's voice sounds sad, but I push the thought away. I'm probably imagining it because why would he be upset? He wants me to leave. Doesn't he?

"When?"

"When it's safe to do so. I thought I made it clear that I would help, but it seems you didn't believe me."

Does he sound hurt? "Why are you taking this so personally? You're the one who told me that you want your solitude back."

"Well, it seems you're determined to do that, so we're even."

"Even? What the hell is wrong with you?"

Silas spins so fast that I almost fall out of my chair. He grits his teeth. "Wrong with me? I saved you multiple times. I gave you my word that I would keep you safe, I had no evil intentions, and that I would get you home. Instead of believing me, you decided to trudge out into the danger and freezing temperatures. You'd rather take that chance than trust me!"

Speechless, I watch him walk over to get a drink of water. I'm not sure what to feel. Shock over his feeling of betrayal? Happiness that he seems to care about me? Anger over him thinking I need to do as he says or I'm betraying him? Annoyance over the fact that he seems to think I have to just trust him while he keeps secrets and I barely know him?

I choose the latter two emotions. "How can I trust a man I barely know? Yes, you saved my life, and I'm grateful for that. But you just showed me that there is so much I don't know and that you're part of it without giving me a shred of information. You live alone in the wilderness and fight every attempt of going to a doctor, which you proved you don't need. You have cougars with a vendetta against you. That's not normal."

Silas takes a deep breath and scratches the back of his neck. "Fine. I concede your point. I was just worried."

"Worried? Why? I would have been out of your hair."

"Maybe your company has grown on me, Greta. Maybe I'm so tired of being alone, even though I also crave it. Maybe the way you look at me sets fire in my veins."

His words stop my ability to speak again. That can't all be true. If so, that's crazy. It's the stress. It has to be.

"Listen," he says with a grunt, "how about we take stock of any injuries you might have, get some rest, and see where we stand when we wake? We are both tired, and you're injured. Let's take care of those issues instead of arguing to make more."

I want to keep arguing, and I think he can see it because he holds up his hands for peace. A few deep breaths lower my adrenaline enough that I can feel the aches beneath the anger. I'm also exhausted to the point my eyes are burning.

"Fine," I say. "But I'm not going to the couch. That's covered in your dried blood."

"Fair enough."

Silas takes some of the makeshift bandages I made and brings over some water. When I protest that I can do it myself, he pushes my hands away, unwilling to allow me the chance to attend to my own needs. I want to fight him, but I don't think I have the energy right now. I've been outside in the cold all night, and everything hurts.

Poking and prodding brings hisses from me as he assesses my possible injuries. I'm already developing a lot of large bruises all over my body. The wound on my shoulder doesn't need more than cleaning because the teeth didn't penetrate all the way through my coat. The bite on my hand has stopped bleeding, but his gentle touch still brings pain. He cleans and bandages that wound first, surprising me with his soft touch. At this point, I'm glad my fingers are numb enough to keep the pain from radiating into them. In fact, I can feel slight tingles all over as my body finally reacts to the warmth of the cabin.

When he reaches my ankle, the pain ignores all lost feeling. I jerk away. "What are you doing?"

"I can see that it's swollen. I need to evaluate if it's broken or sprained. It may hurt."

"A little warning would be nice."

Without answering, he pokes and prods my sore appendage some more, much to my discomfort. He declares it is just twisted and wraps it in a larger bandage.

"So," he says while tying the bandage tight, "I followed your tracks until I saw some with what looked like bear prints. Were you attacked?"

"You should know."

Freezing, Silas looks up at me from his position by my ankle. I can tell I startled him by making the connection. "I'm not stupid, Silas. The bear led me right back here, then you came back not long after. You have a trained bear."

Relief followed by amusement flash across his face. I'm not sure why he'd be relieved. Maybe the trained bear is part of his secret, and he's happy he doesn't need to keep that much again. It's quite obvious he had to send the animal after me.

"You met him?" he asks with a sly grin.

"You sent him after me, so of course. I'm not stupid."

"I never said you were."

"You made it seem that way when we first met."

Silas shakes his head. "I never thought you were stupid, Greta. Maybe naïve. Maybe a little helpless. Never stupid."

Anger rises again. "Helpless? I took on a group of wolves and held them off until your pet found me."

"Color me impressed. It seems there's more to you than I expected."

"You better believe it."

My yawn interrupts whatever he might have wanted to reply. "You need to sleep."

"I'm fine," I argue.

"And you're freezing. Let's get you to bed. Try to stay in it this time."

"You can't tell me what to do." My words are half-hearted because of the exhaustion weighing me down. I will stay in bed, but not because he told me to. I'm simply too tired to fight back.

Silas kindly lifts the covers for me to climb in, then goes about cleaning up the mess left by the table. As I thaw under the covers, my body begins to shiver so hard I feel like I'm having convulsions.

Silas notices. "Are you alright?"

"I can't seem to get warm."

"I can cure that."

He buzzes around the room to make sure the cabin is ready to be left unattended for a few hours, then walks to the other side of the bed. Slipping underneath the covers, he settles in without touching me.

"How is this a solution?" I ask. "What about your heat packs?"

"It would take longer for those to warm than it will for my body heat to create a little furnace under the covers. I promise to stay on my side. Besides, I'm tired of sleeping in my own dried blood."

"Just stay on your side." Inside, my warning means nothing. I find myself glad to be sharing this one bed with him, even with the space between us. Not that I'm not still mad at him, but keeping me warm will help him make up for it. A flutter in my belly tries to hint at other reasons. I ignore it and stay with the safe answer. It's only survival.

CHAPTER EIGHTEEN
LEARNING OPPORTUNITY

GRETA

By the brightness within the cabin, it has to be afternoon or close to it. The fire's almost out, leaving the small space feeling a little cool. Sila's heavy arm drapes over my waist, giving me a hint of that musky scent that I've come to think of as safety and home. I allow my body to snuggle back against his.

The hard planes of his upper body press against my back, inciting a marvelous fire all through me. I've never felt a man like this, and I can't say it's an unpleasant experience. No cold anger could survive the heat this man brings to my skin. I'm not even mad at him anymore.

As subtly as possible, I move to feel the hardness of his muscles more. Something else hardens, and I find my eyes widening at the size poking into my butt. I've never been with such a man. Not for the first time, I wonder what it would be like to release my grip on civility and lose myself in a wild man like Silas.

What would it be like? It has to be different. I imagine Silas brings the wilderness to his sheets, rough and feral. The mere thought brings warmth between my thighs. At this point, I have no idea who I am anymore, but I'd enjoy experimenting to find out.

I carefully roll over to face the man making me question my entire sexual existence. His brows furrow in his sleep before smoothing out into peacefulness. Pulling my hand up between us, I enjoy the feeling of him shivering under my touch. The vibrations send thrills through my body. My hand rests on his cheek.

For a moment, nothing happens. Then his eyes slowly open to stare at me in the haze of recent awakening. My thumb strokes right next to his lips, and his eyes take on their purple hue. I smile, bringing my lips to his.

At first, I'm the only one making any moves. I've shocked this large man, confused him with a completely unexpected direction after our last conversation. His body tenses against mine, but I don't give up, pecking his lips with soft kisses.

I'm about to give up and pull away when his lips part to accept my attention. Strong arms pull me closer, and I rub my soft curves over his hard lines. Silas moans before pushing his tongue into my mouth. This feels good. This feels right.

Thoughts of other kisses come to mind for comparison. After all, this is what I wanted to know; what is different.

So much varies from past experience. Where past kisses were gentle and clumsy, Silas shows me exactly what he wants with an eager tongue and little nips of his teeth. His lips are forceful, knowing what they want and willing to show me. His tongue is wild and quick to touch areas of my mouth that make me shiver.

I want more. Men take what they want without hesitation for who they might hurt. I can't see this hurting anyone. We're just two people, stuck in a cabin in the woods, passing time. It doesn't need to mean anything. Damian surely didn't. Why should I hold back from what I want?

Greedy hands slide down his face and to his chest, where I hold them and marvel at the feeling of his muscles flexing beneath my palms. After a short time of enjoying his chest, I move lower into the lines of his hard stomach. Tracing them elicits a groan from the bear of a man pressed tight against me.

When my hands start to wander lower, Silas encircles my wrists with his strong fingers, halting my journey to the peak I wish to climb. His lips stop moving, making me mourn the taste of him. He puts his forehead against mine and looks down to avoid meeting my gaze. I follow his eyes to see him hard at attention in his pants. My mouth waters.

Silas must sense what I'm thinking. "We can't."

My jaw falls open as he slides out from under the covers. "What? Why not? You seemed enthusiastic."

"It wouldn't be right."

"It feels right," I argue.

His eyes hold frustration when he looks at me. "No, Greta. It doesn't feel right. I can't do this with someone who doesn't trust me."

"Are we on this again?"

"Did you think a nap and a kiss would make it go away?"

I didn't, but then I didn't care anymore about it. Why does he have to hang onto it so hard? Why can't we move on? This argument isn't as important as discovering who I am and what this burly man can do for me.

"I trust you," I say, completely surprised that I feel it's truthful. My defiance from last night is gone, replaced by acceptance of my situation and the strangeness surrounding it. I do trust Silas and his strange bear. They could have left me out there to die last night, but here I am. Silas was even concerned enough to run outside without a shirt on. That's something.

"You're just saying that because of the heat of the moment, Greta."

"No," I argue. "I really mean it. It's strange, but I do trust you. You saved my life."

"This isn't the first time I've saved your life, so I'm going to assume it's not enough this time either. I'm going out to check the traps."

He's gone before I can argue, without a shirt again. I'm shocked he can handle the frigid temperatures half-naked, no matter where he says he comes from. It's freezing out there. I'm sure the sun makes it feel warmer, but it can't be that warm.

Standing, I walk to the window to watch him stride into the trees. I don't even think of asking him to take me because I figure I'm the one he's trying to get away from. Rejection stings. My fingers run across the dirty glass where his figure disappeared.

Not only do I wish for release, my heart aches as well. What am I supposed to do? He threw my words back in my face, so I have no true argument. It's how I did feel. Not now. Now, I want his hard body back against me.

Sighing, I move over to the washbasin and strip. If he's checking traps, I have time to do a quick wash. After throwing a few more logs on the fire to warm the cabin up a little more, I run a rag across my naked skin. The soap is a fresh bar, so I lather more thoroughly. If he wants to deny me release, he can spare extra soap as an apology. Last, I dunk my hair in the water basin and soap it up, worried about how dry it's going to look by the time I'm out of here. Bar soap can't be good for luscious locks.

As I rinse, I notice that running the rag between my legs produces a whimper. That man really got my engines revving. Well, there is one thing I can do, but Mother says civilized ladies don't do those things. Maybe I don't want to be a lady anymore. I slide my hand down my stomach and between my legs. Mother doesn't always know best.

On shaky legs, I dig through Silas' clothes. Another thing he can deal with; me stealing something to wear. My previous outfit smells of sweat and is stained with my blood. I carefully wrap my hand up again, hoping infection holds off until I can get to a proper doctor. Wolf bites probably carry all kinds of bacteria.

By the time I'm pulling his shirt over my head, I'm hurrying to make sure he doesn't walk in and see something he already turned down. That fact still hurts. My ego is only slightly damaged because it's my heart that hurts more. I'm not even sure why.

When Silas doesn't return when I feel sufficient time has passed, I start to worry a little. Maybe something got to him. Maybe he fell in a hole. He could have tripped over a rock or root and twisted an ankle.

Or he might just be blowing off steam.

I decide to put my worry aside for now and use the outhouse. Pausing on the porch, I search the area to make sure nothing's waiting for me. Once I'm sure it's clear, I dash for the outside bathroom, surprised at how little my ankle hurts. It must not have been a bad sprain. There's pain, but not as much as expected.

The trip to relieve myself goes without incident, and I refuse to go back inside until he returns. Maybe I'll see that strange bear again. Where does Silas hide such a large animal? On the other side of the house, I contemplate the chopping block.

Silas makes it look so effortless. Curious, I put a log on the block and reach for the ax. Lifting it causes a grunt to puff out of my throat. I hold it above my head and almost fall backward. Steadying myself, I swing down with all my might, completely missing the log and hitting the block. I try again, this time hitting the log. It must be a tough one because the ax just bounces off the piece of wood.

Giving up, I return the log and the ax. Silas is much stronger than I am. I can’t even break a piece of wood with an ax. By this point, I'm feeling hot from my couple of swings of the ax. I settle myself on the porch to wait. Time ticks by, unknown without a way to tell how much. I miss clocks. I miss my phone. Is Dana worried about me? I'm sure she tried to check up on me not long after the storm. She must be so worried.

The sun is setting when my stomach grumbles to remind me I haven't eaten after my eventful night trip. I'm sick of waiting for Silas. Right now, I kind of hope he fell down into a gorge. Any other excuse for being gone so long isn't acceptable. Grumbling, I stand and walk into the cabin.

First, I take some time in front of the fire—putting more logs on it—and warming up from my time outside. Next, I invade the food bin, finding our stores running low. Silas chooses this moment to finally walk through the door.

I spin and place my hands on my hips. "Where have you been? I've been worried about you."

"Now you know how I feel." Ouch, but I deserve that. "I needed some time to walk and decompress. You seem to have survived my absence. Hungry?"

He holds up a rabbit, and my mouth waters, forgetting my retort to his last statements. "Starving. We don't have much in terms of vegetables. We might want to think of conserving them a bit."

"Take out two potatoes. Poke some holes in them, rub oil and salt over them, then wrap them in the foil in the supply bin. Throw them in the fire. It'll take a while, but they'll taste good."

I do as he says, positioning the foiled potatoes under some hot logs with the poker. Turning, I see him preparing to cut into the rabbit. I consider for a moment before saying, "Wait."

Knife poised to gut the rabbit, Silas turns his head my way. "What?"

"Teach me."

"Teach you what?"

"How to skin the rabbit."

Amusement enters his dark blue eyes. "Are you sure? It's not like you'll need this skill once you're home like you want to be."

I leave the hurt tone when he says *want to* behind. I'm not sure what he's upset about. He can't be sad I'm leaving when he turned down my offer to get closer this morning. Sure, I didn't want to feel any kind of emotional attachment, but it was still a way to have me. He must be annoyed at something else.

"You never know when I might need survival techniques. Please, show me," I say.

"Fine. Come here."

I walk over, ready to act like a pioneer woman. Inside, I tell myself it has nothing to do with bridging the chasm between us or being close to him. This is simply a learning opportunity. Nothing more.

CHAPTER NINETEEN
PEACE AND TRANQUILITY

GRETA

The water turns red as I rinse my hands off, paying special attention to beneath my nails. I frown at how long they're getting before returning my focus to a spot I find between my first two fingers. All thoughts of grooming disappear when I remember what I just did.

I gutted and skinned a rabbit, and I managed to do it without throwing up. I'm not sure how I did it, but I pulled through. Even now, my stomach heaves when I remember the gore that covered these hands. The entire time, Silas watched over me, ready to jump in if I passed out. I showed him by not losing consciousness.

Not that it was easy. There were a few times that my vision dimmed. Closing my eyes and taking a few deep breaths helped, which I don't understand since the air smelled like blood. It doesn't matter in the end. Silas is skewering the naked rabbit on the spit because I'm not quite ready to impale anything.

"Won't it drip on the potatoes?" I ask, drying my hands.

"If it does and is able to penetrate the foil, it'll add some delicious flavor. We have some time to kill while it cooks."

My stomach grumbles in frustration, and I cover it with my hands when he looks my way. "We haven't eaten all day."

"Well, I need to check some bad spots on the porch, and it tastes better if cooked slow. Why don't you come out with me? Maybe it will distract you."

"Okay."

This time, he puts on a sweater. I haven't seen his coat since the day he was first attacked by cougars after my arrival. Shrugging into my own coat, I put the thought in the back of my mind. It's not as if he hasn't adequately proven that he doesn't mind the low temperatures. I'll assume it has to do with his magical nature. I wonder what else in the world exists that I don't know about. What else is hiding from the curious minds of normal people?

Silas is already outside, so I stop thinking about the impossible possible and hurry out after him. While outside, he shows me how to spot decaying wood. I help him carry over some boards that don't look all that fresh and some tools. He gets to work tearing out the old to make room for the new, something I'm no help with.

Instead, I look around at all the high snow. It's not as deep as before. The sun melts the fluffiness down into wet snow that's good for packing. That gives me an idea. Dana showed me how to build a snowman once, but I want to do something more special. I get to work.

By the time Silas is ready to nail in the new boards, I already have a sizable oblong ball sitting before me. It's over half my height. He looks over with curiosity, but I don't have time to talk when I have a head to roll up. With a shrug, he goes back to work, sending the echoes of hammering into the air around us.

This snowball is easier to make. While still big, it's not too heavy to lift. That doesn't stop me from grunting under the weight.

"Need help?" Silas calls over.

"Nope. I got this. It's my project."

"Very well. Just say something if you change your mind."

I glance over at him to see he has two more boards to go. "Keep hammering away. We both have important missions."

"Except I don't know what yours is. I'd say a snowman, but the bottom doesn't look round enough."

"It's a secret."

He chuckles while I lift the heavy ball on top of my larger oval. "A secret mission. Got it. Let me know when its big reveal is ready."

"Will do."

I look at the head, unsatisfied with the shape. Bending, I scoop up a double handful of snow. After I roll it into another uneven circle, I place it on the head and use my hands to melt where it comes together enough for it to stick. Next, I roll four cylinder shapes and place them at all corners of the large piece. Time for the finishing touches.

A smaller cylinder makes a tail. Then I form two half disks to place on the head. Silas walks over, done with his chore for the day. "Bear?"

Disappointment floods me. "Awww. How'd you guess?"

"You got the shape right."

"Well, that's a good thing. I need eyes."

Silas fishes around in his pocket and comes up with two large nails. He inserts them exactly where the eyes should be. I find some sticks to form a mouth and claws.

Stepping back to take it in, I tap my lips. "It needs something. It's supposed to be the bear that saved me. A proper tribute to him."

"Oh, is it now?" Silas says with a satisfied smirk. Well, he would be smug, seeing how it's his pet bear.

"Oh!" I say with a snap of gloved fingers.

I kneel in a more heavily used part of the path and get some mud on my gloves. When I return to my snow bear, I wipe my dirty hands over the body, leaving a smear of brown over the white.

"Perfect," I say.

"A muddy bear is perfect?"

"Well, your bear isn't completely white. It has some brown in it."

"So it does."

Silas frowns, and I look over, confused. "What is it?"

He shakes his head. "Nothing. I was just thinking."

"Of?"

"Nothing important. Food is probably ready now."

The reminder makes my stomach growl again, so I let the subject drop. I'm starving enough to leave the mysteries of the universe alone, as long as something tasty is at the other end. Excited, I practically skip into the cabin behind Silas. The wreath falls again, but he's careful not to step on it. I treat it with the same care and pick it up to replace as I walk by.

"Thanks," he says.

"No problem. I can tell it's important to you."

He sends me an indecipherable look before pulling a chair out and motioning with his hand. Surprised, I lower into the seat and let him push it in. He moves over to the fire to remove the food. It smells divine.

"So," I say as he sets the table, "you do have some manners."

"I'm not all wild adventure man. I'm like an onion."

"Many layers," I say before he can.

"Very much so."

"I don't know what that's like. What you see is pretty much what you get."

"I don't know about that."

"What does that mean?"

Silas gives me a warm smile as he sits across from me. "Oh, nothing. It's just some observations I made. How is your ankle?"

Letting him change the subject because I doubt there are any big reveals about me anyway, I shrug. "Still a little sore, but not as bad as I expected."

"It felt pretty inflamed this morning, but that could have been from you walking on it. I don't think you twisted it that bad, so it should heal quickly. I'm not surprised at the lack of pain."

As it turns out, some of the juice from the rabbit did penetrate my potato, proving Silas right. This is the best baked potato I've ever had. The rabbit is cooked just right. All in all, this is a delicious meal for an empty stomach.

Something is bothering me. "Where do you keep your bear? I never saw him until he took on those wolves."

Silas smiles around his bite of potato and rabbit together. "Oh, he's around. I don't like to cage him in."

"So you just let him wander?"

"Everyone needs freedom, Greta."

That hits home, and I feel myself deflate. What is freedom? I don't think I've ever felt it before. All my life has been me following Mother's orders to try to make her proud. So far, that hasn't happened. It seems like the harder I stretch for the unattainable approval, the further it's pulled away. Pride in my accomplishments seems so impossible to reach, along with the love of a mother.

I bite my lip and push a piece of potato around on my plate. Silas notices the change in demeanor. "Everything alright?"

Nodding, I force a smile and take a bite. "Yeah. I just was thinking that I don't know what it's like to be free. Is that why you're out here alone? Besides the magic thing, of course."

"Yes. It was so stifling where I grew up. So many people expecting so many things out of me. They wanted to set my future the way they thought it should be, but I wasn't cut out to follow in my father's footsteps. One day, I simply told them what they wanted wasn't me and left. Out here, I don't have anyone expecting me to follow their plan. I get to live each day as I want. It's pleasant."

I take a deep breath and chew some rabbit. Maybe I do have a small touch of freedom here. The person trying their best to chain me down is me this time. Instead of enjoying the lack of rules and critical examination of my day, I can build snow bears and read genres Mother said aren't for sophisticated ladies.

It's different here. Besides the vengeful predators, it's peaceful and calm. No heavy traffic. No cell phones ringing. No television blaring in the background. All the things I once thought I'd hate, I now find freeing. While I still wish to know the time sometimes, I can deal without the rest. All I need is good company and the bare necessities, which Silas provides.

Maybe I shouldn't go back? I shake my head. I've left too much behind, and Mother will never let her bargaining chip go. My marriage is the key to expanding the Parks empire. She'll hunt me down if she needs to. If I know her, and I do, she will find me eventually. This is a world that I'm only meant to enjoy temporarily. I wish it was otherwise.

"You seem sad," Silas says into the silence.

"I like it here. I'll miss it when I go."

He leans back in his chair. "I was thinking about that on my walk."

"Thinking about what?"

"I'm not forcing you to stay."

I nod. "Yes, I trust that you aren't. Last night was stupid."

"It was, but I get why you did it. What I want to say is that you're welcome here as long as you want to stay. I won't force you to remain, but I won't kick you out either."

Shocked, I look up at him. "What about your solitude?"

"I'm finding it's overrated when you have the right company."

I smile and blush, looking down at the fingers squeezing my fork tight. My earlier thoughts come back, and my excitement dies. "Truthfully, I'd love to stay. I just don't think it's possible."

"Why not?"

"My mother sees me as a chess piece to use for her advantage. If she finds me, she may turn the law on you. I know you don't want that. She has enough influence to make sure your freedom is shattered forever. I can't do that to you."

"How about this? The offer remains open, even after you head home. If you find a way to get free, I'll still be here for you."

Another smile splits my face. "I'd like that. Maybe I'll come visit at the very least. I do really feel at peace here."

"I'll welcome the visit."

I insist on helping Silas clean up. After everything is tended, we slip into bed to avoid the stained couch and each grab a book. We spend the night reading under the firelight, content in each other's company. It's amazing how the world comes together when I stop being angry at the things I can't change and embrace the little freedoms I have—however temporary. This is the perfect way to spend an evening.

CHAPTER TWENTY
PROTECTING WHAT'S MINE

SILAS

The ax splits the log in half, throwing both pieces off the chopping block. Greta sits on the porch once again, watching me work with a pleased look on her face that makes me feel warm in all the right places. I bite my lip and split the next pieces with a grunt.

I'm not sure how to explain the recent turn of events. During my walk, I felt an overwhelming need to offer her a permanent place to stay. It was almost like I needed her presence with me.

I love my solitude and peace. It took me so long to find it, and now I want to just give it away. This doesn't make sense. It's not who I am. Why would I ask her to stay?

Deep inside, I know it was the right thing to do. Having her close this long has shown me what I've been missing all this time. It's not all company I don't want; it's bad company.

How does that make any sense? She doesn't even know what I am. Even the idea of magic freaked her out badly enough to make her risk her life with a pack of wolves. How would she react if I tell her I can change into a bear? I can't even imagine the amount of panicking Greta will present if shown my inner animal. I'll definitely be uncivilized then.

Glancing behind me, I see her lick her lips. Before I can react, I turn back around. And then there's the kiss. What is the correct interpretation of that?

It's insane. We are two completely different people, so how do we go from looking down on each other to kissing? I do feel I've learned more about her as time goes, but to this point seems unreal. She's stronger than she looks, hidden away due to her mother's suppression of her self. There's also no doubt that I feel attracted to her. She's a beautiful woman.

But there's more. Beauty doesn't pull at the heart like this, making me feel like her leaving will be more painful than the decision to leave home was. There's no denying it; I don't want her to leave. According to her, she doesn't want to either.

In the end, choice is taken from us. I hate that her family wishes to use her as nothing but a chess piece. They suppress her inner strength to make sure she doesn't have the guts to push back, then do as they will with her without a single negative effect on their conscience. Greta deserves so much better than this. Too bad there's nothing I can do. As stated to her multiple times, she's not a prisoner.

I almost wish I could lock her in my cabin without letting her out.

That would cage her spirit as well, the one that's slowly coming out thanks to the lack of her mother. Still, that woman remains in Greta's head. I don't have her caged, but her family does, and I'm at a loss for any way to set her free. It has to be her choice, but I worry she will never be able to make it. How do I help?

Frustrated, I slam the ax down hard enough to startle Greta into a squeak. "Are you alright, Silas?"

I glance back at her. "Yes. I apologize for frightening you. That one looked like a tougher log, so I made sure to hit it harder."

"You're sure?"

"All good."

"Okay."

I turn back to my work, picking up another log. I have plenty already chopped, but I like to do this year round to make sure I never run out if something happens and I can't do more. The pile of unsplit logs is growing smaller, so I'll need to find a fallen tree to chop up soon.

Out of the corner of my eye, I see the snow bear Greta constructed. It's really quite well-done, and I can't help but wonder if she maybe has an artistic side to her that's all buried down deep. I'm sure artist is not a fitting position for one in her social group. It doesn't matter though because I can see it in her, like so much else she tries to hide.

Her reasoning for spreading mud over the snow sculpture stung a bit, reminding me of my imperfections. She doesn't seem to mind the difference, but she doesn't know bears well. My DNA keeps me on the line between two different shifter species. Bear just so happens to be the dominant.

Remembering her idea of what the bear is to me almost makes me laugh. When she first mentioned that she knew what was going on, I was so close to a panic. Never did I expect that truth to be her belief that my bear is my pet instead of part of me. It was a relief to hear her say that, but it also brings amusement.

Since Greta's leaving, she won't need to find out my secret. Even if she does visit, it's not something that needs to be brought up. Only someone remaining in my life permanently needs to know the truth about who I am, and that's not going to be her, no matter what offers of freedom I show her.

My anger spikes at the thought, causing me to hit a few more really hard. When I get through what I wanted to finish today, I stand and pant for breath. A soft hand touches my shoulder. I look back and drop the ax when I see Greta looking at me with concern. Why does she have to be so beautiful?

"What's wrong, Silas?" she asks.

Puffing out clouds of breath, I turn to fully face her. "Nothing important. I'm just frustrated at the situation."

"About me not staying?"

She's perceptive. "A little."

Greta gives me a shining smile that takes the breath that I just got back away from me. "I'm happy to have the offer, and I really would stay if I could. While I didn't like where fate put me at first, I've come to cherish these circumstances now. Life is so peaceful and free out here, so much different from what I'm used to—in a good way. Unfortunately, I can't."

"I understand," I say while wanting to scream the opposite. No matter what happens, I'd keep her safe. This time, she's trying to protect me. Her mother won't let her winning chess piece free.

I reach up and cup her cheek in my palm. She leans into my touch. As she glances behind me, her eyes widen and her body tenses. Without hesitation, I spin to confront whatever has frightened her. It's a brown bear that watches us with curiosity.

"Tell me it's one of yours," Greta says behind me.

"I only have the one."

The animal chuffs at us, sniffing the air to see what we are. It takes a step closer, and I reach behind me to make sure Greta remains hidden behind my back. Not that I think the bear doesn't know she's there, but he'll have to go through me to get to her.

"I thought they usually hibernate in the winter," Greta says. "That's what I learned in school."

"Most species usually do. Something woke this one up, and he's searching for that something. Keep calm. He won't charge if you don't run."

As if our voices aggravate him, he stands on his hind legs and growls. Greta squeaks, but I remain still and quiet. Standing at my full height, I channel my inner bear. Power of the change fills me without transforming my body. If Greta could see my eyes, she'd probably be scared. I'm sure they look like a bear now.

Our curious guest settles back down on all fours. I push with the animal side of me, and he looks shocked and confused. I take a step closer, earning a hiss of warning from the woman hiding behind me. I'm not at all worried. The bear takes a step back.

"Leave," I say out loud while channeling all my dominance into that single word.

The bear shakes his head and retreats, casting one last uncertain look over his shoulder as he goes. The animal in me fades back deep inside. My invisible hackles smooth out, and the satisfaction of protecting my territory swells within. I won this battle without a fight.

"That was impressive," Greta says from behind me, her soft hands gently touching my back. She's peeking around my side to watch the animal disappear.

I rub the back of my neck. "It was nothing. When you live in the wild, you get a sense of how to handle certain animals."

"Except cougars."

"Can't handle what wants your blood."

"Why do you think that bear was out here?" Greta asks, changing the subject.

I shrug. "Could be anything. Another predator may have invaded its den. The den may be damaged. Or it sensed food. Any of those are plausible reasons."

"Guess it will remain a mystery. Let me help you carry some of this wood in."

"I can get it."

She laughs. "I'm sure you can, big strong man. Anyone that can chase a bear away just by looking at it and telling it to leave can certainly handle a few piles of wood, but I want to be useful."

Startled, I watch her lift an armful without protest. My mouth hangs open as I watch her walk by with a seductive sway to her hips, taking a deep breath to inhale her sweet scent. I blink a few times.

Did she just flirt with me?

Her tone suggests yes. Well, I guess it shouldn't be too shocking after the kiss we shared. That doesn't mean I don't have the right to my surprise. Shrugging away the questions, I fill my basket full of wood and carry it inside, casting a side-eyed glance at the bear meant to resemble mine. She will never know.

Inside, Greta feeds a few logs into the low fire to bring it back to full life. She then goes over to the food stores. "Not much here. Rabbit sound good?"

"Rabbit sounds perfect. I don't even need to see the rest of the menu."

She laughs, and I realize I'm using a flirty tone as well. Coughing to hide my surprise, I cover my mouth and turn away.

Greta's voice forces me to face her again. "What are these?"

I examine the can she holds in her hands. "Baked beans. I like to get a few cans for when fresh food grows scarce. That's one of my usual purchases, which is why it was hidden at the bottom of the stores."

Or steals, but I won't tell her that.

"I've never had baked beans," Greta muses.

"Seriously?"

"Yeah. Is that weird?"

"A little, but I'm getting used to that from you."

She scoffs. "This coming from a man that can super heal. What do they taste like?"

"You're going to find out."

I take the can from her and dig through our supplies for a can opener. It's been a while since I've needed the non-perishables, so it's all the way at the bottom. Once open, I settle the grill over the fire and dump the beans into a pot. A few pieces of rabbit go into a skillet. As everything cooks, it leaves a sweet and smoky scent in the air. I sniff it and move closer to the pot, removing the lid to take a long inhale.

Greta joins me. "That smells delicious."

"Doesn't it?"

Turning my head, I find hers right next to mine. Her muttered agreement stops midway as we stare into each other's eyes. When she licks her lips, my gaze travels to them. Remembering the taste of her mouth makes me instantly hard. I open my mouth to say something, but words don't come out.

The beans choose this moment to start bubbling, catching me on the cheek with hot sauce. I jump back on instinct. The moment between us breaks. I wonder if there will be more, and I am not the least bit surprised to realize I hope there will be.

CHAPTER TWENTY-ONE
DESTROYED TRIBUTE

GRETA

It's warm under the covers, and I refuse to open my eyes. I'd rather spend the time snuggled in warm covers than face the chilly morning. Sleeping in is a luxury I'm unaccustomed to, so let me enjoy it as much as possible. No strict schedules. No unbreakable rules. Just simple living in a cabin covered in snow. I never thought I'd enjoy this way of life this much.

Sure, I didn't before, but that was prior to giving it a chance. Now, I find it comforting and something to strive for. Simplicity is best. I don't need the TV or my phone.

Movement of the mattress makes me groan at the insistence of waking. My eyes open to find a pair of dark blue pools in front of my face. Startled, I squeak and jerk back, only to realize I'm already at the edge of the mattress. Starting with my rump, my body slowly slides off the bed. Silas reaches over, grabs my shirt, and pulls me back until I'm flush against his chest.

That's not the only thing that's flush right now. Is it hot in here? I could've sworn I thought the air was chilly. Not anymore. Thinking of the strength and fluidity of his movements sends heat straight to my core. I'm pretty sure my face is pink. I want to know what it would be like to take it further with this wild man.

Silas clears his throat. "I didn't mean to startle you."

"Why were you so close then?"

"I was trying to see if you were awake. It seemed like you were, but you weren't opening your eyes."

"I was enjoying the peace of the morning for a moment."

This earns me a pleased smile that sends a tingling all over. I want to pounce him, but he's already stated that he won't take this further until I prove that I trust him. For some reason, that means a lot to him, which is something else different from what I'm used to. Most men jumped in bed with me if I so much as hinted at the desire for it. They didn't care to know me or earn my trust. Now, I feel a different kind of warmth flow through me, starting in my chest.

Being uncertain about my feelings makes me anxious, so I decide it's time to get up and away from this man that makes me feel so strange. Before I do, I bring my lips to his in a quick peck, careful not to cross the boundaries he set after our heated moment. His eyes widen in shock, which makes me giggle.

I slide from bed. "I need to pee."

"I'll come with you."

"I think I know the way."

"You do," he admits, "but I need to use the outhouse after you."

"Well, there's no arguing that. Let's go."

We dress, me more bundled than Silas. I wish I had his immunity to the cold air. Life would be so much easier if I didn't have to layer myself just to go outside. I lead the way, opening the door and stepping onto the porch.

My eyes scan the area, and my hands fly to my mouth. "Oh, no!"

"What?" Silas asks, instantly alert.

I run down to what's left of my snow bear. "I worked so hard on this tribute. It meant so much. Who would have done this?"

Where my bear once stood lies a mess of snow chunks. Claw marks and bites are evident in the large pieces. It's a ruined mess, not a single recognizable piece remaining. Tears threaten at the thought of the maliciousness that was put into the destruction.

"Cougars," Silas growls.

I look back at him, seeing the anger in his eyes. "You're sure?"

"I see their paw prints."

Glancing around, I can make out what he's talking about. They're faint, but they're there. Not that I could identify them if I tried. I trust him to know better than I would.

"Why would they do this? Is it because it looked like a bear?" I ask.

"It's because it looked like *my* bear."

"They don't like your bear?" That's when it hits me. "Oh, that's how you survive the attacks. Your bear comes to help."

He looks startled for a moment, but it doesn't last. Did he really think I wouldn't figure it out? It's clear he can command that animal, which is pretty neat. I wonder if I'll ever get to thank the bear properly for saving me. He may have been under Silas's orders, but that doesn't mean he doesn't deserve to be thanked.

"Something like that, yeah," Silas says.

"Why do they hate your bear so much?"

Silas' shoulders slouch. "My bear killed one of their high-ranking members defending a kill. It was self-defense, but cats are extremely territorial. We killed prey in their forest. When they tried to take it, we fought back. My bear didn't mean to kill the cougar. It was an accident."

"They really hold a grudge."

"They do," he says with a sigh. "I thought you had to pee."

"Oh, yeah. I forgot."

One more glance at the ruined snow bear to finish mourning it, then I'm hurrying to the makeshift bathroom. As usual, it's freezing in this little box, but at least it isn't windy. Once out, I tell Silas that I'm going to start heating up leftovers. He nods and enters the outhouse to do his business.

Back in the cabin, I throw the last of our food into a pan and place it on the rack above the fire. Silas returns, taking over stirring it while I ready our bowls and get water to drink. While I don't need everything I left behind in the city, I do long for a tall glass of orange juice or hot chocolate. Wants aren't needs though, as I'm slowly learning. It's difficult when I've been given everything I could possibly want in my life, except the freedom to live as I choose to.

Is comfort worth the loss of freedom?

I used to think so, but not anymore. There are more ways to be comfortable that don't require vast stores of wealth. My time with Silas proves that. Here, I'm more comfortable emotionally and mentally than I ever was physically in the city. That now seems more important.

I'm interrupted from my contemplation by food, and I dig in. "What are you doing today?" I ask around a mouthful.

"This was the last of our last catch. I need to check traps."

"A walk sounds nice. Count me in."

"Maybe it wouldn't be a good idea," he says. "The cougars will try to get to you to hurt me."

Taking my last bite, I stare at him. "They're animals. Isn't that too much for their reasoning levels?"

"They're smarter than you can guess."

"Either way, you seem to always know when they're close, and I trust you to protect me." And I do. I no longer question my safety with Silas. I feel stupid for questioning it before.

"I'm not going to talk you out of this?"

"Nope. I'm going."

"Fine, but if I tell you to run, you go in the direction I tell you to."

"I can do that," I say with certainty.

Silas stands and moves to one of his boxes of supplies. After digging around for a few moments, he returns to the table. "Here. Just in case."

I pick up the sheathed knife he places beside my empty bowl. "I don't know how to use something like this. I've never even been in a physical fight before. The closest was the wolves."

"It's easy," he says with a playful smirk. "You slice with the sharp edges and stab with the point."

"I know that much."

"Then you know how to use it. If you're coming with me, I'm equipping you with something to defend yourself with. Either take the knife, or stay in the cabin."

"Fine," I mumble, standing to clean out our bowls.

Before we leave, he shows me how to clip it to my borrowed pants. Once again bundled up, I follow him out the door. We follow the same path as before to check traps, having about as much luck as we did last time. A few have heads in them but nothing else, which makes me feel confused over how other animals pulled that off. Each empty trap tenses Silas's shoulders more.

"What if we don't find anything edible?" I ask, my breath puffing in the frigid air.

"I'll have to hunt. You will not be accompanying me for that. It takes practice to know how to stalk animals."

"I can learn."

He shakes his head. "Maybe when we don't need the meat so badly."

I nod, even though he's too focused ahead to notice. I'm sure my silence communicates my agreement. It's not like I'm willing to kill anything yet anyway. I've just started helping gut already dead animals. Might as well get used to that first.

A few more traps resign me toward the possible need to spend time alone in the cabin. It's almost like someone has gone through a lot of trouble to make sure we don't have anything to eat. I'd suspect the cougars after the destruction of my hard work, but they don't have hands. I can't see claws and paws able to free the animals enough to leave just the head. Something else is going on again.

Does Silas have human enemies in the woods too? Maybe they also have this strange magic. Maybe he's an outcast. He's awfully secretive of his past, so I can see any of that being true. Not that it changes how I feel about him. I'm pretty much an outcast from our society as well. Mother is never happy with me. Father is indifferent. My own fiancé cheated on me.

I don't belong in that world. Once, I thought I did because I was born to it. After spending time living simply in a cabin in the woods, I no longer feel like I belong there. I'd rather stay with Silas than go back to the backhanded compliments and rich politics. This life seems so much better for me. Too bad I'll need to return to the life of an official Parks. I can't risk Silas' freedom to grasp for my own. If only I could think of a way to make it possible. Mother would never let go of her pawn. No one would believe I ran off from such a *glorious* lifestyle.

I'm so lost in my thoughts that I don't realize Silas has stopped until he grabs my arm. My head snaps up to see him alert and searching the surrounding trees. My heart speeds up, and my breathing turns shallow in an effort to make as little noise as possible. I see something move ahead of us, darting from one tree to another.

"Cougars?" I ask.

"Yes. They must have been waiting for me."

"Should I run?"

Silas circles to look all around. "No. There is no safe way for you to flee without running right into one of them. We're surrounded."

As he speaks, the cats start coming out from hiding. There are at least six that I can count, plus one that hangs back. If a cat could smirk, I'd say that one does, but I know they can't. That's just silly to think so. My mind is playing tricks on me.

They circle us, snapping and snarling. My hand reaches for the knife on my waist, but Silas covers my hand with his. "Not yet. If they see it, they'll attack."

"If they're going to attack anyway, I'd rather have it. That's why you gave it to me."

"I'll make sure that you have time to pull it out. They're waiting for something."

This makes no sense. "Waiting for what?"

"For me to defend us."

"That makes no sense."

He takes a deep breath. "Unfortunately, it makes a lot of sense."

Silas keeps me from drawing my knife from its holder, staring down the cougar that holds back. I don't understand. What are we waiting for? What are *they* waiting for?

CHAPTER TWENTY-TWO
A Tough Decision

SILAS

Being surrounded by large, predatory cats is not a situation one wants to find themselves in. At the moment, I'm stuck in that terrible reality with only one way to chase them off, the way that will also chase Greta away. She's the only reason I haven't made that choice yet. By the smirk on Ande's furred face, he knows it too.

How long until he forces my hand?

Because I know that's what he's aiming for. My death isn't even on the table right now. He knows Greta doesn't know my secret, and he's forcing me to show her first hand, which will only scare her away. I feel like she's finally starting to trust me, but revealing that my bear isn't some cleverly trained animal is going to cause that trust to fly right out of the window and not look back.

What woman of class would accept what I am? No amount of acceptance will carry over to knowing that I can change into a bear. Not only does that make me unknown and scary, but it shows that I'm still lying to her. How do I get out of this without backtracking with every concession I've earned from the woman clinging to my fingers? And why do I care?

I shouldn't. I told myself long ago that caring brings pain and rejection, which I'm sure to feel again when she knows what I am. Just like if my so-called friends found out at home. If people used to magic and shifters can't accept me, why would a human without knowledge of our hidden world?

Ande makes eye contact with me, settling down and curling his tail around his front paws. He's simply waiting for his cougars to force me into a decision, one I dread because I know I will face the rejection if it keeps Greta safe. She seems weak and useless, but she's shown me there's so much more to her deep down. I want to explore that inner self more. I'm doomed to lose it before I can gain that chance.

A cat feints in, and I backhand it. The animal snarls and backs away. I'm not stupid enough to think it's giving up. We're surrounded, and everything feels hopeless. They'll force me to shift, or they'll kill Greta in front of this helpless form. There is no doubt in my mind that they will go that far. Ande hinted so during our last meeting. Greta is nothing but a weak human to them. She's so much more to me, which is why we're here right now.

It seems their vengeance isn't going to simply be killing me. They want to drive her away and hurt me in every way possible before moving in for the kill. All because of a misunderstanding that I didn't mean to happen. I know I screwed up. I feel guilt over the incident daily, but I can't take it back. That doesn't mean I deserve this treatment.

"Silas," Greta says beside me.

I pull her away to kick the cougar about to pounce her away. This isn't going to work. There's too many of them. Only my bear form can survive an attack like this, and I'm sure that means losing Greta. Either decision means losing her, so I need to choose the one I can live with most. That's the decision that keeps her alive.

"You win, Ande," I growl at the lazy cat.

He only cocks his head to the side. Greta asks, "Who's Ande?" I point to the cougar waiting impatiently. "You have a name for the cougar."

"No, the cougar has a name for himself. I'll explain it all if you let me later."

"Why wouldn't I let you?"

"You're about to find out."

The next pounce causes Greta to cry out. Red blossoms on her wrist. Fury fills me, and the last of my hesitation melts away. How dare they touch her, particularly when I am giving them what they want. The bastard that did that will pay for it.

My bear comes quickly, inciting Greta to ask, "Silas, what are you doing on the ground like that when we are being attacked by cougars?"

If only I had a different answer to that question. I don't, so I choose to let her eyes tell her what's going on. Her exclamations of shock, followed by the fear I dread, tell me that she sees perfectly fine.

My body grows, forming the shape of her beloved snow sculpture. First, these animals destroyed what she worked so hard on and took so much pride in. Then they threaten her life and destroy the trust I worked so hard to earn back. They will pay for it all.

Greta screams as the fur grows out of my skin and the bones break and reshape themselves. I push the sound out of my mind. There isn't much I can do about her fear besides teach these felines a lesson about forcing my hand in this respect. So much for her going home and never learning the truth about me. I shouldn't have let her come look at traps today.

As if she would have listened.

When I'm fully a bear, they attack. It seems like the second part of their plan has been put into motion. Greta tries to back away from me, but I force her to stay close by following her steps. She pulls her knife, leaving me with a hope that she won't use it on me. One tries to pounce on her, and I swipe powerful claws at the animal. Blood sprays us both, but I failed landing a killing blow. The cat yowls and limps away.

Before I can move in for the kill, two more hit me at once. I stand on two legs and roar my fury at the cats clinging to my fur with claws and fangs. One slips off, landing hard enough to seem dazed. The other decides it's best to dig their back claws into my ribs. I growl and jerk to try to dislodge them.

Greta stares at me with wide light blue eyes. If it wasn't for my attempt to shake this creature off, I wouldn't have noticed that another was readying to take her out. I push past her, knocking her onto her butt with a squeal. The supposed attacker turns and runs when faced with my reaching jaws. The one clinging to me hops off and follows.

Every other cat runs in the same direction, except Ande, who still watches with his tail wrapped around his front paws. I turn on him with a snarl. I know why he doesn't fear me; he's too fast for me to chase. Trying is futile, so I express my anger while sticking close to Greta as she clambers back to her feet.

Ande huffs out of his nose, turns his back on me, and saunters away as if this were a regular outing instead of a way to ruin my life. Running footsteps crunching snow pull my attention back to the woman behind me. At least she had enough mind left to run in the opposite direction of the predators that tried to kill her. Knowing how clumsy she is, I wish she'd put the knife away.

Too bad she considers me one of those predators as well. Sitting back, I let her go for now. I knew this was going to happen, so I'm not surprised. All the cougars went the other way, and none doubled back that I can tell. That's not saying much, considering how sneaky they are. I trust she's safe though. This show accomplished what purpose it had.

What am I going to do?

There's not much I can do besides hope that Greta will see reason. How fast she's fleeing makes that seem impossible. How will I get through to her? I doubt I will. The best I can do is allow her to let me lead her to a town in my bear form. I'm not sure if she'll even agree to that, but I have to try. She won't survive without me.

Again, I knew this was going to happen. Anyone not used to shifters would react this way. People that can transform into animals are pure fantasy to them. They even have books about people with this power, some of them quite dirty. I want to say the first people that wrote about shifters must have seen them in person and understood the fictional value they had at their fingertips. That doesn't make this any easier.

Still, I'd rather her be scared of me than dead, so I don't regret the decision to shift. I simply have to decide on how to handle the consequences. That's a question I'm not sure how to answer. I have no idea how to even approach her now.

Standing, I stretch and feel the strong breeze stir the hair on my back. There's nothing to do but walk blindly into this conversation and go with it. There is no planning to be done when it comes to something like this. She's too frightened to be predictable, and I have no idea how to approach this situation. It's best to just walk right into it and do the best I can.

Her trail is easy to follow, Greta's footsteps clear in the snow. She's weaving frantically, and I can't tell where she's heading. It's not back to the cabin. Of course not. Why would she return to my place of residence? Although, this haphazardly trek isn't going to do her any good either. She seems to be heading in the same direction as the other night, which is deeper into the wilderness. At least the wolves should be gone this time.

As I round a particularly large tree, a buck jumps out in front of me, startled by something up ahead. I'm going to guess that it's probably

Greta. I don't miss the opportunity, swiping open its neck with a sharp claw before it can gather itself enough to flee. He stumbles and falls.

I take a quick interlude to drag him back to the cabin because I passed it not long ago. I'm not sure if Greta knew because she kept moving forward, but I've already decided that she wouldn't head back to the cabin. Hiding the carcass between the woodpile and our shelter, I return to my pursuit of the woman who no longer feels safe near me.

When I return to her trail, I take a moment to sniff the air. I pick up her scent before moving along the path she took. Ambling forward, I keep my nose to the air. Thanks to this, I can tell when she stops running because the smell grows stronger, indicating she's staying in the same spot. Once I feel I'm close, I listen.

There are no sounds of fighting and no scent of blood, so she's not in trouble. I pause, wondering the best way to move forward. It's clear that she's afraid of my bear. Going in furry won't do me any favors. After a brief debate, I push my bear away.

My body transforms until I'm standing naked in the snow, not far from the woman I seek. Frowning, I tell myself that I should have grabbed clothes at the cabin, but I didn't want to leave her alone longer than I have. The deer was only because we need food for when we are done arguing. I'm hoping it's still *we* when I catch up to her and explain myself.

Well, it's better if I appear naked than showing up in a bear's skin. Maybe the nudity will make her feel more on level with me. Anything to give her enough of an advantage to sway her to listen. Sighing, I put one foot in front of the other. Where she should be is empty. I look everywhere, behind all the trees, confused about her possible position.

I lean against a trunk and think. Did she run off again? No, I would've heard if she did. She's near. She must be great at hiding. Sniffing, I catch her scent, as if she's right on top of me. I frown.

A noise above me makes me look up. I grin with amusement at what I find.

CHAPTER TWENTY-THREE
BEARS CAN CLIMB

GRETA

My feet kick up snow as I gasp for breath. My heart pounds in my chest faster than my legs move. Anything to put distance between me and whatever the hell was going on back there. Silas *is* the bear.

How is this possible? Sure, I've heard stories of people that are allowed to read steamy books, but those are fictional. Beast men don't actually exist. Do they? A deer startles me as it crosses my path, fleeing in the direction I came from. Even deer feel the need to scare me.

They obviously do, and I've been living with one since my ill-fated trip into a blizzard. It took me forever to accept his magical excuse for healing, but this is too much. He's a freaking animal. He lied to me. That bear wasn't trained by him; that bear is him. I need a straight jacket. This isn't normal. Maybe I really died in the accident and this is some very strange afterlife. Maybe I'm in a coma.

Anything makes more sense than what my brain is telling me I saw. That is illogical. Who am I kidding? Logic has no place in my life anymore. Did I pass out in my car and wake up in an alternate universe or something? Anything makes more sense than the fact that creatures like him exist in the real world. It's not possible.

I skid to a stop. Running isn't going to help when I have animals at my heels. I look around and find a likely tree. Rushing over, I jump and grab the lowest branch. Pain blossoms in my injured wrist, but I ignore it the best I can while cursing the cougar that bit me. Now I need to worry about supernatural rabies.

My first attempt at pulling myself up, after hiding my knife away, almost throws me back into the snow. I grip the branch with my own supernatural strength to keep from falling. My ankle is better, but I am not twisting it again. I shouldn't have skipped gym on pull-up days. My upper body strength sucks.

I'm surprised when I finally make it up onto the branch. I lay on it, panting for breath before continuing to move upward. Once on this lower perch, moving further toward the top is easier because the branches are closer. Adrenaline keeps me going, despite the fact that my legs feel like jelly and my lungs are burning.

When I'm far enough up, I find a place to settle against the trunk and lean my head back. That was exhausting. Maybe none of the predators after me will look up here. Are the cougars half human too? That would explain their cleverness and their vendetta against Silas. Oh, my. Does that mean he killed one of them? That would be more like murder. Wouldn't it?

I'm not sure how any of this works. Do I think of the cougars as animals or people? Do I think of Silas as a bear or a man? This is so confusing. I kept calling Silas wild without having any idea that he really is.

When we were together, he felt like a man. His body and voice certainly did. They stirred a need in me that a bear couldn't. Would that make him extra wild in bed?

"Damn it, Greta. Stop thinking about that," I mutter to myself.

I'm an idiot if I'm still thinking about sleeping with Silas. Not only did he lie to me, but he's also half animal. He can turn into a bear. That should be enough to turn me off, not turn me on more. My body doesn't listen. For some reason, I still picture myself tumbling around on his lone bed, rutting him like a wild animal myself.

What is wrong with me? It must be something big because anyone else who had this happen to them wouldn't be stuck on sleeping with the bear man. Has he been drugging me? No, that doesn't sound right. If he was and his aim was to get me to have sex with him, he would have taken the opportunity I presented him. Instead, he pushed me away like he didn't want to sleep with someone who isn't sure of him.

Well, I'm sure not sure now. I used to be. Or, at least, I was getting there. I trusted him completely. I knew he would keep me safe from the cougars. Too bad I didn't know what that would entail.

"You have always been an idiot, Greta," I say, parroting my mother's mantra. "You're willful and stubborn. You make decisions based on how you feel instead of using your brain. Always such a stupid drama queen. Look where that's gotten you."

I laugh. If only she could see where I am right now. Hiding in a tree to avoid a man that can turn into a bear. Would she have me committed or hide me away to keep the press from getting hold of my crazy? I sincerely have no true guess for that. I'm going to say the latter, but I'm not completely sure. For once, I can't predict the way my mother would react to my stupidity.

A twig snaps in the distance, and my heart stops. I press as hard as I possibly can into the rough, cold tree bark. It scratches the back of my head. My wrist aches and stings but is growing numb from being out in the cold. Putting it into my pocket isn't an option. I'd rather it be numb anyway.

Silas comes into view. The breath stops moving in my chest. Every part of me is still as I will myself to become one with the tree at my back. At least he's in human form—naked human form. I make sure to keep my eyes away from a certain appendage to avoid more confused thoughts. I don't need those right now. The rest of his muscular body does enough to me. My goosebumps aren't only from the cold right now.

As he checks behind all the trees and doesn't look up, I find myself hopeful. For what? I'm not sure. It's clear I have no idea where I'm going. I'm thoroughly lost, a thought that doesn't bode well for my survival without him. But he's a bear. Bears are dangerous.

My foot slips, and I bite my tongue. Dark blue eyes look up, a smirk showing amusement when he sees me. "Bears can climb."

I open my mouth before closing it tight. What? It takes a few tries to ask, "They can?"

"Very much so."

Damn it. My city knowledge doesn't cover the tree climbing habits of magical bears. "Go away."

He sighs while I do my best not to marvel at the muscles that move in his chest when he does. "I'm not going anywhere, Greta. We need to talk."

"I'm perfectly fine where I am. Thank you."

"It's cold and you have to be hungry."

I laugh. "And you're a bear. I think yours is a bit more alarming and urgent."

"I'm still Silas. I'm not going to hurt you."

"You. Are. A. Bear."

He sighs. "Are you going to be hung up on that?"

"Why wouldn't I be? You aren't human."

"Part of me is."

"Splitting hairs here."

Silence stretches for long enough that I hope that means he's going to move on. I'm wrong. "Greta, can I ask you a question?"

"Depends on the question."

He lifts one perfect eyebrow. "You're stubborn. I'm going to ask. Did you trust me before you found out that the bear is me?"

"Yes..." Where is he going with this?

"I was a bear then too."

I narrow my eyes at him. That's not fair. It's logical, but logic isn't always fair. "I didn't know it then."

"Who I was before is who I am now. I told you I won't hurt you. Please come down. I got a deer on the way over."

Food and answers. Both of those I'm in dire need of. He still looks like Silas. "Okay. I'll choose to trust you, so if you decide to eat me now, that will be really crude and just downright rude. Answers before food."

"Very well."

Getting down sounds a lot easier than it is. Climbing up was hard, but returning to the ground looks even more difficult. Numb fingers are not going to help either. Turning over happens slowly, at which point I cling to the branch and stare down.

"Do you need help?" Silas asks.

"No. I have this."

He looks skeptical, which only makes me more determined to do this myself. I got up; I can get down. My leg reaches for the branch below me, sending triumph through my mind. The next one comes easier. As I reach for the last branch, my confidence grows. That's when I make my first error.

My feet slip. When I try to grab the one wooden surface beneath me, it snaps. With a scream, I find myself plummeting. I land with a thump, right in Silas's strong arms.

"Put me down. I would have landed just fine," I say, squirming to be free of him.

Without argument, he sets me down. My wiggles almost topple me over, but he manages to set me on my feet. I stumble a few steps before turning back to him, keeping my eyes on his face. I do not need to see the rest of him.

"You need clothes," I say.

"I don't exactly have them stashed all over. I'll get new ones at the cabin. Come."

Nervous, I let him lead while keeping a little distance between us in case I need to run again. I said I'll listen to him, but that doesn't mean I'm going to not leave an escape if he wants to go bear on me again. If I see a hint of fur before I get answers, I'm gone.

As we draw closer to the cabin, my wrist throbs a little more. "Uh, do cougars carry rabies?"

"These ones definitely don't. Is this about your wrist?"

"You know about that?"

"I saw it happen, then I noticed it again when I caught you. I was afraid to mention it."

I'm quiet at the thought of him being afraid of someone as small and normal as I am. "Uh, yeah. It hurts, but I think it should be fine. I just wanted to make sure I wasn't going to go rabid. Are they like...you?"

"Yes, but I'd rather talk about this somewhere more contained."

Nodding, I let the questions drop. We will wait until we get to the cabin. Warmth will be welcome, along with the return of the feeling to my fingers. Although, the return of feeling may make the pain increase. Right now, it's a dull throb as long as I don't try to use it. Thawing it out may make it do more than throb. It doesn't matter though. I won't let him touch my wrist until I get answers—if I let him touch it at all.

Even if I forgive him for what I found out, he still lied to me. The fact that it was most likely a justified lie doesn't matter. I was finally beginning to trust him. Oh my gosh. I thought he was a trained bear. How stupid does he think I look for that guess? Now I'm not in such a hurry to get him alone.

Will he bring that up? Not if I make sure the focus stays on him. In the end, my accusations bear more weight because he lied and hid things from me. My guess may look absurd, but he went along with it, so he's as much to blame as I am.

My thoughts stop circling when the cabin comes into view. The relief overwhelming me is unexpected. Despite the fact that I wanted to escape not long ago, this still feels like coming home. My feet still slow, not ready to face what's to come. Silas opens the door, then replaces the wreath that falls off.

He turns to me. "Are you coming?"

I take a deep breath and nod. Time to get answers.

CHAPTER TWENTY-FOUR
PICKING UP THE PIECES

GRETA

Silas starts walking toward the couch, frowns at it, then changes directions for the table. I remain by the door, the mush slowly sliding from my boots and my arms crossed over my chest. The cabin welcomes me with open arms, and oh, how I want to snuggle into that embrace. It's almost like part of me has already forgiven Silas.

That's just stupid and impulsive when I haven't even heard his explanations yet. What is it about this man that lets me release my guard? My shell crumbles in his presence, and I'm not sure I like it. This is absurd.

"Are you going to sit?"

I jump at Silas's voice with a gasp, cursing myself for not paying better attention in the presence of a bear in human skin. The homeliness of this cabin is a cover for the strange danger that lingers within. I need to keep my wits about me.

I frown at the man sitting at the table. "I'd rather stand, but you might want to put some pants on if you want me to be able to focus."

Silas looks down. "Oh, yeah. Nudity never mattered much to me, so it's still strange to dress as soon as I come back after shifting. Give me a second."

Doing my best to avoid gazing at his glorious backside as he finds clothes, I look around the cabin once more. Not that there is much to look at. My gaze travels up, finding that our resident spider roommate has made a very impressive web.

The chair creaks, and Silas says, "Better?"

My eyes find him again. His bottom half is covered, but his top half is still out in the open to distract me. What am I supposed to tell him?

Can you put a shirt on? Otherwise, I'll get lost in your hard muscles and may jump you.

Yeah, that wouldn't be a crazy thing to say at all. Swallowing hard, I find his eyes with mine again, seeing the familiar twinkle of purple. The look in his eyes is smoldering, and I wonder if he can read my mind. This won't do at all.

Change the subject our minds seem to want to discuss. "You changed into a bear."

The purple disappears into the dark blue. It occurs to me that I only see it with strong emotion. Interesting.

"This would be easier if you would sit down." When I only hug myself tighter, he sighs and continues. "Very well. It's called shifting."

"That's a real thing?"

"Yes, and there are lots of different kinds of shifters. I will tell you all that I can, but I can't speak of my home. No, don't argue. That's one thing that's forbidden to me because no human can ever know about it."

My eyebrows draw together. If he won't tell me everything, how can I trust that he isn't leaving out something important? In the end, I can't and have to learn to simply believe him. Silas hasn't steered me wrong yet, besides pulling me into a war he has with shifting cougars.

"So, if you killed one of them, is that murder?" I ask.

"It's still self-defense. Since then, I've done my best not to fatally injure another one of them. I was so starved then that I couldn't stop my bear from defending our kill with everything we had. I didn't even know he was a shifter when I killed him. That knowledge came later, and I deeply regret it. Not just because they are now determined to make me pay for it, but because of the death on my conscience. Today was the closest I've been to killing another. I would have without thought."

"Self-defense again?"

He leans back, crossing his arms over his chest to match my stance from a sitting position. "In defense of someone I don't wish to lose."

It takes me a minute to follow his train of thought. My eyes widen. My heart skips a beat and soars. Tingles run over me. Then reality washes over me once again.

Sighing, I walk over and practically fall into the other empty chair. At this point, my wrist is starting to throb harder. Silas notices it and gets the last of our first aid supplies and makes new bandages.

As he works, I say, "You know nothing can—"

"I know. You need to get home to keep me safe."

The tone he uses makes me wince like I've been slapped in the face. "I would stay if I could."

"For me or for the peace of the place?"

Silence falls between us while I consider. He's professing an attraction for me. I refuse to say love because it's too soon, but he's at least fond enough to keep me here and determine if it might become love.

How do I feel? Attraction is definitely there. Even when frightened of him, I'm ready to jump him like a cat in heat. Maybe a bad analogy right now. Love? No. Fondness? Yes.

It's not enough. I want him. I want the simpleness of this place. I have so much more I need to do at home. Mother will make sure to drag me back at the earliest convenience. If he fights back, which he may, she'll find a way to destroy him. I've seen it happen to those that have stood in her way before.

"I can't, Silas."

His jaw clenches, but he doesn't say anything else. I begin to feel guilty for hurting him, but then I remember everything. I may be comfortable here. That doesn't mean I belong. This is a world I'm not even part of. What will happen to me if I stay? Besides, he's the one that has lied to me continually since I got here.

"Tell me more about shifters. Are they all fast healers?" I say a little colder than I expected my voice to be.

He flinches but continues to clean the bite on my wrist with extreme gentleness. "We have the magic to change from birth. It comes from the world around us but is usually genetic."

"So your parents were bears," I say, thinking I understand.

His jaw ticks for a second before he continues. "One is a bear shifter. The other is a different kind. I'm a hybrid and basically a mistake."

The bitterness of his voice robs me of my dignified anger for a few moments. "You're not a mistake."

When Silas looks up at me, the expression in his eyes conveys pain. He truly believes he is a mistake. Something has broken him, and I feel a little kinship with him over that, more than I've felt since I've been born.

"You're not a mistake," I say again with more conviction.

He laughs, but it's a laugh that isn't born from amusement. "I am. Where I'm from, there are people that can control magic but aren't shifters. My parents actually led those people and kept their animal side secret. Those that don't need to shift to access the magic tend to look down on those that do with disgust and superiority. I'm worse because I was born between two different shifters. I always felt different and left as soon as I was old enough."

"Have you gone back?"

Silas shakes his head. "Not once, and I don't plan on it. I hated my other half so much that I looked for a place without magic, hoping my bear would disappear."

"You can't rid yourself of who you are," I argue.

"I figured that out when I fell into a state of heavy depression and felt empty inside. I moved on until I found a place secluded and still full of magic. Too bad others had claimed it as theirs first."

"You built this cabin. Why do you stay here?"

He's silent for a few minutes while he focuses on wrapping my wrist. He then cleans up and settles into his chair again, staring into space. I'm about to ask again, but I'm not sure if I should.

Silas saves me from the need to decide what the best course is. "I don't know. Maybe I think I deserve the punishment that the cougars dish out. Maybe I'm afraid I won't find somewhere as good as this."

"You deserve peace, Silas."

"Do I?"

"You do. I fully believe that. You took a stranger in to avoid her death. After stuffing your true self down, you fought off cougars and kept her safe. You're more than you could ever understand."

I'm not surprised to learn how much I believe those words. Silas may aggravate me to no end, but he's the best man I've ever met. Maybe that's why I'm so conflicted. I'll never meet another like him. That thought makes my heart ache. Despite all I've been taught, I finally met a true gentleman, and he's nothing like my mother said he would be.

Silas still hasn't looked at me, so I try one more thing to snap him out of his internal darkness. "Can I see it again?"

This time, his head turns to me. I almost flinch at the pain and uncertainty I see in his eyes. He needs me to not fear him. He needs me to tell him he's worth more than he thinks. I have the ability to seal some of the cracks in his damaged sense of self.

"Are you sure?" he asks. "I don't want you to be frightened of me anymore."

"I won't be. You'll never hurt me."

And I know that to be true. All I need to do to prove that is one simple thing. At least both bites were done on the same hand. Standing, I reach with my good hand. He follows my lead, and I pull him toward the door. I know he can't change in this cramped space. His bear is too big.

When cold air blasts me, I'm happy to have kept my winter clothes on. I stop on the porch, but Silas moves down into the snow. After one last pleading look at me, which I meet with an encouraging smile, he strips his pants off. I grab them and fold them until they're needed again. Keeping my eyes in a polite place is getting harder and harder.

This time, I get to watch it happen without the danger of circling cougars and the surprise of not knowing. First, his snout lengthens as hair grows over his entire naked body. His body enlarges while his fingers fuse into massive paws with sharp claws on the ends. Within a matter of seconds, the large white and brown bear stands before me. I didn't notice it the other night, but he has purple eyes.

With a deep breath, I take the couple steps down and hold my hand out. He hesitates before coming forward to sniff my palm. The bear nudges me with his nose. Slow enough to make sure I'm not crossing any boundaries, I stretch out my fingers and touch his fur. It's fluffy and soft. The brown spots are a little coarser but still pleasant to touch.

Silas closes his eyes and grumbles a pleased sound, making me bolder. I practically pet him while combing my fingers through his hair. When I get to the top of his head, I feel two lumps by his ears. They feel like some sort of bony protrusion. The mood of the moment changes before I can blink.

He pulls away from me, eyeing me with uncertainty. I can tell whatever I felt is a sore spot for him. Maybe that's a product of his hybrid status. Silas shakes his head and begins to shift back. As he changes, I feel a wave of something hit me and make me tingle. Is that magic? I didn't feel it before, but things were a little more complicated.

I take a few steps back to give him room. My feet now rest on the step right before the top of the porch. Silas stands naked before me once more. When he points to the pants lying on the wooden surface behind me, I merely look at them and turn back to face him.

My eyes rake over his body. He's broken, like me. He thinks he's a freak that doesn't belong, like me. This man is hotter than any man has any right to be. A wild animal lives within his body.

And I'm alone with him.

Silas looks confused. As he starts to walk up the steps to grab his pants, I stop him with my hands on his shoulders. He looks into my eyes, and I see the purple flash again. I slide my hand to the back of his neck and devour his lips with a hunger that surprises even me.

The bear of a man pulls my body into his, exchanging the heated kiss with even more fire. When he pulls away, I feel breathless. "What brought this on?"

I gasp for enough oxygen to make my voice work right. "I trust you, Silas. I want you."

"But you can't stay."

"Let's live in the today. We don't know what the future holds, so let's do what we can now. I can't give you my heart, but I'll show you how much your presence means to me until I have to separate from you. Please. I need this."

His lips capture mine again, and I feel myself pushed backwards. The wreath falls as he closes the door. For the first time, he doesn't replace it. Instead, he maneuvers me backwards around the table, pulling off my coat as we go. I almost fall kicking off my boots, but his strong arms keep me from harm, as expected.

At the bed, he removes his clothes from my body. I have nothing to remove from him, so I use the time to run my hands over his hard curves. Feeling brave, I wander further south and take his stiff cock in my hands, making him groan and push into my touch.

Once I'm naked, he picks me up as if I weigh nothing and tosses me onto the bed. I gasp at the sensation of falling before I bounce on the firm mattress. Before I can recover, Silas is on top of me, licking and sucking on my collarbone. I moan and squirm at the attention.

Silas continues to move his mouth downward until he comes to my breast. He's slow and methodical, worshiping every inch of me. I've never been so thoroughly aroused. He's paying my body more attention than any man ever has before.

This fact is making me wet between the thighs as pressure builds within me. When he sucks a nipple into his mouth, I cry out and arch my back, forgetting everything in the bliss I feel in this split second. I groan and press into him.

Silas's other hand moves over my stomach, and I feel my legs parting without command. An eager thumb finds my clit. I'm no longer capable of sound. Shocked at myself, I find my hips moving to encourage his efforts. When a finger enters me, I find sound again.

"Silas," I say through my pants. "That feels so good."

His mouth is too busy with my other nipple to respond. A burning starts between my legs and travels up through my body. I'm trembling with the need for release. When I decide to listen to my body, he removes his hand. I cry out in despair.

Silas moves back up to my pleading lips. Between kisses, he says, "Not yet, my sweet. I want to feel it happen."

I'm about to argue, but then his length is pushing deep inside. I orgasm right then and there, prepped by his careful ministrations before. My nails dig into his arms as I cry out and shudder. It's like a gush of relief like I've never felt before. I tremble and shake until spent, collapsing beneath the burly man over top of me.

"I'm not done yet," Silas whispers into my ear before pulling out and pushing back in.

My body is instantly ready to do this again. I gasp and writhe beneath him, moving my hips to make him thrust faster. He complies, and I'm soon rising again. There is so much pressure building in my core that I feel ready to explode. I moan with the effort to hold back.

Then Silas is growling and grunting his release. I allow myself to take that leap with him, yelling his name. This time, I'm not the only one to collapse. Silas falls to the side and pulls me into his arms.

I don't know what the future holds for me, but this is right where I'm supposed to be at the moment.

CHAPTER TWENTY-FIVE
BROKEN SOULS

GRETA

It's blissful in his arms, and I take the time to suck in the feeling of belonging that I've never felt before. Too bad I have to give this up soon, as long as the weather holds. I feel right here. Leaving is going to suck.

At least I have the here and now. I can revel in this feeling and lap it up until I can't anymore. My stomach chooses this moment to rumble in frustration at its emptiness.

"Well, I guess that's our cue," Silas says, taking the wonderful feeling away by moving. "I need to feed my snow princess."

I prop myself up on my elbows. "Snow princess?"

"That's what you looked like when you were making the snow bear. I like that image and choose to keep thinking about it."

I blush. "I doubt it's much to look at."

"It was. Your cheeks were pink with the cold, as was your nose. The smile on your face was beautiful and happy enough to take breath away. I need to gut this deer. Would you like to learn how to do it with bigger prey?"

And there goes the bliss. "No thank you. I think I'll wash up and get dressed. Maybe use the little girl's room."

"You mean the outhouse?"

"Whatever you want to call it."

"Well, I don't want to think of myself going in a little girl's room, so let's keep it as the bathroom or outhouse."

"Buzzkill."

He simply grins, grabs his knife, and steps outside. I decide to stay in the warm blankets that smell like him for a little longer. No matter how thoroughly he changed the subject, I want to live in this a little longer. I don't need him to do that. Although, it is easier with his arms wrapped around me.

Groaning, I give up and slip out of the covers to wash. Once clean and warm in a new set of stolen clothes, I bundle up and step outside. The wind is gone, and the sun is out, bright and warm. Snow drips from everything in sight. I sigh as I take it in.

I'll need to leave soon. If this thought would have been possible from the beginning, I would have been happy. No longer. Instead of joy, I feel a heaviness in my chest, as if my heart has turned to stone. I don't get this feeling at all. That was just mind-blowing sex. Wasn't it?

When I turn the corner in search of Silas, I find him bent over the frozen body of a deer. As I watch him saw at the meat to free what he can, my stone heart plummets into my stomach. I don't get it. Why do I feel like I'm losing the world?

It's only been a couple of weeks, so why do I feel like I've known this man my entire life? Not only is our companionship new, but he lied to me throughout the whole thing. Yes, I've forgiven him. That still doesn't explain these strange feelings. What emotion is this? It's something I'm not familiar with.

Silas turns to notice me standing at the corner of the cabin with my gaze on him. The smile he sends me cracks the hard shell around my heart. Whatever this feeling is, I think he feels it as well. Otherwise, why would he smile at me as he does?

"Come to help?" Silas shouts over to me.

"I'll just spectate today," I reply with a warm smile. "Are you going to cut up all of that?"

"No. That would be a waste. Even two people can't eat all this meat before it'll spoil. I'll take what I think feels realistic, then I'll drag the rest into the trees. Another hungry predator will take it."

"Feeding the cougars?" We both know those are the main predators that are obsessed with this spot area of the forest.

He shrugs and places more meat in a sack he has next to him. "If it's them, then so be it. As long as it's all used up. I'd rather feed the enemy than waste the bounty of the forest."

This man is too sweet for his own good. He even still feels guilty over a kill made in self-defense. I can see his anger over how the cougars won't leave him alone, but I could also see the disgust he had for himself while talking about the fate-changing incident. Like I have room to talk. I'm the queen of conflicting emotions right now.

Silas walks over and hands me the sack. "I cut a couple steaks; they're on top. Rub a bunch of seasoning over them and slap them on the grate over the fire. I'll be back once I dispose of the rest of the animal. Anything left in the sack can be put away."

"What seasoning should I use?"

"Whatever you would like. I doubt you can ruin this."

I huff. "You underestimate me. I have no idea how to cook."

"Well, this is a good time to learn. Experimenting is a great way to learn new flavors."

Sighing, I nod. I stand and watch him drag the deer into the forest before heading back in. After taking the raw steaks out, I put the rest in the box. It needs more snow, so I do that real quick. Then I start to dig around in his spices.

Garlic powder and onion powder are favorites of mine. He's used them a lot in other dishes, so I decide that's a good start. I also remember him saying everything could use a little salt and pepper. He said a bunch, and I make sure to smother the meat in it. After perusing the box of supplies a little more, I pull out some green flakes that lost their label. Shrugging, I dump some of them on.

Like I've watched him do before, I rub the spices into the meat before throwing them on the fire. Silas returns as I clean my hands. He waits his turn to clean up, and I'm mesmerized by the process for a few minutes.

"Can you flip the steaks?" he says with a glance my way.

"Oh, yeah. Sorry. I was distracted."

His smirk warms my cheeks better than the flames can. I'm sure he knows what distracted me. My mind goes over what we did, and I wonder when it would be proper to do it again. I want to soak this man in before I have to walk away from him. That thought cools the heat rising in me.

This sucks.

The meat sizzles when flipped. Silas digs through the pockets of the pants he left on the floor and pulls a few green tubular plants out. "What are those?" I ask.

"I found some wild onions in a sheltered area while looking for somewhere to dump the deer. It's a rare find, and it may not be the best side dish, but we don't have a lot of veggies left."

"I'm willing to try it."

Another smile melts my heart, then he works on chopping the wild onions up. He places them in a skillet with some oil and other seasonings. Once the pan is crackling on the fire, I start setting the table. Not that it takes long with limited dinnerware and only two people. I return to flip the steaks.

"I could have gotten those," Silas argues. "Sit and relax."

"And miss my cooking class? No, thanks."

He chuckles and pushes the onions around in the pan. It's not long until the food is done. We sit and dig in. I'm reluctant to take the first bite, but I find the meat surprisingly delicious. I follow Silas's idea to put the onion on the steak and feel that makes it even better."

"You did well. This is really good."

"Thank you," I say with another blush.

We're silent as we eat, enjoying each other's company without the need for conversation. I always thought simple food looked boring and unappetizing, but I'm developing a preference for it. I do miss fruit.

I can't help but ask. "Do you ever find fruit in the forest?"

"I try to, and I sometimes acquire it outside the trees."

"How do you make the money to buy them?"

He grunts and lays the fork on his plate. "Since I'm being truthful, I tend to sometimes take things from the farms in the area. Never much, but enough to supplement what I can do myself. I've never been good at growing my own."

Shocked, I let my mouth hang open for a while. Silas is a thief. After some deliberation, I decide I can't judge whatever brought him to relying on others for survival. I do ask, "Do you ever offer to work for food?"

Silas seems surprised at the question. "Do they do that?"

"Some do. If it's a bigger farm, they'd be happy to pay in leftovers instead of cash. You should try it."

"I will. Thank you. It never crossed my mind to ask. I'll be happy to not need to take it without asking."

Feeling a little better now, I give him a bright smile. "What's your favorite fruit?"

"I'd have to say blueberries. You?"

"This store near us sells organic strawberries. They are the sweetest because they're vine-ripened. I go there often just for a carton."

"Are you going to run there and get some right away?" he asks, looking down at his empty plate.

I almost choke on my last bite of steak, and I feel the conversation sour. "Probably."

"This fiance you talked about; what is he like?"

I flinch, glad my meal is done, or I would be unable to eat it. "Terrible. Mother arranged the marriage because it's beneficial for the family."

"And you just went along with it?"

"My mother doesn't take no for an answer. I'm so used to following her orders that I didn't even think to do the opposite. It's not like I had many prospects anyway."

Silas narrows his eyes. "What do you mean? You're beautiful and come from a well-to-do family. I thought people always ate that up—so I've heard."

"You think I'm beautiful? You haven't even seen me with makeup on."

"You don't need it."

My heart aches once more. "Mother tells me I do because I'm plain without it. No reputable man would want me."

"She's full of it. You're a catch. This fiancé didn't seem to cherish you enough. You deserve someone so much better."

My mind immediately jumps to the fact I have him right now, but I push it away. No need to make this harder than it already is. "He cheated on me with his boss, so there's that."

"What's she like?"

It takes me a moment to understand what he's saying. "Oh, no. His boss is a man."

"Really? He gave you up for a penis?"

I choke on the water I'm trying to sip. Laughter echoes from me. "I don't care who he slept with. Penis or not doesn't bother me. It's the fact that he did it to begin with. I broke up with him, and he basically called me homophobic."

"You're not, I'm assuming."

"Not in the least. I've had friends that married the same sex. What about you?"

He shrugs. "Not my business who loves who, but your fiancé is a moron to give you up. I'm glad you didn't put up with it."

Looking down, I take a deep breath. "I broke up with him, but I almost went back to his condo to beg him to take me back."

"Why would you do that?"

"Mother told me to. She insulted me and reminded me that I'm not good enough for anyone else. My best friend, Dana, told me she doesn't know what she's talking about, but what if she's right? That's why I was out in the storm. I was trying to get to Dana's to keep myself from listening to my mother. I didn't make it."

I hear Silas's chair scrape across the floor. He grabs my hands and pulls me to stand in front of him. I refuse to look at him, not wanting him to see my tears. The choice is taken from me when he takes my chin in his hands and lifts it up. He sweeps away my tears with his thumbs before leaning in for a sweet kiss.

This isn't my playful peck I used before. It's not the hungry desire I experienced the other two times. It's slow. His lips caress mine as if afraid to ruin them; as if they're the most precious thing in the world. My vision blurs more.

Silas pulls away and braces my face in his hands. "You are so much more than you've been led to believe, Greta. You even showed this grouchy bear what it's like to care about another. I hate that your mother did this to you. I agree with this Dana. You are so important to me. Your tears break my heart because you deserve so much better. I wish you could stay with me."

"I wish I could too," I whisper.

That's all I can manage before my pain takes over. Silas takes me in his arms to let me sob away all my trauma. I could recognize his trauma because I have my own. We're both broken souls.

CHAPTER TWENTY-SIX
A LITTLE TOUCH OF HEALING

GRETA

The burning in my eyes brings me back to consciousness. They feel dry and sticky from my cry. Silas held me until our legs grew tired, then transferred us to the bed. I must have cried myself to sleep.

Opening my eyes hurts, but I manage to do it without waking the dreaming bear whose arms are wrapped around me. My cheeks feel raw, and my head hurts. Waking to his embrace makes it all worth it.

I've never told anyone about what my life is truly like, except Dana. Silas was patient and understanding, knowing the exact words to say. In fact, I can't believe he said those words. Sure, Dana says them all the time, but it feels different coming from a man I have budding feelings for.

I shake that thought away. No. I can't develop feelings. Feelings mean more heartache when the time comes to leave. This isn't anything more than two broken souls comforting each other and enjoying the company that comes with it. It doesn't hurt that we are enjoying something else as well.

But he told me so many things earlier that I can't push out of my thoughts. It's then that I realized he has feelings, but the thought of breaking his heart hurts. I don't want to cause pain. Yet, staying isn't an option. Not if I want to keep him safe. He's spent all this time keeping me safe, so it's time for me to reciprocate.

I may not be able to protect myself from my mother, but I can do for him what I can't do for myself. Shield him from her wrath.

Taking a deep breath, I tell myself that this isn't what I want to be thinking about right now. My last days need to be cherished before I'm forced to leave. Every single second I have left with Silas needs to be worshiped. I won't dwell on the things I can't change.

Silas rolls onto his back, pulling my head onto his chest without waking. I don't fight the movement, happy to be his teddy bear for now. My injured hand is free, so I use my fingertips to lightly trace the muscles on his chest and stomach, wondering at how well-sculpted he is. This man is glorious, any woman's wet dream.

And he's mine for a little longer.

According to the window, it's now night. What time, I'll never know. It was still bright and sunny when we ended up here, so we slept for a few hours. It can't be too far into the night yet. I wasn't physically tired, only emotionally.

My fingers trail further down, brushing across the area over his waistband. He hums a soft sound of pleasure, still not waking. Frustration grows in me, but I push it down. He worshiped my body the other day, so I need to repay the favor.

I move back up his torso, circling his nipple with my thumb. A growl reverberates in his chest, and tingles shoot through me with the sound. I'm not sure if it's the feelings he admitted to or his animal side, but he's better than any man I've ever had. He's selfless and hungry to please. Sex isn't just for his benefit.

Turning my face more toward him, I run my tongue over his other nipple. Another rumble vibrates my body, and I decide I need more. Silas's arm tightens, his hand squeezing my hip and raising my shirt to expose a little skin. Still not enough.

My hand dips low again, teasing along his pants one more time before dipping even lower. He squeezes again, a feeling that leaves me begging for more. I wrap my fingers around his hard shaft. There is a little pain from my injury, but it's more than worth it.

When Silas's breath hitches, I say, "You're awake. Aren't you?"

His chuckles cut short when I do one quick pump. "I wanted to see how far you'd take this."

"Are you satisfied?"

"No."

"Well, then, let's keep going."

I push Silas back down when he tries to roll toward me. Sitting up, I remove the covers from his body and pull his pants down. His cock shoots up as soon as the waistline of his pants releases it. The sight of him ready and needy makes my core burn for him to be inside me.

Instead, I take my time to finish pulling his pants off, then remove mine. My shirt comes off next. I crawl back up his legs, stopping to nip his hip with my teeth. He hisses and jerks, but it's not from pain. His cock brushes my neck and chin, so I decide to taste it.

My tongue moves up the shaft, making him moan in pleasure. At the tip, I move back down and take him in my mouth. He gasps and tenses at the feel of my mouth's heat. I only move up and down three or four times because all I want is a taste. There is another fate in store for his cock.

Crawling further up, I settle on his hips, his wet shaft against my backside. He takes my breasts in his hands and kneads, and I arch into his touch with a groan of pleasure. When he runs his thumbs over both nipples at the same time, I let out a small whimper. Desire pulses through the entirety of me. I need him now.

I reach back with my good hand, grab him once more, and slide over his stiffness with a moan. His squeeze of my breasts is almost painful, but it only fuels my desire more. I lean forward on my hands to adjust my angle and start moving my hips up and down.

Silas's head flying back toward the headboard is reward enough for my efforts. His hands squeeze my butt as he moves his hips with mine. Breathing becomes difficult with the mounting pressure and burning insides. Silas grabs my shoulders and pulls me down into a kiss.

Our tongues dance in fiery steps of pleasure. He bites my lower lip and braces the back of my head with his hands. Through all this, we both keep moving until kissing is no longer possible. The edge is coming close for both of us. I straighten and move faster while Silas's fingers dig into my hips. We both take the plunge over at the same time.

I cry his name while he roars like the bear he is. We ride back down, and I collapse on top of him. Silas wraps his big, strong arms around me as if he never wants to let me go. I lie against his beating heart until my hips start to complain. Rolling off him feels like I'm losing something important.

"Thank you," I say when I can talk again.

He laughs. "I think I should be the one to do the thanking."

"I mean from before. Your words."

"I only spoke the truth from the bottom of my heart. That's nothing you ever need to thank me for."

"This is coming from the man who gave minimal conversation when we first met."

"You might have been a threat."

I laugh. "I'm like half your size."

"Never underestimate the little people."

I smack him half-heartedly in the chest with the back of my hand. That's when something occurs to me. We've gotten so carried away that I never considered it. "Do I need to worry about a little bear cub?"

"No," Silas says with a sigh.

"You're sure?"

"Shifters and humans don't mate well. Not that I mind that at all because I don't want to bring another of me into this world to feel like they don't belong. I've heard it's possible if the human is subjected to the magic of the land over years, but this won't cause anything that needs to be worried about."

"Well," I say, "I think the world can use more men like you."

"Hybrids don't fit in anywhere."

"Neither do some humans. I know I don't."

"Maybe you're simply looking for the feeling of belonging in the wrong place."

I crane my neck to look up at him. "Maybe you are too. I need to cut this little piece of healing short. I need the lady's room."

"You need to stop making me feel like a perv."

"It's not like there are any ladies using it besides me."

He sits up with me. "I'll come with you."

"I think I can still find it in the dark."

"The forest is a lot more dangerous at night."

Right. I've been lost in this blissful existence that I almost forgot about cougars and wolves. Apparently, disgruntled bears too, but I trust Silas when he says that's extremely rare. I wonder whatever happened to the one we saw.

Shrugging, I get dressed and bundle up. My white-furred knight escorts me out into the darkness. I go first, relieving the painful bladder that's begging for attention. Silas follows but leaves the door open to be ready to defend me at a moment's notice.

As he does his business, I scan the darker shadows in the trees. Nothing moves. No sounds come to us. Are they out there? Are they mad they didn't scare me away from Silas?

It didn't take me long after the adrenaline wore off to understand the cougars forced Silas to go bear in front of me. They wanted me to see what he is. If they were expecting to have me turn him away because of it, they're sorely disappointed. Although, it almost worked. Silas is too trustworthy to fear for an extended period.

That means their plan failed, so they're going to need another. Will the next one involve me as well? What more can they do to me to get to Silas? My throat closes at all the options. It's best to leave those hidden in the back of my mind.

When Silas finishes, he takes my hand. We walk onto the porch together, and he opens the door before frowning at the empty hook. I bend down to find the wreath to hand to him while also grabbing the pants we left outside. As he puts it back in place, I take another look into the darkness.

A smaller shadow moves between trees. This close to shelter, I don't worry because I can easily get inside before anything could think of reaching us. I need to know what I'm seeing. A twig snaps in the distance, and Silas pulls me into the cabin.

"I was trying to see if it was them," I say.

"It is."

"How do you know?"

"I have better vision because of my bear side. They rarely come into the clearing, but I wasn't letting you risk yourself."

I scoff. "I was three steps from safety. I would have been fine. And they came into the clearing to destroy my snow bear."

The way his gaze jerks to mine tells me he almost forgot about that incident. "That's right."

"And I loved my bear."

"It was a magnificent bear."

I smile. "Not as magnificent as your bear."

He grins, pulling me into his arms for a kiss. It's not difficult for me to decide to oblige. He tastes divine. How will I ever live without this?

No, Greta. No thinking about that part of this.

The sound of something scratching glass pulls us apart. Silas tenses, and I follow his gaze to the window. A cougar stares in at us, propped up on the outside sill with its front paws. I yelp as Silas puts me behind him and snarls at the cat. It bares its fangs and disappears. We hear a yowl not far away.

In an instant, Silas is stripped and heading for the door. I chase after him, grabbing his arm. "They can't get you here."

"I'm not dealing with their threats, and they will learn the consequences that come with scaring you."

"Please, don't go."

Silas kisses my forehead. "This is necessary. Trust me. I will be fine."

"Silas!" I yell as he jerks his arm from my grip and barrels out into the cold darkness.

I call for him again before shutting the door when his bear runs into the forest. He shouldn't be out there, but following will only put him in more danger because he'll need to worry about me as well. Dividing his attention could end up with us both seriously injured, or worse. I can only wait for my bear to return.

CHAPTER TWENTY-SEVEN
A LITTLE TOUCH OF HEALING

SILAS

On four paws, I trot through the forest, chasing the tail of a cougar, who keeps himself slowed enough to let me keep him in sight but not close enough to harm him. I know this. He's obviously leading me, but my fury over the continued threats to Greta make me reckless. I don't care who I come across; they'll regret focusing their attention on her.

I'm sick and tired of these games. If they want to come for me, it's *me* they better harass. Greta is more than a game piece that they can move around to get to me. I'll make sure these beasts know that. They'll rue the day they set their cruel sights on her.

The cat in front of me picks up speed, quickly distancing itself from the lumbering bear behind it. Whatever the chase was for must be at an end. Nervous energy ripples beneath my fur. Running out blindly was a stupid idea, and I should have listened to Greta. What if they're attacking her as I stand here like an idiot? Does she know enough to use the lock on the door? I don't know if I ever showed it to her. It sticks and is hard to work.

Worried about the rest of their plans, I turn to make my way back. A voice stops me. "Fancy meeting you here, Silas."

My fur stands on end at the familiar tone. I turn and survey my surroundings. When I don't find the wretched beast of a man, I start scanning the trees. Sure enough, the bastard sits out of my reach. I bare my teeth in a snarl.

Ande only smirks down at me. "If you're worried about your female, don't. I simply wanted to talk to you, and I wanted it to be on my terms. Would you like to shift, or do you just want to listen?"

Like hell I'm turning back into my more vulnerable form. I can smell his cougars circling us, on the alert for any hint of weakness. There's no way I'll give it to them. My sharp teeth and claws stay. It's the only way I have a chance of surviving an attack. I don't have anything to say to Ande that I can't say in bear form.

"Well, I guess it's this form then. You really need to learn to trust more."

I growl at him, picturing tearing him limb from limb. The man doesn't deserve a quick death after all the threats and his fixation on Greta. I'll make it slow. All he needs to do is come down to my level. A fall would be nice, but even in this form, he has a cat-like grace. He sits in the tree as if he belongs in it.

"It seems that she didn't react to your true nature as expected. You must be *very* convincing."

His smirk and knowing look throws me into a rage. Roaring, I charge his tree and scar it with my claws. I can't reach the cat before he could shift and leave, but my rage needs an outlet. The tree is my target.

"Temper, temper, my bear friend. There's nothing wrong with enjoying the woman cooped up in your cabin. That's all females are good for anyway, as weak and fragile as they are. It's strange that her fright didn't warn her off your savage nature.

“My men circled around and were waiting for her to come down from that tree, but you got there first. I was curious if she'd stay up there and freeze to death if she saw us. Although, I doubt my cougars would have been that patient. You had to ruin the fun."

I'm going to rip him apart. Roaring, I attack the tree again, sinking my claws in and shredding it as I would Ande. Screw this. I'm going up.

As soon as I dig all four sets of claws in, Ande stands on his branch. "Do you really think you can reach me before I hop to the next tree? I don't even need to shift to do it either. Bears can climb, but we both know they're not suited for treetop chases."

Snarling, I let my body stand on solid ground again. I need to keep my cool and hope he makes a mistake. Keep him talking and wait for a good moment. I can only hope that moment comes.

"Smart bear. You see, we didn't lose. We've only been waylaid. Do you think I'd only have one plan? There is more to come. I figured that I'd give you warning—let the idea stew for an indeterminate amount of time."

That's it. Before I can stop myself, I'm growling while shimmying my way up the thick trunk. Ande simply laughs, shifts, and moves along the branch. He jumps to the next tree, and I allow myself to drop to the ground. My paws hit the snow at record speed as I chase him from one branch to the next. He's more likely to slip while jumping, so I've made my own luck.

It ends with a solid weight hitting me from the side. I stumble and turn in time to swat the cougar across the face. Two more come from behind to nip and claw at me. I spin, but they jump out of reach before I can even think of hurting them. Then all three are off.

My sides heave with my exhausted breath. A few trickles of blood tickle my haunch, but I ignore it. Small wounds heal quickly. My eyes continue to scan the trees. Ande is gone. Maybe the circling cats were really just a protection detail, not looking for a way to attack me. It seems like he wants to cause as much pain as possible before finishing me off. Sadistic, as always.

Turning, I amble back toward the cabin, no longer in a hurry. They ran away from my safe-haven, so they're not after Greta tonight. He simply wanted to gloat and add fear of losing her to my list of troubles. Now, I need to brace for an attack against her at every turn. Great.

There's no other way to think about this. Greta needs to go home. She needs to spend the rapidly approaching Christmas with her family. It's only about a week away; I can feel it in my bones. This bear is better off alone. I only bring danger to those around me.

I pause to look at my surroundings. The snow barely covers the ground, more mush than pristine white. The pile she drove into probably remains, but my strength should be enough to remove it as well. It will most likely be partly ice, so it'll be tough, but I can handle it. Then I can lead her out. She'll have no problem walking to her car in the little snow that's left.

I have no excuses left to delay her rescue. I have plenty of reasons to send her on her way. Although, it won't be that easy for my heart. All our time stuck in a snowy cabin has let me see what a truly wonderful person she is. That's only more reason to let her go. She deserves better than me.

Huffing a puff of breath out of my nostrils, I continue on, drawing closer and closer to the cabin that holds the woman I have to let go. I was always fine on my own, but the thought of my small home without her presence hurts. It's for the best for both of us. She can get away from killer cougars that want to hurt her to get to me. I can go back to fighting them on my own.

One thing's for sure; I'm done playing nice. Before, I wanted to mitigate further harm. Now, all bets are off. These cougars need to pay for the pain they put Greta through.

I reach the cabin, its welcoming warmth feeling chilly. This will be my last night with Greta, so I better cherish it. It's time for us both to move on to what we are meant for in life. My lonely existence and her hopefully learning who she truly is. She deserves better than me. She deserves so much more than a cheating fiancé. She deserves more than her awful mother. I'll have to put my reliance on her mother. Greta is beginning to feel more confidence, so maybe her mother's pushing will finish showing her the right way.

Shifting, I trudge up the steps to my final goodbye. As I walk through the door, Greta runs into my arms. I squeeze her tight, trying to memorize the feel of her small body against mine. Her scent fills my nose, and I try to embed it in my mind. Anything to make the parting easier. Anything to make her presence linger once she's gone.

She steps back and looks up at me. "I was so worried."

"No need to be. I'm back, safe and sound."

"Why do you sound so sad?"

I sigh and walk over to the table, sitting down with the rough wood of the chair scratching my bare behind. "I'm tired."

Not a lie, but not the truth either. I need to tell her. I need to make her understand. Soon. At this moment, my heart aches too much.

"Did I wear you out?" she teases, making me smile.

"I can never get enough of you."

"Maybe some food with help. I found a few more potatoes in the bottom of our stash. That's the last of them. I figured you might be hungry when you returned, so I fried them up with some of the leftover wild onions and venison."

Our stash. Soon to be just my stash once again. That thought makes my stomach bottom out, but I make noises that tell her I agree as she plates the food. She's learning to cook for me. This has gone on for too long. I push the grief down.

"Are you sure you're alright?" Greta says as she sits.

"Not really, but let's not ruin this great meal you made. We can talk after."

Her comforting smile falls. "Is it bad?"

"Just not what I want to think about right now. Let's eat. It smells delicious."

She looks at me with suspicion while I take my first bite and hum my pleasure at the good food. She's learning well. I watch Greta take a deep breath and turn to her food. The deer steak is cut into strips, and everything is fried together, so the flavors all mingle perfectly. I'm learning she likes garlic a lot. Another piece of information to file away in my Greta box to dwell on when my nights are empty.

Once done, I can't put it off any longer. "I'm going to take the shovel to your car tomorrow. I think the snow should be melted enough to get you out."

Greta freezes halfway to standing. I see a brief look of pain before she reanimates herself again to wash our plates. "Won't the pile still be there?"

"Yeah, but it should be small enough to work with."

"You don't want to wait a few more days to make it easier?"

Oh, how much I wish I could do that. Never would be acceptable as well. "It's not safe."

She pauses while wiping my plate and turns to me with wide eyes. "What do you mean?"

"That cougar was meant to draw me out. Ande, the cougar that leads the annoying felines, wanted to have a word with me. He threatened you."

She finishes the dishes in silence and sits on the bed. "Why me?"

"To hurt me."

"But I never did anything to them. Why punish me?"

Standing, I walk over and join her on the bed. I take her hand in mine. "It's all to punish me. They can tell we've grown close, and he knows your pain will cause mine. He's an evil bastard. This is why you need to go home. They can't get you within your bright lights and rich crowds."

Greta looks at where my hand clasps hers. The bandage on the other wrist reminds me why this must be so. They've already injured her once. When she sniffles, I can tell she's holding back tears. I lift her lips to mine, giving her a small kiss.

I don't have plans to take it further, but she makes the decision. Her tongue enters my lips, and I accept its presence. Greta devours my mouth in a feeling of desperation. Tears threaten at the thought of her pain. I bury the terrible emotions in the taste of this incredible woman.

Her good hand wraps around my cock, and I gasp at the sensation. The feel of her never disappoints. Feeling my own desperation rise, I pull her borrowed shirt over her head. Perfect breasts find their way into my hands. I squeeze, rewarded with a moan from Greta.

I spin, ending with her under me on the bed. Her scent of arousal spikes with my position over her, which makes me harder than I've ever been. I pepper kisses along her jaw and down her throat. My lips continue to move down, worshiping every bare inch of her. A perky nipple enjoys the feel of my tongue circling it.

She arches into me, and I cherish that I can make her feel like this one last time. My hand moves to her waistband, but she pushes me away. Shocked, I look at her with hesitation. With a grin, she pushes me over and takes the position on top after removing her pants. This may be the only sense of control she feels she has over her situation, and I won't begrudge it to her.

In fact, I'll enjoy it.

As her wet heat slips over my stiff shaft, I groan and throw my head back. She orgasms immediately, telling me how much she needs the closeness that comes with this. I reach up and fondle her breast as she rides me with speed that shocks. The pressure builds enough to hurt, but I don't release until she does for a second time. My pain is worth her pleasure.

Greta collapses on top of me, her heaving chest pressing against mine. I simply lie on the bed, arms outstretched as I enjoy the feeling of pleasure that still wracks my body. I'm unsure how long we remain this way, but she soon starts to kiss my chest and throat. I grow hard while still inside her from the last time.

This time, I roll her without extracting myself. She squeals and giggles, urging me on. If this is what she wants, I'll give it to her. She deserves the world, and I will let her have whatever she wants. We will enjoy our last night together. I'll revel in the taste, smell, and feel of her for as long as she'll let me. She's mine for a little longer.

CHAPTER TWENTY-EIGHT
LIFE'S A TEASE

GRETA

Stretching, I roll over to cuddle against my bear. When my grasping fingers meet empty blankets, I shoot up to find the other side of the bed void of life. Wakefulness assaults me as I look around frantically. I don't find Silas in the cabin at all.

Still groggy, I stumble from the bed, ignoring the soreness caused by all the action in it all night. The light looks weak, so it must still be early in the morning. After all that happened last night and this morning, I need a little more sleep. Silas should as well. Maybe he just went to the bathroom.

I open the front door, blinking at the light, to see Silas tying a pair of pants to a shovel. All worries and complaints forgotten, I stare at him with my eyes narrowed. "For some reason, I don't think we need to be worried about the shovel feeling cold."

Silas gives me a sad grin. "I'm going to walk the shovel up as a bear. I'll need pants when I shift back because I'm sure a naked man shoveling a car out of a pile of snow will turn a few heads."

"So one would think. You're heading out?"

"Yeah. I'm not sure what it looks like at the road, so it's best to get an early start."

"You seem to be in a hurry." My heart falls, and my eyes sting. He's already ready to send me off without any hesitation. It's not even full daylight, despite the observation of my tired eyes earlier.

Silas must notice my thoughts because he hops up the steps and wraps his arms around me. "I'm not in a hurry to be rid of you, Greta.

Ande didn't give me much to go on, and their attack can happen at any point. For your safety, we need to get you on the road before they realize you're gone. I don't want you to leave, but I'm not willing to risk your life because of my wants."

"I'm going with you."

He pulls away and looks me in the eye. "No."

"Well, if it's dangerous, you may need help. Give me the knife back."

"No. For all we know, the cougars may be waiting at the car." He moves back to dressing his shovel.

"Then they'll attack later as easily as now. I can help. If things get dangerous, I can jump in the car and lock the door."

"You're safer here. It's going to be hard to keep an eye on everything if you're there."

I feel my stubbornness surfacing. "Then I can be your lookout."

"No! I will not risk it. Cougars are versed in stealth. You wouldn't know they're there until they were taking a bite out of you. It'll be safer for me to walk you to your car as a bear right when it's time to leave. Please, just do this for me."

"Fine!" I say, stomping back into the cabin like a petulant child. It's not that I don't believe in his strategy—I do—but these are my last few hours with him. I'd like to be by his side. Besides, I feel like I really could help. Yet he's pushing me away.

Silas follows me in. "Let me show you how to lock the door."

"I noticed that the door locks last night, but I couldn't get it to work."

Silas closes the door behind him. I didn't even realize how cold I was until he cut off the stream of wintry air. Shivering, I rub my arms and make sure to focus.

"You have to lift the door up just enough to line the bolt. I didn't get it just right. You also need to pull out a little. Like this," Silas explains.

I watch him do as he said, then try it myself. Silas makes me do it over and over until I could lock the door blindfolded. He leans down and kisses the top of my head, embracing me for a minute and inhaling deeply. He then gives me a secret knock, demonstrating on the door frame; two quick raps and a third about three seconds behind those. I memorize this in front of him too.

"I'll be back to escort you as soon as I'm done," he says, pulling away. "Lock the door behind me."

Silas steps out without waiting for me to answer. I stand in the doorway with my hands rubbing my arms, watching him strip. He stops before he shifts.

With a glance my way, he says, "Lock the door."

"I want to watch you leave."

"I want to make sure you don't have any trouble. It can be tricky, and I won't let you here without the proper protection."

"We just practiced it and our secret knock until I can do them in my sleep."

"Greta, just do it."

"Whatever," I say, slamming the door behind me. Without thought, I position the door properly and slam the bolt into place. I then give the door two quick knocks and a third after counting out three seconds to be a smartass.

I can hear Silas mumble on the other side of the door, but I can't make the words out. Probably not complimentary, but I don't care. I know he's worried about my safety. Does he have to be so cold? The embrace and kiss were the only warm things about him. It would be more heated riding a motorcycle in the winter.

Sighing, I pace the small cabin before looking out the window. I see a white and brown bear disappear with a shovel in his mouth. Another shadow follows, and my breath stops. I want to warn him, but he'd only yell at me. Besides, I didn't actually see what it was, so I could be anything besides a cougar. Silas's caution just has me on edge.

I'm not sure how much time has passed, but I think it's been a while. The sun is much brighter now. I've lost all track of time while circling my small space. The spider watches me from the ceiling corner, a fresh egg sack next to her. I grimace and finally stop my pacing.

At least I won't be here for the infestation that comes with those hatching. What am I supposed to do while I stand here and worry? I tried a book. That was laughable. After a quick sniff, I decide I could stand a wash.

Pausing, I look over at the washbasin, then down at my borrowed clothes. Silas probably needs these. I hang a large pot of water over the fire and place a few more logs to increase the heat. Next, I throw a piece of soap in it and submerge my clothes with the poker. I'll let those warm up, then scrub them as best I can.

While waiting, I go ahead and wash up, putting Silas's clothes back on before gingerly removing mine and tossing them in the basin. I do my best to clean the body odor and mustiness off of them. When I finish, I wring them out. I hang them to dry before Silas returns to take me to my car.

With that done, I feel like I have nothing else to do, so I go around sorting through some of the mess. The couch is a ruin of dark red stains that I can do nothing about. Instead of even attempting to clean it, I throw a fresh blanket over it.

I then use the rest of our indoor water supply to wipe things down as best I can. The old broom has seen better days, but it works well enough. When I get the dirt pile into the pan, I look around. Normally, things like this go outside. I'm not allowed to step foot through that door.

Shrugging, I put the dustpan by the door. A look around tells me it didn't do much, but it did keep me busy for a little. Maybe I should eat. The thought makes my stomach flip. It's hard to find an appetite when someone you thought cared is pushing you out the door like his life depends on it.

That's not fair of me. Sighing, I collapse onto the chair and let the tears fall. I don't get this. Going home is what I wanted. Why am I so upset about it? I know Silas would keep me here if he could, so why am I turning him into a villain for trying to protect him?

Maybe it's the coldness. Is that his way of letting go? He'll feel less pain at the expense of me. This is ridiculous. There shouldn't be any pain on either side. This isn't a relationship. We have always known we must part ways. It's stupid to think of our companionship as anything other than that.

So, why do I? Groaning, I bury my face in my arms on the table. This shouldn't be so hard. Sure, I've felt freedom. That doesn't mean it's meant to last. I should know this because I've never in my life been allowed freedom. Soon, it'll be back to galas and balls; smiles and waves; cameras and flashing lights. Let's not forget a mother that is so narcissistic that she can't feel love.

That thought surprises me. Before, I would have never had the courage to think that, no matter how much Dana told me so. After so long living in the wilderness without her, I've come to see the truth of it.

And I'm going right back into the lion's den.

Am I stupid for doing this? Couldn't we just run away and find an even more remote location? That's a fantasy that I can't indulge in. Silas is sending me home, afraid of the cougars that have threatened my life to get to him. This all feels surreal, and I have to keep it to myself in civilization.

Silas will probably move on now that I'm not holding him back. He'll leave the evil felines behind, even if he promised I could visit. There's no question that he doesn't want me to anymore, so that's a point that doesn't matter.

I already feel so empty. The weight of my status already drags at my shoulders. Mother will make me beg Damian to take me back, like she tried to before. I'm sure that during the press conferences, she'll be nothing but the relieved mother, happy her only daughter is back. Behind closed doors, I'll be slapped and lectured. First, for trying to defy her. Then, for getting lost in the woods. More for embarrassing the family by daring to disappear.

Maybe the cougars would be more merciful. They'd only claw and bite until I died. My mother does the same and will do so for the rest of my life. The cougars would be quicker and less painful.

I snort at my thoughts. Like I have the guts to walk out and offer myself to them. Just the thought of the pain in my wrist is enough to make me stop. That hurt and letting them take actual chunks out of me would be worse than that. It's not a thought to even consider.

It looks like I'm doomed to a life of being bullied and unloved. Maybe that's all there ever was for me. I'll have to ignore Damian's many mistresses and smile for the cameras like a happy housewife. Pop out a few kids and be the model mother. Live a loveless life forever.

This was only an interlude, showing me what I could have if life was different; kinder. Silas was only meant to show me what I can never have and make me more miserable than before as I remember what could have been. All his beautiful words to me, the touches and caresses, the kisses, and the mind-blowing sex were only a tease. Life wants to make sure I understand how thoroughly it hates me.

Two quick knocks, then the last sound on the door. Despite my melancholy and the fact that I know better, my heart flutters. I'm an idiot. Like always.

That doesn't stop me from almost skipping to the door. After a brief struggle, I yank it open. A lithe man with light brown hair and golden-brown eyes stares back at me. "Thanks for demonstrating the way to get you to open the door before locking yourself inside. My name is Ande."

Gasping in recognition, I try to slam the door shut on him. He hits it with enough force that I fly back and roll across the floor. Before I can recover, Ande grabs my hair. Sharp, blinding pain explodes in my temple, and consciousness flees.

CHAPTER TWENTY-NINE
UNLEASH THE BEAR

SILAS

Opening my jaws, I drop the shovel into the thin layer of slush. This recent unexpected warmth is helpful for melting the snow, but it's not comfortable when you're sporting fur thick as a polar bear. I quickly shift and put my pants on to walk the rest of the way on two legs. While unexpected, it's not so rare that this warm bout is anything to worry about. It happens from time to time.

The look of hurt in Greta's eyes has been haunting me the whole way here. I feel guilty for hurting her, but it's for the best. She needs to leave to get away from Ande and his miscreants. I won't have her killed because of me. This pain will be easier to handle than a group of cougars attacking her at the same time.

I can't stand seeing the tears in her beautiful light blue pools. It's better than seeing the red of her blood on the ground and her cold, dead eyes. No matter how much this hurts both of us, it needs to be done. She needs to return to the human world, where she belongs. The middle of a supernatural battle is not a place for a being without magic.

Her car comes into view. As expected, it's mostly free. She's still embedded in the pile, but it doesn't look like it's going to be an issue. In fact, this shouldn't take more than an hour or two to shovel free. The issue is going to be the large rock I see behind her front tire. The snow must have made it easier for her to go up and over it without damaging anything.

I begin work around the car, which will be the easiest part to clear. Most of it is mush, making it heavy, but it still comes away easily. It helps that I have a bear's strength to work with. As I go, I check all her tires to ensure they're still good. They look a little low. They should still get her to the town down the road, and she can fill them somewhere there. I don't have any way to help with that part since I don't drive. In fact, I only know as much as I do thanks to a stop I made in a small town when I was trying to avoid magic. My strength made me useful in a local garage in the area. Not that I know much, but I know this.

She should be fine, as long as she doesn't hit anything nasty on her way. At worst, she'll make it to town and need to call for assistance. With that done, I move on to the leftover pile. Her bumper is only slightly snagged in it. Like I thought, it's icy. Worse than I thought, I'm going to need to chisel it.

First, I work what I can free, then search for a sharp rock. It takes longer than expected to work enough free that I can see the edge of the bumper. Thanks to my partial immunity to the freezing cold, my hands are only a little numb. I use the shovel to scrape the leftovers away from the front of her car.

Now, it's time to turn my attention to the rock. This will be more difficult.

As I kneel to get a better look, I notice something in her front wheel well. I reach in, freeing it from its spot, and lean back to look closer at it. It's smaller than my palm and covered in mud and mush. It also looks a little banged up. Whatever it is, I've never seen one before.

I click the displaced casing back into place and bang it off my hand a few times. A small light gives three weak blinks before it goes out again. Clueless, I shrug and place the strange device on the passenger seat as I slip into the driver's. I left the keys in her ignition after I turned it off, so I'm happy to see they're still there. Since the car is free, I'll remove them and carry them with me.

First, though, I turn them to make sure it starts. Glad to hear the engine, I also check her gas level. Everything looks good. Now to move back to that stupid rock. Another look under shows me it's right in the middle. Reaching allows me to touch it, but I need to get behind it to pull it out. I check her trunk to find a jack.

Once the car is high enough, I'm able to wiggle under and grab the large stone. It takes all of my strength and lots of grunting, but I finally pull it free. I return the jack and lock everything up.

Before heading back, I take a moment to stare at the vehicle that will take the woman I want to hold close far away. Last night was wonderful, and I'm glad I had it. Too bad I'll never have that again. I'm not sure what exactly it is about Greta that makes me want to spend the rest of my life in her presence, but something makes me desire to keep her close.

Sure, I found her annoying at first, her naivety and lack of survival skills. Then I learned there's so much more to her. She buries her strength down deep, probably a survival mechanism I didn't notice at first. She's quick to learn new things and help where she can. Her soft-spokeness comes off as weakness at first, but I've noticed it's more politeness and reservedness causing it. Greta likes to be kind. Yet, she wants to fully understand someone before opening up.

I've never met another woman like her. She feels like a kindred spirit that I don't want to let go. I don't have a choice, and I probably never did. My enemies became her enemies the moment I pulled her from the front seat. It's best for her if she moves on.

Sighing, I take a look at the sky. It's only been about an hour and a half, judging by the change in light. There's still plenty of time, and I'm not ready to bring her to the method of distance yet. I'll walk back on two legs. It's slower than four, but it'll give me more time before the inevitable. Anything to keep what's coming as far away as possible.

I pause partway into the trees, sniffing the air before crouching to examine the muddy ground with a covering of mush. The paw print has four tows with the imprint of claws. The M shaped heel, coupled with the scent on the air, can only mean one thing.

"Stupid cougars," I mutter. "Why can't you just leave me be?"

If they'd simply leave me in peace, I'd leave them alone as well. Isn't it enough that they have tortured me as long as they have? They've injured me countless times. They've hurt Greta. Why can't they just accept that I've had enough?

A twig snaps in the distance, and I scowl. Felines are silent hunters, so I know that sound was for my benefit. They want me to fret over their presence, but I refuse to. I've beaten them countless times, even in human form. They won't win this. In fact, I'm no longer worried about not causing fatalities. They've gone too far.

"Bring it on," I mumble, watching the landscape for any movement.

My bear is ready, right beneath my skin. Let them try it. They'll be lucky to return to Ande only missing a couple of legs. My rage and protectiveness overrides all of my passivity. Let them try me.

When none attack, I scoff. "Cowards."

Turning back towards the pull of home, I start walking, my senses straining for an attack I'm sure will come. They're circling me, not being at all careful about the noise they make. They're cocky, but I'll knock that right out of them.

Greta came into my life and made me feel something besides shame and pain again. I grew close to her. They're taking it all away. They threatened her to no end. They tried to frighten her away with knowledge of what I am, forcing my shift to protect her. Her wrist bears one of their bites.

I will take no more from them. My nerves are in overdrive, and I'm ready for blood. The next cat that tries me will learn just what they've awoken inside me. I'll do more than knock them out and scratch them up. They'll pay for it all. I just need one to take the risk.

None do. A few times, I catch glimpses of their feline bodies. A tail here and there. A supple brown body moving tree to tree. A hiss following me on the air. None of it amounts to anything, but I know they're there. What do they want? Are they trying to goad me? All they need to do is come closer to learn how much I'm ready for a bloody fight.

Instead, they continue to circle the whole way. I walk slowly and warily, but they never draw close. It's almost like they're escorting me. I could change. That will make it seem like I'm frightened of them. I'm not in the least bit. I'll take them all on if I have to.

They back off a little when I enter the clearing containing my cabin and the woman I need to escort far away from me. I pause, thinking about the possible danger of doing that while they're following. Maybe they're waiting for the right moment to attack. Bringing her into the open may be that opportunity. What choice do I have? I can't keep her prisoner.

When my eyes reach the door, my heart stops at the sight. It's hanging open, the door and the framework busted up. My wreath lies in pieces in the snow. I jump over it without thinking.

"Greta?!"

I enter the cabin and see the destruction wrought upon it. The fire is out, Greta's clothes hanging over the fireplace. The bed is torn to shreds while the table lies on its side. All my supplies are destroyed and strewn across the floor. The smell of cougar urine wrinkles my nose in disgust.

None of that matters. "Greta?!"

She doesn't answer me, which leaves me terrified of what I might find. I rush around the small space, looking for any sign of her. I'm partly relieved to find no trace of blood or her body. She's not here. That can only mean one thing.

I run back out onto the porch. "Damn you, Ande! If you harm a hair on her head, you'll be begging me to tear you to shreds!"

Yowls, growls, and hisses ring me from the trees. Those bastards are here to see my reaction. Well, they won't like what I'm about to show them because I know exactly where this ragtag group dens. Ande keeps them in a cave system like actual animals. If he wants a feral beast, he's about to see one.

My bear comes without prodding, and I roar my rage into the air. It bounces off the trees, scaring the circling cats into the forest. They won't go far, but they're about to learn what comes to those that take what's mine. I may be letting her go, but Greta will always be mine. They'll rue this day if they can survive it. I'll take this right into the cougar's den if I have to, and those mangy felines will regret the day their mothers gave birth to them.

Starting with Ande.

I barrel into the trees, continuing to bellow my anger. I catch the scent of cougars all around, but the sounds only come from the direction I'm heading. They know I'm coming for them. Let's hope I'm not too late.

CHAPTER THIRTY
HOPELESS

GRETA

Whispers make my head ache worse, so I scrunch my eyes tighter, not ready to wake into a world of head-splitting pain and nausea. Tears fight against the walls of my eyelids, but I refuse to let them through. All the books and movies I've read and watched show people forgetting what happened. I don't.

I remember exactly what happened in the cabin. Ande showing up at the door. Me trying to slam it shut, only to be thrown and dazed. The sharp pain of my hair being pulled back and the larger pain of something hitting my temple. Then the blackness taking over.

Silas's musty smell is absent here. All I can catch a hint of are unwashed bodies, blood, and decay. Oh, and stone. Judging by how hard the surface beneath my tortured body is, I'm guessing I'm lying on some kind of rock. I don't want to look.

My bear fought so hard to keep me safe and get me away before something like this could happen. He failed. Not that I blame him because I'm not his responsibility. I'm also sure they had no thoughts about giving up easily. Maybe they were waiting for us to make a move. If so, we played right into their hands.

I can hear Ande's voice over the whispers, making me even more reluctant to open my eyes. I'd bet my entire wealth that he will gloat over the fact I'm in his custody. He'll say terrible things about Silas. He'll do whatever he can to turn me against the man that saved my life before slaughtering me before him. I won't do as he wants. I'll die with dignity.

The man in question shouts at someone, which startles me enough to force me to open my eyes. Another pair stare directly into mine, and I scream before jerking upright and regretting the movement instantly. As I hold my head and moan, a small naked child runs into the arms of a woman in the back of the cave.

Ande stomps over to the woman and yells at her. "I told you to keep your damn kitten away from my prisoner!"

The volume of his voice sends sharp agony throbbing through my skull. I clench my teeth and scrunch my eyes shut while pressing into my temples with the heels of my hands. I swear every word he yells produces a splash of color behind my eyelids. I think I might throw up.

When a hand yanks my hair again, I do just that. The fact that I can just make out Ande jumping back from my stream of vomit gives me some satisfaction. I hope I got him, and I hope it's disgusting. This hurts so bad.

"Stupid human bitch," Ande growls. "Females are always so useless, particularly human ones. It's disgusting. Someone get me a rag and water. She got my feet."

It's hard not to smile at the end of that. He thinks I'm disgusting now? If he messes with my head again, I'll make sure to aim higher. As the agony eases slowly, more sounds break through my fog. Feet pattering on stone. Fire crackling. Running water echoing.

This time, the pain is much less when I open my eyes. It still hurts, but I need to know my surroundings to figure out the best way to get free. That doesn't make it easy to force myself to take note of what's around me. Nothing is easy right now.

Ande watches someone clean his feet by the fire. Mean looking men pace around one side of the cave I'm in while other strong ones gut a bear. It takes a moment of fear before I realize the bear is brown. Not

Silas. He's still safe, and I hope he stays that way, but I highly doubt he will. Silas will come for me. They'll attack him.

I need to do something, but I'm stuck. There is a group of what I'm assuming are all cougar shifters surrounding me. Even the youngest member could kill me in this condition. I need to feel better. Too bad I don't know the way out.

Looking behind me, I see more people who look depressed and afraid. If I have to guess, the strong, mean guys are probably guarding the way in and out. That's something. It still doesn't help me get out of here, not with so many of them watching my only exit. Cougars are a lot faster than I am.

The only women in the cave are behind me, as well as the children and some smaller men. Ande keeps all his strength in the front, which makes sense to me. The people in the back seem subdued and jumpy. I can't blame them. From what I've heard and the little I've seen of Ande, he is not a good leader.

I rub my eyes in an attempt to dispel the swirls swimming across my vision. They come and go, but the pain is still there. When Ande is done, he stalks over to me.

"Let's try this again, woman. Look at me," he says.

The demand in his voice is clear, and I am in no condition to fight it. I look up. "Let me go. I've done nothing to you."

"Oh, yes you have. You've given my enemy a will to live, so you're going to take it away from him."

"Screw you. I'm not doing anything to hurt Silas."

He chuckles. "Do you think you have a choice? Your death will affect him more than anything else ever could. Stupid bear fell in love with a human."

My head jerks as I stare at him with wide eyes. "He has never professed love to me, so I think you're misjudging it. Silas simply saved my life. He's in a hurry to send me on my way."

Ande rolls his eyes and looks at the smirking men behind him. "I knew humans were stupid, but did you ever expect this level of blindness?"

The mean men up front laugh. I feel a mixture of shame and anger. Anger for the insults. Shame for wondering if they're right. They can't be. Otherwise, Silas wouldn't be pushing me away as he is. He'd want to keep me and continue to protect me. You don't throw away someone you love.

"Whatever you believe," Ande says, bringing my gaze back to him, "this will hurt him greatly. It's going to be painful; just to warn you. The more you scream, the more he'll die inside. I'll break him before ripping his throat out."

I can't let that happen. Too bad I don't know how to stop it. The only chance I have is to convince them otherwise. "You're crazy if you think I'm the means to your desired end."

"Then you're no use to me."

I swallow hard, already knowing this train of conversation would lead to this. I'm dead either way. Without me, they lose their lure. I'll do this for Silas for as much as he's done for me. It's not like I want to go home anyway.

Ande startles me by breaking out in a laugh. "Look at this human. She's already figured it out. Maybe not as dumb as I thought, but that's not saying much. Even my weakest are much, much smarter than you are, Greta."

As he says the last part, he waves his hand toward the group huddled behind me. I glance back again, examining them with clearer vision. They're all skinny and pale, avoiding looking anywhere near Ande. I reevaluate his leadership. He's not a leader. He's a sadistic tyrant. Even the children look sickly.

On the contrary, his fighter males are all strong and well-fed. I bet they eat first, and the rest have to fight over the scraps. Despicable.

"Do you know what that smelly bear did to me and mine?" Ande says, bringing my attention back to him.

"Killed one of your cougars in self-defense."

Ande snarls. "He killed my successor for rightly trying to chase the intruder out of MY land. You know nothing."

"Your successor? Your child?"

"Please," Ande says with a scoff. "My mate gave me only females and weak males, neither fit to rule. My second mate did much better after I killed the first, but that boy is too young yet. No, he killed my oldest daughter's mate. She was a beauty, and the perfect trophy for the future leader of my cougars. She's weak like all the others. Ran off when her mate was killed. She hides in the city, but I'm prepared to bring her back and punish her—remind the wretches behind you why I'm in charge."

"Because you're cruel?"

"Because I'm strong. Cruelty doesn't factor into it. I lead by fear because that's the best way to keep everyone in line. You're too weak to understand that."

"Only the weak lead by fear," I mutter.

His hearing is apparently impeccable. Ande backhands me, and I fall back hard enough to hit my head off the stone. I cry out as the colors flash again. I roll over to throw up once more. The man that keeps damaging me grunts his disgust at my weakness.

"Pathetic," he says. "In my world, you would've been killed at birth, not fit to be even in the group of my weakest. The bear is more desperate than I thought if he fell for you."

Tears threaten, but I hold them back. The insults hurt. Not as bad as my head though. My head is pure agony, a container that holds pain and dizziness. There's no way I can get out of this without help. There's also no help to be had. I'm doomed to be nothing more than a lesson for a man I don't want to hurt. I can't be the reason he breaks further.

Ande is wrong. Silas is so strong. He's endured so much. I can see it in his eyes. Silas is already broken, but he still goes on. That's strength. Having to beat people into submission is a weakness because the only thing of value you have is your physical strength. Silas is so much more of a man than Ande is.

The smell of searing meat hits me, and my stomach rumbles. It seems that losing everything in my tummy empties it too thoroughly. Even my dizziness and light-headedness can't make me less hungry. I'm in no state to do much of anything, so I just lie on the hard floor of the cave and watch them cook meat.

As I thought, they feed the fighters first, then the other group. Even there, the men go first, then the children. The women go last, eating so little that I wonder how they can even stand. I take a breath and push the pity down. No use feeling sorry for them when I'm in an even worse position.

Once the carcass is clean, it's dragged from the cave by one of the weaker males. Ande doesn't understand the truth. His physical strength makes him a bully, not a leader. A true leader lifts those under them up. I have plenty of experience with cruelty, so none of this really surprised me. It's hard to feel shocked when meeting the crude male version of my mother.

A cougar runs in and shifts to a man, making me shiver. A world of magic I never knew existed, and I'm surrounded by it. This is a world I don't belong in.

"The bear is on the way," the new man says.

Gasping, I sit up and try to stand. Ande sits beside me and pushes me back down. I'm feeling stronger, but not strong enough to fight his touch. I have to do something. I must warn Silas of the trap. That's assuming he doesn't know it is one. He's smart. He has to know. Those thoughts give me a little hope. Another look at the number of enemies in this cave dashes them again.

"It's time, my weak human. Thanks for helping me destroy the plague in this forest. It's almost time. We'll make sure to make it hurt."

CHAPTER THIRTY-ONE
A Dangerous Choice

SILAS

The scent of cougars grows until it's overwhelming. My paws slow in the slush, and I walk with caution. With the smell being so strong, it would be easy to be snuck up on. From this point on, I must take care.

All senses strain for any hint of an attack, but none come. I'd frown if my bear was capable of it. What game are they playing at?

The opening to their den comes into view. Two men stand at attention, ready for an attack and eyes locked on me. They're in human form, tensing while they wait to see what I do, but they make no move to shift. Either this is a trick, or they want me here for another reason. I can guess what that reason is, and it makes me want to go into a murderous rage.

I hold back my need to attack. Wait until I know what's happening. Going in without thinking will put Greta in more danger. Patience and strategy are what I need now. Deep breaths and calm.

One of the men stomps on the muddy ground. "Shift, bear. Ande wishes to speak to you."

I cock my head to regard him for a few moments. Human form will put me at more risk, but I doubt they'll let me in without complying. I'm wanted for whatever torture they've prepared, so I highly doubt they'll attack me yet. It's best to do as they say.

The man raises an eyebrow, and I huff in annoyance at his lack of patience. Cougars are annoying. I will my form to change back to that of my two-legged human. I'll put myself into any danger I need to ensure her prolonged life. This may put me at risk, but it lessens hers.

If she's still alive.

"Greta?" I say when I have the use of words again.

"Alive and waiting inside. Go in. We have all our fighters inside, so be on your best behavior. The attacks you've had before are nothing compared to what will happen if you attack here."

"Just give her to me, and I'll be on my way. I'll move on if that'll help. She isn't part of this feud."

The man speaking sneers. "What you want doesn't matter. You killed one of ours and will pay for it. Ande waits for you inside. Don't make him any more impatient, or the woman will pay for it."

My mind only hesitates for a moment before propelling my feet to follow his direction. Entering most assuredly means my death, but not entering will hurt Greta. I need to do this. If I'm lucky, I'll be able to find a way out of this scenario. All I need to do is stall until I locate that opening.

The two men separate from my path, allowing me to walk between them without bumping either. They look at me as if I'm riddled with disease and decay, but I only have eyes for the way forward. The trap has sprung. Let's hope I can free myself in time to make a difference.

Another group of men stand at the opening to a larger cavern. They smirk at me and step away to let me in. A few smaller cougar shifters huddle in the back, but I only have eyes for the figures I see in the center. My instincts threaten a growl. I swallow it in hopes of keeping Ande from the attack. Not with her so close to him.

Greta makes to get up and dash for me, but Ande has his arm around her shoulder. He sits hip to hip with the woman I came here for. Her beautiful light-blue eyes are wide with fear while her blonde hair is in disarray. A black and blue mark covers her right temple, but she's otherwise unharmed. I need to keep it that way.

"Silas," Ande says, making me frown. "You seem to have lost something."

A few others snicker around us. My lip twitches with the need to snarl. I keep it under control while I gaze around the cavern. The only way out is the way I came, through too many fighters. Who knows what the cougars in the back will do if I turn hostile. I need to play it cool.

"And I'd like her back," I answer.

He shakes his head. "That isn't how this works. The time has finally come for you to pay for past deeds. Isn't that exciting?"

I take a deep breath to push down my anger. "Let her go. I won't fight you."

"I'm expecting a fight and looking forward to it. Try again."

My teeth clench hard enough to make my jaw hurt. "Let her go. She has nothing to do with this."

"Oh, but she does. This woman has been *thoroughly* claimed by you. I can smell you on her—inside of her."

Greta flinches and blushes under his very obvious hidden thoughts. The fact that he's using what we shared against me makes my blood boil. Holding back hurts. Every muscle in my body clenches with the need to rip him into tiny pieces. I'm envisioning it.

"That doesn't mean she has a part in this," I say as calmly as possible.

"You hurt me and my cougars grievously, Silas. I need to return the favor. What better way than the female you've been rutting with?"

Greta locks my gaze with hers and opens her mouth. Whatever she's about to say is silenced when Ande squeezes her shoulder and pulls her even closer to him. Her lips snap shut, and she sends him a glare he ignores. It's clear he sees her as no consequence, besides a tool to teach me a lesson.

"Do I need to beg?" I ask, hating myself for stooping to this level.

"It may help."

Sighing, I kneel. "Please, let her go. I beg you to. What happened was a terrible accident that's been on my conscience since. I didn't mean to kill him. I was only trying to scare him off of my kill. It went too far."

Ande looks at me with his head cocked. "Nah. It didn't help. Why would I be moved by you telling me that you didn't mean to kill him when you shouldn't be in my territory to begin with? Think about that."

He's heartless, and I shouldn't have thought any less. Begging won't help; it's all for amusement. Ande doesn't care about what I want. He doesn't even care about dirtying his hands with innocent blood. To him, Greta is nothing more than a means to an end. I need to make sure the end is not what he expects.

While his fighters snicker behind me, I have to fight to keep my temper in check. The only way I'll have even the slightest chance to gain the upper hand is to remain calm and collected. I must be able to think clearly. Thinking brings only one choice to me, and I have to make it count.

"Let's settle this between us, Ande," I say.

"I already told you I'm not letting her go."

"That's not what I'm saying."

Ande narrows his eyes, but I can't help but see the pleased gleam in them. "What are you talking about then?"

"A one-on-one fight. Me and you. If you win, I'll be weakened and still have to watch what you have planned. If I win, you let her go, and I'll still stay to deal with your wrath. Take out your vengeance on me now and enjoy more later."

I'm not stupid. I know he won't hold to the deal, but neither will I. This won't be a fight until one is down for me. I plan on taking him out alone and hoping his cougars walk away when their leader is dead. It's a small chance. Any chance is welcome.

"I don't know," he says. "I kind of like my original plan."

"You still have a chance at it. This is just a little proposition."

"I think I'll stick to killing her in front of you, then killing you."

Greta tenses more under his arm. Having him repeatedly speak of her death like it's nothing can't be easy. I'll skin his cat alive if I can for what he's doing to her. I'm sick of this evil bastard.

"Well, if you think there's no chance you'll win, I can understand," I say, letting my fear show for however he wants to interpret it. Showing weakness now can only help me.

The wicked expression on his face is enough to tell me he took it in a way that he thinks can't be good for me. To be truthful, I don't think it is either, but I'm trying to talk him into a fight between just the two of us. Even if he agrees, I'm not even close to being clear. He will be a formidable opponent. Him joining the previous attacks would have ended them quickly. If he wasn't playing with me, I would have been dead long ago.

I'm not stupid. He's their leader for a reason, and they obviously fear him. Any shifter in charge of a group of others is strong enough to handle himself against most threats. I can only hope that my rage and desperation are enough to give me the edge over his ruthlessness. I'm no leader, no matter how much my father wanted me to be. I'm not a fighter unless my life is in danger, or someone I care about. Right now, it's both.

"Very well," Ande says, standing from his relaxed seat next to Greta, who releases her tension a little with the loss of his touch. "I'll beat you senseless before I finish the rest of my plan. A single bear doesn't stand a chance against one such as me. It'll be a nice show of dominance. You can't even shift like a proper shifter, dick swinging all over the place."

Greta scoots back on her butt until she's almost in the group huddled in the back. A young child tries to run over to her, but the woman I assume is his mother yanks him back and whispers in his ear. Greta doesn't notice, worried eyes only focused on me. I try to give her a confident smile, unsuccessful through my own concern.

If it seems like I might lose this, I plan on trying to make him kill me. I can't watch what he has in store for her. Even if I win, our position will be precarious. There is no way to tell how his fighters will react to his death. I can only hope I'm not too injured to hold off any that plan to complete his goals. I'm sure the cougar I killed had friends.

First, I have to get through this fight. As soon as I notice Ande preparing for the change, I call my bear forward. I barely get my paws under me before the cat hits me. I fall to my side and hear Greta scream my name. I push her fear from my mind. If I want to have a chance of defeating Ande, I need to focus only on my own emotions.

I let the rage flow.

Ande gets a scratch in, but no more. I position my back paw under him and kick with enough force to push him off me. He yowls as he flies across the cavern. Climbing to my feet, I immediately turn to face what I know is coming. Cats are fast, which will be his main advantage. He proves this by pouncing as I turn on him.

I swipe with my paw, catching him on the side. Ande doesn't waste a second. He darts under my next swing and sinks his teeth into my back leg. I growl with pain, trying with all I have to shake him loose. The cat hangs on while biting and scratching enough that I feel blood run down my paw.

Bracing myself on three legs, I use my free back claws to dislodge Ande from the other. He growls, jumps away, then climbs up my side.

I can hear Greta yelling in concern, and I let her fear in this time. It fuels my fury.

With a roar, I feint to the side. Ande scurries out of reach, but I expect that and fall in an attempt to land on him. He moves. Not fast enough. I feel his leg under me. Before I can do too much damage, he pulls free with a loud hiss. As expected, he's already launching himself at me, so I roll and catch him in my paws.

Long back claws dig into my stomach, bringing searing pain. My thick fur keeps him from disemboweling me, but that doesn't mean it doesn't hurt. I manage to get my back feet under his hind legs and use as much force as I can muster to try to throw him again.

It doesn't work, but it still gives me an advantage. As his rear end flies up, he latches on with his front claws. His body flips instead of flies. I'm able to grab his back in my jaws. Standing, I prepare to throw him into a wall. Through his own pain, he curls forward and swipes across my eyes with a claw. I drop him and take a step back, stumbling on my injured leg.

I can just see him through the blood running into my eyes. He's readying another pounce, but his injured hindquarters throw him off. I am able to hit him mid swipe and shake the blood from my eyes. Ande rolls across the stone floor. I lumber over to hit him before he can climb to his feet.

My opponent stumbles to his belly, and I move in for the kill. Grabbing his head in my jaws, I lift and shake until I feel his neck snap. I drop him, biting into his throat to ensure he's dead. The people huddled at Greta's back stand with shock and a little hope in their eyes. Hisses and growls sound behind me. I spin in time to take the first attacker out with a swipe, but more come.

Some try to slip past me, probably to get to Greta for their own revenge. I block one and grab another with my teeth, but I can't stop them all. Greta's scream makes me roar in fury. I have to get to her.

CHAPTER THIRTY-TWO
COUNTERATTACK

GRETA

I only have a moment to stare at Ande's limp body in relief. Gasps sound behind me, but a glance back shows me no one feels the need to avenge their tyrant. That doesn't mean I'm safe. Silas desperately tries to hold back the fighters. There are too many. I stumble back into the group, looking for any weapon I can find.

The group parts behind me, not wanting to be near me when the cougars charging at me reach us. The child from before runs behind and trips me during my backwards step, dropping something at my feet. A rusty knife lies right in front of my toes. I grab it before the large cats are on me.

I manage to stab the first one in the throat. It falls on me, making me grunt. Wiggling frees me in time to stand before the next two move in. I hold the knife out toward them. They take one look at their fallen comrade and throw their ears back, making no move to come closer. Instead, they spread out. Another comes from behind them. There's no way I can defend myself against all three of them.

My back hits a wall, giving me a small relief. At least they can't circle behind. Turning my back to them wouldn't go well. I have that going for me. Not much more.

The three cats all hesitate, waiting for an opening I refuse to give them. I don't stand a chance with three cougars, but I won't go down without a fight. A few deep breaths are all I have to brace for the incoming pain before one of them pounces.

I throw my bad hand up as a shield and thrust the knife out. The first time, my knife hits nothing but air. The feline pins me against the stone wall, causing pain to shoot through my hand as its neck pushes against my bad wrist. I jerk my head back to keep its snapping jaws out of my face and thrust the knife into its side. The cougar yowls and pulls away.

My knife stays in my attacker's side. The other two hiss their anger at me, but their eyes soon notice my empty hands. I no longer have a way to defend myself, and they now know that. Swallowing, I ready for what is about to come, the undeniable and sure agony of murder by large cat. They crouch for a unified attack.

Silas barrels into them, stepping on one and knocking the other aside. His purple eyes meet mine for a brief second before he turns on the cat he threw. Taking a few deep breaths, I check the one he crushed under his massive paws. It's doing its best to climb to its feet.

Another look at my bear shows me his movements are slow and pained. Two may make it too hard on him in this state. Looking around, I find a pointed rock. I pick it up and charge the struggling cat. It sees me at the last second, but it's too late. My rock comes down on the hard skull. The cougar tries to fight back. It can't win this one.

My enemy falls under my repeated blows to the head with the pointy edge of my makeshift weapon. Even when it's limp, I slam my makeshift weapon into the bloody skull over and over. A bloody mess covers the floor by the time something furry touches the side of my face. With a yelp, I fall back, brandishing my gory rock in as threatening a way as possible.

Silas watches me without a hint of blue in his eyes, which makes me wonder if the purple is his bear coming out. I look around to see a bunch of dead cougars. No more attackers remain. We did it. Somehow, we came out of this alive.

My rock falls from dead fingers as I take a bunch of frantic breaths. Silas doesn't change. I can only guess it's to make sure no one else comes for us. Although, it doesn't look like he can take much more. Almost all of his fur is covered in red stickiness. His body sags with exhaustion, maybe loss of blood. Or both.

Climbing to my feet proves difficult because of jellied legs, but I make it and throw my arms around his thick neck, not a care at all for the blood I'm covering myself in. Silas is alive. I'm alive. We made it through this ordeal.

A small weight hits my legs. The young child that was there when I woke hugs my knees. "Thank you."

My brows furrow as he runs back to his mother. Someone else steps forward. "Thanks to both of you. We've been under his control for so long and didn't have the courage to fight back. If we did, there's no way we would have won. We are now free from his abuse."

The man's voice sounds raspy from disuse. "All we did was defend ourselves. Silas here wouldn't let him kill me, and I wouldn't let them kill him."

"It doesn't matter. You helped us by helping yourselves. We are in your debt."

They all look at me as if waiting for my terms. Confused, I turn back to the man. "I want nothing from anyone. You owe me no debt for doing my best to stay alive, so you are free to do whatever you want to."

"Then we will search for a better leader. One is close. They escaped him, but they'll be a much better leader than Ande. We wish you the best of luck. Take care because a few of the fighters ran off. We can take them if needed. Your bear is badly injured, so please, we will lead you back to your cabin."

Nodding, I simply stand and stare in wonder. A snort behind me reminds me that Silas is there. I turn to him. "Can you walk back?"

He nods, his head sagging. I run my hand over the sticky fur on his cheek and over his neck. My hand comes away wet, but I don't care. I didn't think I'd ever touch this man again.

"Do you want to shift?"

He shakes his head in a no. I don't know if it's because he's tired, too injured, or still on alert. After a few more minutes, the others are ready to leave. We walk in their midst, them unwilling to leave us where we will be attacked easily. The little boy hums to himself and keeps looking back at me with huge smiles. They're free, and they believe it's because of us. I've never had anyone show me this kind of gratitude.

Despite our weariness, we receive no attack, which I'm immensely grateful for. Silas moves slowly, and the cougar shifters match his pace to keep us safe in the middle of their ragged group. His back leg seems to have taken the worst of the damage. He nurses it and depends on the other three paws to keep him moving.

Not that I'm much better. Everything hurts, and I'm sure I'm going to be covered in bruises. A few deep scratches on my shoulders pain me, making me realize I was hurt more than I thought when the one pinned me against the wall. Adrenaline must have kept me from noticing at the time. My entire body is sore and tired. All I want is the bed.

When the cabin comes into view, I'm more relieved than I have ever been in my life. It takes longer than it should to cross the small clearing, an eternity. The cougar shifters part to let us through. Silas stops before the porch, huffing in the chilled air.

I turn back to him. "Can you shift now?"

He nods but doesn't move to do so yet. I see his sides heave as if taking deep breaths. After a few of those, his fur recedes, he shrinks, and he reshapes. As soon as Silas is on two legs, he collapses into the mud. A few of the men come forward to lift him up. I follow them in, waving at the child before surveying the damage they did while I was unconscious. It's a mess.

Even my beloved bed is torn to shreds. Rushing over to the couch, I put what's left of the cushions back on. Silas directs them over to it, and they lay him down gently. My bear man groans as his body falls the short distance to the ravaged cushions.

The men thank us once more and say their farewells. Closing the door, I realize it won't latch anymore, so I find a few boxes and broken pieces of furniture to hold it closed. My work won't do much if someone wants to force their way in, but it will at least give us warning.

I hurry back to Silas. "Are you okay?"

His large hand engulfs my cheek. "I am now. I was so worried he'd win or not take the bait."

"Ande really did a number on you."

"Nothing I can't heal from. As long as you're safe, I'm happy."

Leaning over him, I brush his lips with mine. When I stand again, I say, "Do you need me to clean these wounds?"

"No. They'll heal fine, even with the mud. Your shoulders need to be looked at though."

He tries to sit up to help, but my gentle touch holds him down, telling me just how exhausted and injured he is. "I can handle cleaning these. Get some rest."

Too tired to argue, Silas's body relaxes, so I restart our fire. I move outside, through my mess in front of the door, to gather a little bit of the melted snow from the roof that he collects in a bucket. By the time I get back into the cabin, he's asleep, snoring fitfully.

It takes a few minutes to warm the water, and I feel my eyelids dragging. While the water heats, I put my barricade back in place. My water is ready when I'm done. I strip, biting my lip as the shirt pulls over my wounds. Damn, that hurts.

A glance at Silas shows me I didn't wake him. The gashes are deep, so I try to use some of the butterflies Silas has left in his kit. It's hard with one hand and doesn't look the best, but it'll do. I'm too tired to fret over it.

Pulling my clothes on is harder because they're tighter than Silas's. Every movement of my arms brings agony and pulling. I probably will need to see a doctor for proper stitches. With the possibility of other cougars remaining, I doubt Silas will change his mind. If he does, I still can't stay. If anything is evident after all that's happened, I owe him a huge debt. It's my turn to protect the bear.

Next, I poke the fire, add more logs, and try to find somewhere to sleep. Getting close to the bed brings the scent of cat urine, hard to decipher from further away. Even if it was still whole, I'm not laying down in that. I sniff some of the blankets scattered around and find them clean, if a little worse for wear. I bundle them in front of the fire and stretch out onto my back.

From here, I'm closer to our resident spider roomie and find that I'm not as nervous about it as before. I guess spending time watching it spin the web takes away some of the anxiety caused. Or maybe it has more to do with the fact that I've gone through so much worse than a spider bite recently. No arachnid can compare to a fierce cougar anxious to take a bite out of me.

My gaze travels back to Silas, roaming over the hard line of his jaw, his soft lips, and further down. Losing him hurts, but it's better that I go. That doesn't mean I'm not going to try to find a way to visit. I'm not sure how that will go over. Mother is going to be watching me like a hawk after my defiance and disappearance. She needs to protect her assets.

Sighing, I decide to keep watch. If someone wants to break in, one of us needs to be alert. I need to hold them off while Silas prepares for attack. I hope it doesn't come to an attack, but if it does, he needs to be healed as much as possible. I'm not sure how many ran off or if they'll continue Ande's vendetta. They may not. The most loyal probably were the ones that we fought after Silas killed him.

Despite my desire to stay awake, I feel my eyelids grow heavy. I fight them. After recent events, I don't stand a chance. I drift off into nightmares of vicious cats and nagging mothers.

CHAPTER THIRTY-THREE
SOMETHING TO HOLD ON TO

GRETA

When I next open my eyes, I do so with a massive groan. Silas bustles around the small space we reside in. A glance at the window shows light, but I've lost all track of time since Ande showed up at the door. The gashes on my shoulders ache as I sit up. I think I may even feel a trickle of blood. I need a doctor.

"What time is it?" I ask, ignoring the other important details.

"Sometime in the morning. We both slept through supper and breakfast."

"I think we both needed it. How do you feel?"

Silas waits until he puts some venison strips on the fire. Most of our supplies were destroyed by the cougars, but I guess we had a little left. My stomach grumbles at the thought of eating. He forgot that we missed lunch too.

"I'm good as new," Silas says. "I'm sorry about the meager breakfast. All we have is a little deer meat left. How are you? You were injured pretty badly?"

I'm not sure if the last part is a question or a statement, but I'll treat it as a question. "The meat is fine. My shoulders are a little sore, but it's nothing to worry about."

The lie is easy because it's partially true. While the wounds feel raw and like they might be bleeding, the butterflies and torn shirt pieces are holding me together. I can survive until I can get to a town with an emergency room. At the moment, I'm alright and will be for a while.

Getting up is difficult, and my muscles complain about the action. It's probably a mix of yesterday's activity and a long sleep on a floor. The blankets leave much to be desired, as far as comfort is concerned. They're meant to keep us warm, not to be used as a bed.

Silas escorts me during my much needed trip to the outhouse. Nothing moves outside but birds. All is quiet and still. If there are any rogue cougars out there, they aren't giving themselves away. I mention as much on the way back.

"If they would have attacked, it would have been last night. I was weakened, and we had no way to lock the door. The more I think about it, the less I expect any more attacks," Silas says.

"Why's that?"

"I want you to know this is only speculation. For all I know, they're simply licking their wounds, so we still need to get you out of here. Although, the way I look at it is that they're less loyal to Ande than the ones that attacked us. Those that wanted us dead are most likely his main men. Anyone else was only fulfilling the duties to keep him happy. As soon as he was gone..."

"They tucked tail and ran, so to speak," I say.

"Or quite literally. They'd be faster as cougars. The others attacked as soon as he was dead. If all of them joined in, I doubt we would have gotten out as we did."

We walk into the cabin. Silas is quiet while I contemplate all that, placing our meat on plates. I consider it all, and it makes sense. One thing bugs me.

Silas puts my plate in front of me, and I wait for him to sit before I say, "So, why didn't they attack while Ande was in trouble? If they were so loyal, wouldn't they have?"

Now that the actual event is over, it's easier to consider and speak of it. I'm actually surprised at how calm I am while discussing it. Inside, the memories of my capture roil around inside. I push them away to look at this more objectively.

"It happened too fast. I did my best to kill him as quickly as I could without giving it away until it happened. Even so, his men were already starting to change. Otherwise, they wouldn't have hit me as fast as they did."

That makes a lot of sense, so I don't ask more questions about what happened. There's no need to live in that memory longer than necessary. I'd rather think of good things during my last however long I have here.

Silas doesn't seem to think the same. "I saw you wielding a knife. Where did that come from?"

"A little boy gave it to me. He was staring at me when I woke up, which made Ande angry."

"Then he saved their lives more than we did. Their thanks should have been to him."

"It seems that you had it handled."

Silas shoots me a quick glance I can't read before picking up our empty plates to clean. I watch him move about the cabin. When he passes by me, I can't hold it in. "You didn't?"

Silas pauses by the couch, leaning on the back of it. His bulging muscles tense and relax over and over. I'm about to ask again, but his sigh stops me. I wait a little longer.

"If you would have died, I would have lost the will to fight," he whispers, just loud enough for me to hear.

I stand from my seat and walk over behind him. When my hand touches his bare back, he twitches but doesn't turn. My heart both breaks and leaps at the admission. I can't allow myself to believe it.

"I'm not worth your death, Silas."

Now, he whirls. His strong hands frame my face. "That's not true, Greta. You. Are. Everything. Don't you dare let anyone tell you differently. Not your shrew of a mother. Not that poor excuse of a man you were engaged to. No one. You are worth death and more. I won't give back this time together for all the peace in the world. Everything is worth it when it comes to you, and I'd die a thousand times if it keeps you safe."

My mouth drops open, but I have no words. At this moment, this time where Silas bares his soul and heart to me, I have no voice. There are so many important things to tell him. There is so much that needs to be said. All gets stuck behind the lump in my throat.

I decide that if I can't use words to describe how his speech makes me feel, I'll do even better. My lips crash into his. He reciprocates, careful to be gentle enough to avoid hurting me. My hands slip around his waist, bringing his hips to mine. His arousal presses against me, and I feel warmth grow from deep within.

When my hands slip into the back of his pants, he pulls away. "You're still hurt."

"Not so much that I'm willing to keep my hands off of you. I want this more than I want to be pain free. Give me the love you say I deserve. Give me something to remember you by."

His hand strokes the hair over my temple. When a sharp pain makes me jump, he apologizes. I can only imagine what that part of me looks like. It's where Ande hit me to knock me out. Before he can balk further, I pull his mouth to mine again, pushing him into the back of the couch and rubbing my thigh up to his hip.

A growl rumbles his chest, and I bite his lip to gain entrance. He gives it to me before lifting me up and setting me on the table. It takes a lot of care, but we manage to get my shirt off. Silas kisses down my collarbone, his thumb grazing the soft skin below my breast. My breath hitches with a small whimper. He doesn't stop. I never want him to stop.

As his tongue slides around a taut nipple, my head falls back with a moan. He sucks, which makes me gasp as lightning shoots through my body. The heat of my core rises to meet the electricity of his tongue. My entire body trembles with need.

When he presses closer, the table putting me at the perfect height to feel him against my clothed sex, I can take no more. "Get these pants off me."

"I can do that."

I slip from the table as he works the button on my jeans. While he works with my pants, he nibbles at my neck. I grab fists full of his hair. His next words are spoken into my neck.

"It's easier to get my pants off you."

I laugh, wiggling to make it easier on him. Once I'm free, he lifts me gently back onto the table. The movement gives me a little pain in my shoulders, but I barely feel it through the pleasure coursing through me.

Before he can try more foreplay, I use my legs to bring him to where I need him. He enters without hesitation, making me gasp and groan. Fire shoots through my core and further up as he slides inch by inch into me. His thrusts are gentle and loving, and I've never felt this way before. Sure, this man is an animal, but he's so much more than that.

My back arches as the pressure grows too strong. I release, followed closely by this bear who is mine for a short while longer. I treasure this, locking the feeling and sound of him away into a vault in the back of my mind. Silas is not a man to be forgotten, and I plan on making sure I don't.

Breathing out, I lay my forehead on his shoulder to hide the threatening tears in a moment of needed closeness. I don't want this moment to end, but it has to. For my safety. For his. That doesn't make this any easier.

I've never felt love before, not even from the person who is supposed to give it to me unconditionally. I've finally found it, and I need to walk away from it. Life is cruel. Life is as painful as everything that happened yesterday. I'm losing the one thing I've longed for my entire life. I'm leaving it for those that make me feel like I'm nothing.

Silas places his fingers under my chin and lifts my gaze to his, kissing my tears away. "Greta, I'd keep you forever if there was any way I could do so safely. Losing you is the last thing I want to do."

Nodding, I give him another soft kiss. He lets me down to get dressed. Emotions swell in my chest, ready to burst it. This man bared his heart to me, but I'm still too scared to. All my life, I've had my feelings thrown back in my face. I don't expect him to do the same. That doesn't mean my self-defense mechanism doesn't kick up subconsciously.

"I don't want to go either," I say.

Silas stares for a moment, giving me a soft smile. "If it could be any other way, I'd really keep you prisoner. As it is, we need to get on our way to make sure you can make it back before nightfall. You'll always have my heart, Greta."

Mine breaks as he bustles around the cabin again. The urge to tell him all grows. I can no longer hold it in.

"Silas, wait." When he turns to face me, I almost lose my courage. I push on before I can. "You're not some freakish screw up. Wait, that came out wrong. You're so much more than you think you are too. To me you're... I...

"I'm screwing this up. Let me start over. I've never felt the way I do with you. I've never felt important or wanted. Only you have made me feel these things. I know you don't like who you are, but I *love* who you are. You're strong and courageous. You're caring and gentle. You're great in bed. I don't want these feelings to end. I don't want to leave them behind. I wish there was more we could do."

There I go, crying again. Silas wraps his arms around me, my last time of feeling truly safe again. I wrap my arms around him too and hold tight to what I will soon have to let go. For the first time in my life, I have something to hold on to.

CHAPTER THIRTY-FOUR
UNWANTED LIFE

GRETA

Hand-in-hand, we traverse the muddy forest. Silas watches our surroundings, including up in the trees. I examine everything as well—for a different reason. If I can find my way back to him, I will. All I need to do is memorize the way back to the cabin. As I have proven multiple times, I'm good at getting lost in the woods, so I take a better look at our path, committing it to memory.

There's a tree that splits in three ways. We are walking to the right of it, which would mean left coming back. A pile of three large rocks over to our left. Oh, and there's a fallen tree, leaning on the fork of another. A small patch of pine trees here. Lots of pine cones in the mud.

Silas pausing brings me from my memorization. When I look up at him, he's intent on the way forward. I look in front of us but see nothing. Still, I know that alertness anywhere.

"What's wrong?" I whisper. "Cougars?"

"I hear voices."

My brows furrow. "Who would be crazy enough to be walking around out here?"

"We are."

"Well, yeah, but I'd be lost without you. This place is completely wild."

Silas shrugs and lets my hand drop. He moves from tree to tree, and I follow in his footsteps. The look he sends back that tells me I should stay put is met with a scowl to tell him I want to see as well. Once we are close enough, my mouth falls open as I step out of the forest.

"Mother?" I say loud enough for her to hear.

She looks over at me. "There you are, Greta. You've caused quite a lot of trouble you need to account for."

Silas steps out from behind the tree that he barely fits behind with a scowl. Mother jumps at his not-so-sudden appearance. I place a hand on his arm to keep him from saying something in my defense. With my mother, it's best to not start an argument.

"Who is this?" she says with the corner of her lip drawn up. Her dark brown eyes move up and down his body, and I can tell she finds him wanting.

I feel the hair on the back of my neck rise. "This is Silas. He saved me after I drove into the snow pile and gave me a place to stay until he could shovel me out. How did you find me?"

"Who's Silas?" comes a voice I wished never to hear again.

"Damian?"

I feel Silas tense beside me, so I squeeze his arm harder. It's best to keep the peace for now. I can argue later. Right now, I need to keep Silas from placing himself in my mothers sights. She's a mean and vicious hunter, as cruel as Ande but without the killing part. She ruins lives in other ways.

"I already explained who Silas is. I would have died if he hadn't found me after the accident," I explain again, my voice sounding a little short.

"Why are you still with him?"

"Not that it's any business of yours, but the snow was too much until yesterday. He didn't return to the cabin after shoveling until late, so he is leading me back now."

"Greta!" my mother scolds. "Watch your tone. I did not raise you to have such an attitude. While this conversation is fascinating, you've been gone for far too long. It's almost Christmas, and we have appearances to make. Move along. You need a long shower and proper clothes. Thank you, Silas. We can take it from here."

From the look on her face, I can tell the shower isn't just because of my dirty state and the thank you isn't heartfelt. Appearances are everything to her, so she must appear gracious to the man that kept her daughter alive, even if there is no one out here to see.

I sigh and look up at Silas, who is sporting an impressive glare directed at Damian. He speaks through gritted teeth. "Her car can only make it to the nearest town. She needs gas and new tires."

Mother waves her hand as if it's of no consequence. "I already called a tow truck. She will ride back with us."

This time, I'm the one that tenses. Silas must sense it because he moves to put himself between me and the two unwelcome visitors. I step out ahead of him and say, "How did you find me?"

Mother rolls her eyes, an action I was always yelled at for. She pulls a small box out of her purse. "It's a bit banged up, but I found it on your passenger seat. It wasn't working until yesterday. I had given up hope, but decided to check one more time this morning. Imagine my surprise when your signal showed up."

"You put a GPS tracker on my car?"

"Of course. With the way you make decisions, I thought it best to know where you are to avoid any embarrassments."

Again, her eyes stray to Silas, making it clear she sees him as one. My back stiffens at the insult to a man better than any I've met in the past. I want to defend him, but the words stick in my throat.

"Let's go," my mother says, not sparing us another glance before walking to the black SUV parked along the road.

Damian refuses to walk away, scowling at Silas. I turn to my bear. "I have to go. Thank you for everything. I really mean everything. You've kept me alive and showed me a side of life I've never known before. I'll always be grateful."

"Remember what I said before," he replies with a sad smile. "Always welcome."

I want to kiss him, but I can't with an audience. "I'm sorry for my mother and for how we have to part."

"I understand. Remember who you are, Greta."

Smiling, I let my hand fall down his arm until I can squeeze his fingers. Turning, I walk up the small slope, trying to leave a wide berth between me and Damian. He tries to walk over to me, but I move away. He sends another glare to Silas before opening my door.

Huffing at the familiarity, I slide into my seat beside my mother. He takes the front seat next to his driver. As we pull out, I look out my window and watch Silas, who doesn't move until we are far out of view. Tears threaten, but I hold them in. I'm no longer in my safe place. Crying means scolding, and I have enough of that coming as it is.

"What were you thinking shacking up with a man like that, Greta?" my mother questions as soon as I settle into my seat. "I thought I taught you better than that."

"Would you rather I had frozen to death, Mother?"

"Don't you dare take that tone with me. Remember who you're talking to. Can you imagine the bad PR we'd receive if word got out?"

I remember quite clearly who I'm talking to, and I hate it. "No one in here is going to say a word."

"And you're lucky about that fact."

So lucky.

Mother straightens her tight bun, bleached to match Father's light blond hair. She says it makes them look like a power couple, even if it's clearly fake. Her sharp nose is so far in the air that I'm sure she's going to puncture a hole in the roof of the vehicle.

"Did you sleep with him?" Damian asks, startling me.

"It was a small cabin. It's not like I could sleep outside in the snow."

"That's not what I mean, and you know it."

I narrow my eyes at him. "What business is it of yours?"

"Greta! Attitude!" my mother says.

"You did, didn't you?" When I don't answer Damian, he gives me a disgusted look. "Why would you sleep with a man like that? My fiance no less."

Anger rises up, but I keep my tone civil, even if my words might not be. I need to remember what I've been taught to survive in this life. "So, you can screw everything on two legs, but I can't keep warm in a snow covered cabin with one man? Besides, we aren't engaged anymore. I broke up with you."

Damian rolls his eyes. "Like you can break up with a man like me. Here's the ring you forgot at my condo. By the way, your mother found that disgusting filth on your phone and deleted it for me."

He tosses the ring at me. It bounces off my window and falls to the floor while I look at my mother in shock. When I make no move to pick up my shackle, she does and holds it out to me.

"I don't want it," I say.

"You'll wear it. This marriage is best for all."

"Not for me. I deserve love, Mother."

Her dark eyes darken further. "Greta Ann Parks, you will put this ring back on your finger if you know what's good for you. Love is an unnecessary complication. Marriages are nothing more than a business transaction. Like all business transactions, personal feelings don't matter."

"She probably loves her neanderthal back there," Damian says with a sulk.

I turn to say something particularly nasty to him, but Mother's hand on my shoulder makes me look back at her. I don't see the slap coming until my cheek is stinging hard enough to make me bite my lip to keep from crying out. My vision blurs.

"Don't you dare try to use your tears on me," my mother scolds. "A single tear falls, and you're getting another one."

My gaze drops to my lap. "Yes, Mother."

"That's better. Put this love nonsense behind you and wear your ring."

She places the gold monstrosity in my lap. Keeping my head down to hide the flowing tears, I slip the ring back on, feeling trapped once more. I never thought a ball and chain could be so small and so sparkly, but this piece of jewelry proves me wrong. With it on my finger, I feel like a weight is dropped onto my shoulders from a great height.

The driver hits a bump, and my seatbelt rubs my shoulder. I wince. "Can you take me to the ER?"

"What for?" Mother asks.

"We were attacked by cougars yesterday. I have some scratches that need to be stitched up and looked at."

I can almost hear my mother's sneer of disgust. "Seriously, Greta? People are going to think I didn't raise you right. I've told you to stay away from wild animals, and here you are, traipsing through the woods and letting them attack you."

"I didn't want to be attacked. They surrounded us. Silas chased them off."

"And there is this Silas again. I refuse to listen to anything you say if his name is involved here on out. Whatever you had or did with him is in the past. Keep it there. No, I will not take you to the ER.

You'll get cleaned up and dressed, then we'll go to a private doctor that understands discretion. I'll make sure you're checked for diseases. As it is, we are going to need to go in the back way to hide the mess you are."

My breath hitches, and I turn to look out the window. From the reflection, I can see Damian staring at me, completely satisfied with what's going on in the back seat. She deleted the proof I have of his affair. She forced me to accept his marriage, so he can move up in the ranks by showing he has put the family name first. He's won.

And I've lost. So much is stolen from me. My freedom. The man I have come to love. My life. There's nothing left in my life to bring joy. All that I have is duty, plus the threats that remind me who's in charge if I don't do as I'm told. It's all so hopeless. Locked in a life I don't want, forced to leave better behind.

Silas, I miss you already, more than you can ever know.

CHAPTER THIRTY-FIVE
REALIZING POTENTIAL

GRETA

Mother's fork creates an annoying ringing when she taps the champagne glass to gain all the attention. Thoughts of how much she likes attention flutter through my head, but I keep them contained. Now is not the time.

"We would like to thank everyone who has met with us to celebrate the re-engagement of Damian and Greta. After her shocking and harrowing absence, we can now continue with our plans to unite our two very powerful families into an unbreakable alliance. Tomorrow is Christmas and the day these two become one entity. We hope for all your blessings and well-wishes."

Clapping echoes around the banquet room our little party is in. My body freezes. "Tomorrow?"

Despite my voice only being a low whisper, Damian must have heard. "We decided to wait until now to let you know. We didn't want you running off again. After shacking up with the wild man for so long, we didn't know what to expect from you."

My mouth grows tight as I look around. No one heard a thing, thanks to Damian leaning in close to my ear. The official story is that the engagement was put on hold due to my disappearance. With my return, we are back to being the loving engaged couple all the media says we are. It sickens me, but I'm not sure I can do anything about it.

Spending the rest of my life with Damian and giving him as many children as he wants with me sounds empty and absolutely terrifying. Never knowing love again. Never tasting freedom. Raising my children in this snake pit that is the higher end of society. I deserve better. Too bad I don't get what Silas says I deserve.

"I'm still angry that you were sleeping with another man all that time," Damian goes on. "I'm willing to forgive you though. All you have to do is prove I'm your one and only."

I'm about to snap at him about his affairs, but I notice my mother scowling at me and click my mouth shut. Part of me wonders if there are enough people here to announce my true feelings and be able to flee without retribution. Everyone here is part of one family or the other, so I'm sure it would all be kept hush. Silas would then be put in danger because I'm sure they know exactly where I'll head. I need something bigger.

Too bad bigger is so difficult.

"That's a good girl," Damian says into my silence.

I clench my teeth and look down the table to my only ally. Dana watches me with sad eyes. This is too much. I can't handle this. I can't breathe.

"If you'll excuse me," I say with false calm, "I need to use the restroom."

"Just make it quick. We have people to impress."

I clench my fist, feeling the skin on my wrist pull. Mother did take me to a doctor, so all my injuries are taken care of. They're healing and rarely hurt more than a dull ache anymore. Standing, I keep composure the entire way to the bathroom. Once in the stall, I lose it.

Tears stream down my face, and my nostrils fill with snot. Sniffling, I barely hear the door open and close. My breath hitches. Damian wouldn't follow me in here. No, he wouldn't, but my mother would. Just what I need.

"Greta?"

My neck straightens when I recognize the voice. "Dana?"

"Are you alright?"

"Yes."

"I can hear you crying."

I give a low giggle. "At least you're not trying to convince me that over text."

"I could hear it then too. Let's talk. I haven't had any alone time with you since they abducted you."

Hysterical laughter bubbles up, but I push it down, choking on it. I blow my nose and wipe my eyes. I've talked to Dana over the phone, and Mother consented to inviting her tonight in hopes of keeping me domesticated. She doesn't understand that Dana is the least domesticated person on the planet.

I told Dana everything that doesn't involve magic or shifters. She's furious that I had to leave Silas. Hence, what she called my abduction. She's been trying to talk me into running away again. We both know that isn't a good idea.

I exit my small shelter. My best friend wets a paper towel with cool water. "Put this on your eyes. No, don't argue. I can redo your makeup. Damian is a real bastard."

"He truly is."

Dana lets her eyes widen. "I'm not used to having you agree with me so vehemently."

"I had love, Dana."

The tears start again, and I find myself dissolving into a weeping mess. Dana grabs me and pulls me into a hug. The familiar feel of her embrace helps calm me. I can't count the number of times we've ended in this position.

"Silas treated me like the world," I sob.

"I need to meet this Silas sometime. He looks good on you."

"Dana!"

"I don't mean like that, but I'm happy you got some from someone who wants you for you. It's the best feeling. This is why I keep telling you that you have to go back. Despite how rustic it sounds, that place and that man made you happy. You will always deserve happy, Greta. Who cares what your mom thinks."

"My mother would claim he kidnapped me," I say. "She'll insist he brainwashed me and use all her connections to get him put in a cage for the rest of his life."

"You need a grand public gesture."

"Mother keeps a close eye on me now. I can't go anywhere without being seen. How am I going to manage that?"

For the first time, Dana looks defeated by my pessimism. "I don't know. All I know is that you can't marry that wretched excuse for a man. You have so much better waiting for you. I'd miss you, but I want you to be happy."

"If it was possible, I'd find ways to call and visit. He's not that far from your house."

She laughs. "Just in the only giant spot of wilderness between here and there."

"One that he knows. I'd never forget about you."

"I know." Dana squeezes me tighter. "You are worth so much more than you will let yourself believe. You deserve Silas."

Her sentiment reminds me so much of Silas's. He told me not to forget who I am. I lost that so long ago that I'm not quite sure I can grasp the Greta I hid so deep. How do I change my thinking and my life in an instant? How do I get what I want for once?

Dana pulls out her purse as someone else walks in. "I have eye drops in here to reduce redness, then it's time to fix your makeup and get back out there."

I avoid looking at the woman who makes her way to the nearest stall. She's recognizable from the banquet, but all I know is that she's somehow related to Damian. She doesn't need to know I was crying. My mother can't find out.

Once presentable, we move back out into the wasps' nest.

The hostess brings everyone's coats. Excited voices talk about the wedding as Mother and Father flank either side of me for an escort. Father doesn't bother to look at me, which is pretty typical. Most of my parental interaction has gone through Mother my entire life.

Lucky me.

Damian slips his arm around mine, strictly for appearances I'm sure. Father takes a step forward, and Mother takes his arm as well. Our party files outside in a long line with us at the front. Outside, I smile and wave at the cameras I didn't know were going to be here. Before we reach the limos, I pause.

Can I say something in front of the cameras? If I out what's truly happened, there's no way my mother can contract the mob to go after Silas. I may be able to garner enough sympathy that leaving again won't be retaliated against. My eyes find Dana's in time to see her nod at me. She knows what I'm thinking.

But that won't work either. Mother has most of these media companies in her purse. They'd simply edit the footage in the most unflattering ways and make any other reports sound fake. It's hopeless.

Damian tugs at my arm, and I take a few more steps forward. Hearing a few of the reports use the word *live*, I freeze again. They can't edit live footage as it's being recorded. This might actually work.

"Greta, move to the car." My feet take an automatic step forward at Mother's command. She's the one big roadblock I have. I've defied her once, and I can do it again. I don't want her in my life anymore. I don't want her exerting control over my actions.

You will always deserve happy.

Remember who you are.

I don't take another step. "No."

"Excuse me?" Mother says.

"I said I will not get into the car." I make sure my voice is loud enough to catch the attention of the reporters. "I will not allow you to force me to marry Damian."

Gasps echo all around. Mother sends me a warning look, but I hold my ground without flinching. Mother's eyes narrow. "Get in the car. We will discuss your cold feet at home."

There she goes, making it all seem like it's my fault. I'm not being unreasonable. I'm refusing to be a pawn any longer. Damian tugs my arm, but I pull my hand away. I'm done with this.

"Why? So you can threaten and slap me into submission?" I ask. This brings more shocked noises from the crowd. Reporters move closer. "I'm through being bullied by you. I deserve better than a marriage with a man who sleeps around, and I'm taking it."

I can see Silas's name on her lips, but she pulls it back. "He is your loyal fiance, Greta. You have childish notions that need to be unlearned for your own good."

"Just because you erased the video of him screwing his supervisor doesn't mean it didn't happen."

"Please, we don't even know who sent that video. It was probably someone with a vendetta against such an upstanding young man."

"I sent the video," comes the voice behind Mother.

My mouth drops as we both turn to my father.

"How dare you?!" Mother yells. "Why would you spread filthy lies like that? I expected better than that from you."

At this point, everyone is tuned in to the family drama unfolding in front of them. This is turning out to be a very effective grand public gesture. I spot Dana smiling like an idiot off to the side.

"Because I'm tired of you trying to push Damian on her. I caught him having sex with that man and wanted to make sure she knew about it. One of us needed to tell her some truth."

"Some truth?"

Father looks around at the crowd and shrugs. "Many of our businesses are failing, Greta. This alliance is your mother's wet dream to bolster our image and our pockets."

"Why would you admit that in front of the world?" Mother says in horror.

"Because I'm not willing to destroy lives to line my pocket. I may not have been the best father to Greta, but I'm doing something for her now."

Mother sends me another glare. "Let's go home."

I shake my head. "I'm not going with you because that's never been home to me. I'll be going elsewhere."

"You'll be going back to him, you mean," Damian says, causing more gasps to circle.

"Where I go is no one's business."

With that, I walk away. Wide-eyed reporters part to let me through. Dana runs to catch up to me. "That was awesome. You are my hero."

I giggle as my heart starts beating again. "I can't believe I did that."

Dana stops me for a hug. "Don't forget me."

"Never."

"Good. Now, go get him."

She practically skips away as I watch with a warm smile. Mother is pushing Father into the limo while Damian's parents argue with him. I call a cab. My work here is done.

CHAPTER THIRTY-SIX
SURPRISES

SILAS

Sweat drips down my back as I grunt my way to the front door. The legs of the couch scrapes across my wooden floor. It smells like a mixture of cougar and old blood, and I simply can't take the smell anymore.

At the door, I pause and take a few deep breaths while wiping the sweat from my brow. Even with my enhanced strength, this thing is heavy. I resume my task until I manage to get the weighty piece of furniture outside. I toss it onto the newly fallen snow. I'll haul it further later.

Entering the cabin again, I stop and look around. Everything in here reminds me of Greta. The bed, where we cuddled and enjoyed each other. The table, where I took her last. Cooking together on the fire and having meals. Even the outhouse holds memories of her. There's nowhere in my home that's safe from remembrance of her.

I walk over to the clothes near the washbasin. Lifting them, I place them against my nose. Her scent flows into my nostrils with my strong inhale. I let the pleasure of her fill my lungs and will it to spread through the rest of me. Anything to feel her again. Anything to feel something besides regret and longing.

"I never should have let her go."

My voice echoes in the small space, as if taunting me. I had to let her go. I had to keep her safe. There was no other choice.

Still, the sight of her riding away from me, looking through the window to watch me in return, tore my heart to pieces. In the time since she left me, the days have blurred. I only know that today is Christmas because of the ingrained feeling I have in my heart. So long without the woman that makes life worth living. I have no desire to be festive, no matter whose blood flows through my veins.

And not a cougar in sight. I have seen no sign of my enemy since the fateful fight for our lives. I gave everything to make sure she lives, even sacrificing my beating heart to do so. Now, she's in the arms of a man that doesn't deserve her. She's under the control of a Mother with no maternal instincts. This is the life I condemned her to, but at least she's alive.

I feel like I'm not anymore. I knew I loved her, but I let her go. I knew it would produce agony, but I put her safety ahead of my desires. And I'm paying for the consequences of my actions.

At one point, I longed for the solitude I have now. Greta came into my life and threw it into disarray. I resented her for that, but I kept the woman I pulled from the car instead of letting her die in the cold. She changed me forever. I'm no longer content to stay alone.

But what can I do about it? If I leave in search of companionship, I risk missing Greta if she returns. What would happen if she came here and saw the place empty, cold with the lack of my presence? Would she wait for me? For how long?

And if she never returns? Will I spend the rest of my life waiting for Greta? The answer will always be yes. I can't leave. The likelihood of her return is slim, almost nothing. That doesn't mean I'll risk not being here if that small chance presents itself. She changed me from the cold man locked in his solitude to the warm man who needs her touch.

I'm not going anywhere.

Sighing, I sit on one of the table chairs to pity myself, sniffing the clothes she last borrowed. I've already cleared out the bed that the felines peed all over. My possessions were few to begin with because I didn't need much. I do need more than what I have. Time to figure out how to get it all.

Greta's idea of asking the farmers to let me work for them sticks in my head, but what would they need with me in the middle of winter? In the spring and summer, there are planting and harvesting. In the winter, it's simply survival. Maybe I can make my own furniture from fallen logs. I've done it before. Everything else might need to be taken, as much as I know she wouldn't encourage. It's not like she's here to tell me how to get things.

Maybe I should get a clock. It's not like I particularly need one, but that was always Greta's biggest complaint, even whenever she got used to my minimalism. For some reason, she always wanted to know what time it was. I should get one.

My mind imagines the joy she shows when she walks through the door and sees the clock, and I shake my head at the daydream. One, she's not likely to come back. Two, even if she does, it won't be for a clock. I'm hopeless.

Standing, I walk back outside and over to one of my ruined boxes of supplies. I found some venison stashed under the floorboards to rot. The cougars may have not expected me to return, but they wanted to make sure to make the cabin unlivable if I did. I'll live in any misery for the small hopes of seeing those light blue eyes smile at me again. Any stench is worth the chance of feeling a small body writhing in pleasure under me or the sounds made as I lick certain sensitive areas.

It's all a dream that doesn't stand a chance of fruition. I lift the box and walk into the trees, giving up on hopeless thoughts and unlikely futures. Far away from the cabin, I dump all the rotten meat for any animals that don't mind it rank. No use wasting food when something out there may eat it. Even the buzzards circling above.

Box hanging in my hand, I begin the trek back. As I grow close, I hear the noise of footsteps on wood, so I slow to a creep. I drop my box and move from tree to tree. The sound of a thud reaches me next. I can judge distance well enough to know someone's at my cabin. I can't help but wonder if letting my guard down was a terrible idea. Maybe they haven't given up the vendetta.

Peeking around a tree, I open my mouth in shock. It can't be. There's no way. I rub my eyes to remove the apparition from my sight. This isn't possible.

Then the light blonde head turns to reveal crystal blue pools I thought I'd only see again in my dreams. "Greta?"

The woman holding my heart smiles with such radiance that I gasp. "I see you fixed the door. I got something for you."

I don't care what she got me, so I ignore her last words. Instead, I cover the remaining space in seconds and sweep her into my arms. She giggles that wonderful sound as I spin her around. Before she can protest, I connect my lips to hers, devouring the mouth that has never faded from my mind. Greta tastes as heavenly as the last time I got to taste her.

I'll never get enough of her.

Greta pulls away. "That's the best welcome back I've ever gotten."

"I didn't expect to ever see you again. I can't believe you're here. How are you here?"

"That's an interesting story. Let me show you what I brought first."

I want to argue, but she turns away from me with a gesture toward the door. In the place of the old wreath that I had to dispose of is a brand new ring of pine. Plastic berries and red ribbon are placed in strategic locations around it. She replaced my destroyed wreath.

"Do you like it?" Greta asks. "I wasn't sure which one to get, but this one looked the closest to what you had. The old one was a bit ragged, so it was hard to tell."

"It's perfect," I say.

When I reach for her again, she walks through the door. "I brought other stuff. It was all hard on my own, but I managed. Come see."

"I'd rather spend the time seeing you."

"You'll have lots of time for that. Come look."

Sighing, I follow her into the cabin. It looks better but is still a little disorganized. She pulls out a box from a container with snow melting from it and hands it to me. I read it. "Beanbag couch?"

"Yeah. There's no way I could have gotten a real couch down here, so this is the next best thing. We need a new one."

"How does an entire couch fit into this box?"

Her laugh makes my heart leap. "It's compressed and will expand when we remove it from the wrapping. I also brought an air mattress with a hand pump. Lots of blankets too. I have canned goods and snacks, plus my own clothes. And guess what else?"

Her excitement is contagious, and I can't help but chuckle. "What?"

"A clock with lots of batteries."

"How did you get all this down here?"

"As I said, it was difficult. I thought ahead and bought a large sled to pull it over the snow. The cab driver thought I was crazy for wanting to stop in the middle of nowhere, by the way. I think he was ready to call the mental ward of the closest hospital."

"Is that everything?" I ask.

"What else do you think I could drag?"

I pull her into my arms. "Nothing. I just wanted to do this again."

My lips meet hers again. This time, it lasts longer. Greta melts into me, breathing out in a sound of relief. I share that feeling, having her close to me again. This is perfect, but I need to know what brought it about.

I pull away. "Again, how are you here? Not that I'm not grateful. I just can't believe to see you again so soon. How long are you staying?"

"Forever if you'll have me."

My heart stutters. "Always. How?"

Greta launches into a story that makes me feel shock and pride at the same time. I'm angry at what she went through in that short time and surprised at how well her plan worked. Most of all, I'm proud of her for standing up for herself. It's hard to break a cycle, but she is strong enough to grasp freedom. I knew she would be. It was only a matter of time and the right motivations.

She wraps her hands around the back of my neck. "I stumbled before, but I know my thoughts better now. I've never felt love until I felt it from you. Everything I thought was it before doesn't even compare. No one cares about me the way you do, except maybe Dana. Your love gave me the courage to do what I never thought I could. You changed my life because of how wonderful you are.

"Because of you, I was able to face my demons. I came here with judgment, brought on by my upbringing. You showed me how wrong my mother was. You aren't some freak of nature. You aren't a mistake. You're the greatest man I've ever met. I love you."

My heart swells with her words. I pull her in for another kiss. "I'd offer a little fun reunion, but I no longer have any furniture."

"Let's fix that."

She removes the compacted couch first, and I still find it hard to believe it's an actual sofa in that small package. Greta assures me that it will puff out, but it may take a few hours. I do the pumping for the air mattress. She also shows me a bunch of cash she said she removed from her account before her mother could lock her out.

When everything is done, I stretch out on the mattress. I'll get something more permanent later. For now, this is perfect. Anything with Greta is how it should be. I'll never want with her in my arms.

Greta rolls over. "How about we break this in?"

"Sounds good to me. Merry Christmas."

"The best Christmas ever."

As my lips meet hers, I only have one thought. *Life is perfect.*

EPILOGUE

GRETA

"Hey, girl!" Dana yells as she opens her door.

I step in to give her a hug. Silas comes next. Dana's little two-year-old runs over to join in the hugs, as cute as ever. It's been four years since I walked away from my family. Things have settled well, and I've kept my promise to keep in touch.

Once a week, Silas escorts me into town to make a phone call. We chat for hours while he shops for supplies, then we head home. He's found a farm that keeps him as help for all the time they can. Once a month, as long as it's possible, we visit my best friend. Dana absolutely loves Silas.

Tonight, we're here for Christmas dinner. It's taken me this long to realize that family isn't always what you're born into. Sometimes, you have to make your own. Where my first family failed me, these two have come through for me.

As far as I know, my parents divorced, and my father sold most of his companies. I haven't had much contact with my father and none with my mother. It's for the best. Family is those that love you unconditionally for who you are. They don't try to use you or change you. Right here is all the family I need.

Dana's husband calls for supper, and we all crowd around the dinner table. This is the perfect way to spend Christmas, full of love and joy. There's nowhere I'd rather be.

Later, in Dana's guest room, I snuggle against my bear. Bellies and hearts full, we take a moment to breathe. My drawing supplies sit on the nightstand. Silas bought them for me for our first full Christmas together. I didn't even know I loved to draw until he got me the set.

His chest rises and falls beneath my head. My heart flutters with the thought of the next conversation, but it needs to be had. It's against what he told me he wanted so long ago. Does he still think that way? Will he be upset?

"So, do you ever miss your solitude?" I ask.

"I once thought I did, but I don't anymore. It just seems that I didn't fill my life with the right people. I have them now."

I sigh with contentment. "Do you have room for more?"

He chuckles. "Dana has enough personality to fill the circle. Too many people are never a good idea around magic."

I nod, running my hand over his chest. Anxiety eats away at me because he already told me how he feels about this. I'd like to think things have changed, but my nervousness is heavy.

Dana doesn't know about his secret other half. She never will because I agree with him that the less that people know, the better. That doesn't change the direction of this conversation. It needs to be had. Dana will be waiting for the details tomorrow.

I take a deep breath. "No humans then. I think I've been soaking up the magic around me for plenty of years."

"Are you breaking up with me?"

His teasing voice makes me laugh. "No. Remember when you told me that humans living with shifters sometimes absorb their magic?"

"Mhmm."

The sleepiness in his hum tells me I'm about to lose him, so I decide to just blurt it out. "I'm pregnant."

Silas jumps into a sitting position. "What?"

I panic. "I know you said this isn't something you want to bring a child into, but we haven't exactly been trying to avoid it."

"No. It's alright."

"This might not be what—It's alright?" I don't know whether to be insulted or relieved.

"Listen to me before you react. Before, I didn't want to bring another hybrid into this world. I could only think of the pain in my past. Now, I realize my past and what I am doesn't matter because I found a life that accepts and loves me as is. As long as the child is part of you, I'm excited. There is no one to ridicule, and there will only be love. I want this."

Laughing, I bring his lips to mine. I'm not sure what I expected, but it wasn't this. Life is perfect.

Follow the Author

For more information on Kiera A. Reynolds and upcoming titles, please visit:

Facebook: https://www.facebook.com/kieraareynolds

Instagram: https://instagram.com/kieraareynolds

TikTok: http://tiktok.com/@KieraAReynolds

Newsletter: https://subscribepage.io/IA2DJe

Kiera A. Reynolds can be contacted at kiera@kieraareynolds.com

www.ingramcontent.com/pod-product-compliance
Ingram Content Group UK Ltd.
Pitfield, Milton Keynes, MK11 3LW, UK
UKHW010822200825
7484UKWH00028B/352

9 798230 807179